Praise for **CHARMING A**

New York Public Library Best Teen Books of the Year

Chicago Public Library Best Teen Fiction of the Year

SLJ Best Young Adult Books of the Year

YALSA Best Fiction for Young Adults

Quill & Quire Books of the Year: Books for Young People

White Pine Award Nominee

Junior Library Guild Selection

★ "Henri's narrative swagger effortlessly charms the reader, but it's his growing self-awareness that gives this delightful novel its depth. An intelligently narrated romance with plenty of witty banter and a diverse cast."—**BCCB**

★ "A witty, well-developed bildungsroman that presents a Black teenager carefully attempting to navigate systems that disproportionately disadvantage him." —***Publishers Weekly*** (starred review)

★ "Philippe's book touches on racial and class struggles experienced by students as they apply to college. A budding romance between Henri and Corinne is the icing on a rich and decadent cake. A must-have for all YA collections."—***SLJ*** (starred review)

"Morris Award winner Philippe turns up the charm in his sophomore novel. From its dynamic, easy-to-love characters to the endearing prose, this novel easily embodies Henri's cultivated suaveness, and his unusually confident persona, brings a fresh perspective." —**ALA** *Booklist*

"This humorous first-person narrative with a conversational, almost con⋯

"A v⋯
young people fa⋯ ⋯orable,
multifacete⋯ ⋯s,
and socioeconomi⋯ ⋯r others.
Refreshing, romantic, and at times laugh-out-loud funny, the book is satisfying and, yes, charming."—*The Horn Book*

"Packed solid with freestyle wit, real bestie charm, and the everyday diverse glory of New York City." —**David Yoon,** *New York Times* **bestselling author of** *Frankly in Love*

Other novels by Ben Philippe

The Field Guide to the North American Teenager

BEN PHILIPPE

BALZER + BRAY
An Imprint of HarperCollins*Publishers*

Balzer + Bray is an imprint of HarperCollins Publishers.

Charming as a Verb
Copyright © 2020 by Ben Philippe and Alloy Entertainment
All rights reserved. Printed in the United States of America.
No part of this book may be used or reproduced in any manner whatsoever without written
permission except in the case of brief quotations embodied in critical articles and reviews.
For information address HarperCollins Children's Books, a division of HarperCollins
Publishers, 195 Broadway, New York, NY 10007.
www.epicreads.com

alloyentertainment

Library of Congress Control Number:2020936276
ISBN 978-0-06-282426-4

21 22 23 24 25   PC/LSCH   10 9 8 7 6 5 4 3 2 1
❖
First paperback edition, 2022

TO THE NEW YORK CITY SUBWAY SYSTEM AND ALL THE
BREAKUPS I'VE EAVESDROPPED ON WHILE RIDING.

ONE

The first hustle, if you want to call it that, is also the simplest: Smiling.

Now, please don't be one of those douche-nozzles that go around telling women to smile more or anything, but as far as the daily life of a seventeen-year-old Black guy of above-average height goes in this city, I learned a long time ago that smiling goes a very long way.

Not smirking, not grinning. An earnest Smile.

In a place like New York where everyone—8,550,405 people as of 2019 and rising with every breath—is shoving their way through the masses (see: unwashed and running late), Fight Face at the ready, the combination of Eye Contact + Smile is like pointing a flashlight into someone's eyes. You can almost see their retinas dilate sometimes.

Case in point.

"Hi, Henri!" Mrs. Ponech smiles back as she opens the door

and adjusts to the megawatts awaiting her on her doorstep. "Goodness!" she exclaims. "Look at you two, both so happy. It must have been a good walk!"

"Yeah, Pogo and I have our own routine," I say as I remove the nylon harness in two quick unbuckles. "Riverside Park is our domain, ain't that right, Pogs?"

Pogo is a nine-year-old mutt terrier with some pretty advanced tooth decay that occasionally requires some free-of-charge brushing. He is now ignoring me entirely, too preoccupied with wagging up a storm at the overwhelming sight of the owner he saw just half an hour ago. Terriers are an "out-of-sight, out-of-mind" breed when it comes to their thrice-weekly walkers.

"Have a nice day, Mrs. Ponech!"

"Wait, wait one second." She disappears into the railroad hallway of her apartment and comes back a moment later, now cradling Pogo, and hands me a neatly folded little green square.

"You don't have to do this, ma'am. Like I said—"

"I know the app says they tip you guys, but we all know that's BS." She smirks conspiratorially, nodding to my Uptown Updogs T-shirt as if this transaction places us both firmly on the outside of rampant capitalism. Tip your dog walker: stick it to corporate America.

"Well, thank you very much, ma'am. I'll see you on Saturday, Pogs."

In the case of Mrs. Ponech, every five Smiles or so get me an envelope with three crisp twenty-dollar bills. I will happily take it.

My half-trade is dog walker to the twenty-five-block radius that stretches from 96th and Broadway to 121st and Broadway and, horizontally, from Riverside Drive to Morningside Drive. That rectangle delineates the Uptown Updogs official zone of service. It's all I can manage with my senior year schedule. Last year, even with the SATs, I could easily clear between twenty to thirty hours per week—give or take a mug of Dad's sludge coffee. (Haitian beans, ground by hand in his old-timey coffee machine that echoes around the entire apartment when he gets up at four a.m. It's a concoction that could send a horse out of cardiac arrest.)

Senior year, however, comes with too many balls to juggle.

Between attending FATE Academy, staying on top of the ridiculous amount of homework typical of FATE, the mandatory extracurriculars, and helping Dad with his superintendent duties around the building, I've had to narrow my clients to our neighborhood and go the extra mile to make sure they get nothing short of the best service possible. I really can't afford to lose on the income. No with college around the corner.

That's where the second hustle comes in: a brand. In our case, a branded website and matching T-shirts. See, I'm not just another dog walker: I am a dog walker of UptownUpdogs .world.com. The walkers of Uptown Updogs can easily be spotted around the Upper West Side by their lime-green T-shirts with deep blue cursive writing on the front and back.

I step outside and turn left onto West End Avenue, tightening my scarf. New York City is still hungover from the holidays and slowly getting the legs of its new calendar year under itself. On every other street, you'll find stacked in front of brownstones Christmas trees still green with bits of silver tinsel glimmering between their branches. They're right at home next to the poorly folded boxes from brand-new electronics and the recycling bins swelled with boxes from toys and colorful wrapping paper that has served its purpose of being torn apart by happy hands. All the joys from the holidays are now a set of household chores to get through as quickly as you can or put off as long as possible. It was a snowless New Year, preceded by a snowless Christmas, and a mostly snowless December. The big snowstorm little kids were waiting for this year so they could swarm Central Park and make fashionable snowmen never came. This whole winter might end up being a matter of bare trees with occasional trash bags at their branches, cloudy afternoons, and the chilled breaths of those of us who wake up early enough.

"No dogs for you today, H?"

Gigi, one of the late-afternoon dog walkers of the 110th dog run, greets me as we both find ourselves standing at a streetlight and trading Smiles of recognition before falling into synced steps. Some people get competitive, but I don't mind Gigi. She's cool. She's wearing her City College sweatshirt underneath her open winter coat. Most dog walkers in this area are college students or what I like to call Aspirers. (People who moved here to pursue comedy, writing, theater, TV, and need to make ends meet every month until they make it big or move back home.)

"I already dropped them off. I'm just going home to change and then headed back to school."

"School? It's almost six!"

"FATE has strict extracurricular requirements," I bemoan. "Class doesn't actually end when the four p.m. bell rings. The computer labs and art facilities are open until, like, eleven. It's dystopian."

"Jeez," Gigi says, not even bothering to hide her disgust. "No wonder all those little bundles of privilege go on to rule the world. Present company not included."

Oh, make no mistake: I fully plan to rule the world, Gigi-anne. The Haltiwanger dynasty is a House on the rise.

"Is that a new T-shirt?" she asks, pointing.

"Maybe?" I shrug. "I, um, I have a box of them. They don't pay us well, but they keep us well stocked in swag."

She suspiciously narrows her eyes but keeps focused on her own set of leashes. Gigi likes to triple-book her dogs, which is too dangerous for me. The Berjaouis would have a heart attack turning a corner to find Buddy entangled with other dogs.

"God, I have to get my toe through those Uptown Updogs doors," Gigi continues as we keep walking toward the Wyatt, my apartment building. "My best clients got priced out of the neighborhood, and I'm not going to freaking Queens. Did you tell them about me?" Gigi presses, and I start to feel bad. It's not the first time she's asked me.

"I did," I lie. "The boss isn't hiring at the moment. Says the pile of prospects is yay high."

"Yeah, the website says they're full. You lucked out."

"I'll put in a good word for you when I can," I say, turning toward the Wyatt's lobby. "I promise!"

Sorry, Gigi. There's no central Uptown Updogs office. The entirety of Uptown Updogs exists on my laptop.

You see, for all the Mrs. Poneches of the world, people still love the safety of a faceless corporation, as opposed to a random kid on Craigslist—especially when it comes to their dogs. And I say this as a former random kid from Craigslist who could barely rub three dogs together.

Since "joining" Uptown Updogs, I've become a lot of small dogs' second-favorite person around the neighborhood of Morningside Heights. Twenty-one dogs, to be exact. And it goes hand-in-hand with the Smiling: each of these pup families gets a personalized version of the Smile. That is another mistake people make: giving the same smile to everyone they come across, regardless of circumstances.

There is no such thing as a universal smile.

And while I've considered letting Gigi in on my scheme because she is always very nice and attentive to her charges at the park, the risk of blowing up my spot is too big. The dog walks are just a stepping-stone, and I won't be renewing the URL for Uptown Updogs come college acceptance letters. There's a master plan in the works—and it is wrapped in Columbia University ivy.

So, yeah, there's no circumventing that this is a bit of a scam. But what can I say? Dad calls it "the Great Hunger." That thing that draws everyone around the world here, to America, to New York City. Whether you're the worker scraping off the gum from a monument, the busy CEO that looks to the monument in question on their way to work every day, or the philanthropist tycoon worth billions and chiseled into marble for all the money they've donated to the city. Where you fall between the three, in America, the land of opportunities and blockbusters, depends on how hungry you are for it. How much gusto and hustle you can muster in pursuit of your goals and for that better life for your children.

Haltiwanger Hunger is its own brand of Hunger.

"Ma! I'm home for exactly nineteen minutes!" I shout, hanging the spare leash, ball thrower, and bag of dog treats in the doorway of our apartment.

Our building is a classic Upper West Side institution that also offers the amenities of the modern midtown high-rise building. As the super, my dad is responsible for running the day-to-day of the building, fixing things when they break down, and dealing with the demands of the wealthy tenants. It's a pretty thankless job, but we get to live in this apartment rent free, even if it is by far the smallest of the bunch. An aboveground basement, really, considering the limited sunlight, leaks, and cold drafts in the winter.

I grab a Pop-Tart from the pantry while stripping off today's Uptown Updogs shirt, which goes into the laundry pile by the hallway. Luckily, FATE does not require a uniform for after-hours extracurriculars, but in my case, "everyday attire" actually requires more preparation.

"Henri," Ma mimics, mouth full of pillow, pronouncing it the French Haitian way: Uh-ree.

"You asked me to wake you up. So I'm waking you up."

Light snoring.

"MA!"

"Just . . . give me, like, mmm'ten."

I roll my eyes and disappear into the bathroom, still smelling of dog and now running late.

"Yo, Ma! Do you have the good leave-in conditioner?" I shout, purposely slamming the medicine cabinet a little too loudly.

"Don't 'yo' me, Henri," she grumbles, getting up and pushing past me to get into the bathroom. Her tattoo, a faded peach ("before the emoji"), is visible on her shoulder. Like I said, very close quarters. There's something very strange about witnessing your 5' 6" Haitian mother slowly get more ripped than you. All her firefighter training has paid off. The woman is dangerously close to getting deltoids on her deltoids.

When Mom became a firefighter—or rather, became the sort of paralegal that tells her husband and son over dinner that she wants to become a firefighter, complete with a three-page plan of how it is all within grasp for us as a family in the next four years—I hadn't predicted that I would become a live-in alarm clock. She's currently a "probie" (probationary)—see also: firefighter in training, rookie, runt, worst schedule, and all kitchen duties. Her hours at the station are, by design, all over. There's a pecking order. "Probies" are expected to adjust quickly, be they nineteen-year-olds still living at home or middle-aged women with a son and husband.

"Have you ever seen a burnt body?" Dad had simply asked, quieting the table. To him, it was a nonstarter—but all three of us knew even back then that that's just how things go in this house. Somewhere between what Ma wants and what Dad wants, well, it's not even a contest. The Haltiwanger household is a matriarchy.

"I'm not due at the station until tomorrow," Ma explains. "I want to cook us a meal tonight so we can have a good family dinner and plenty of leftovers for you and Dad. So, tell me: what's next on your busy schedule, then, son of mine?"

I catch the kitchen oven clock through the bathroom mirror's reflection.

"Debate practice, meeting up with Ming, and then interview to walk a new dog."

She shakes her head, chin resting on her hand. "I read an article that most kids your age consider six p.m. the end of the day. Free time to play video games and chat on the phone and worry about their crushes."

"Those are only the kids boring enough to agree to take a survey of what they do with their free time, Mom. Who wants to be that?"

She shakes her head, now fully audibly peeing.

"Mom! Gross!"

"I'll see you later tonight, okay! Don't eat out!"

I let the apartment door close behind me, shaking my head and smiling—I still have a few private ones left, no capital *S* Smiles, no Smile™—and head back toward school.

TWO

I attend FATE Academy on the Upper West Side. For the uninitiated, that is the Fine Arts Technical Education Academy. Around the streets of Manhattan, you might recognize us by our gray slacks and skirts, purple blazers, and navy ties. FATE is a very woke school, very woke. We pride ourselves on our *wokeness*. The student body is diverse and amassed from all corners of the city. There's a giant photo of Barack Obama in Freedom Hall. Freedom is the south wing, Voice is the east, Action is the north, and Mindfulness is the West. (All that is missing is a recycled, environmentally conscious Sorting Hat to bring it all home at this point.)

Dad had pinched me when I made that joke during our tour.

"You're only laughing at it because you're inside it now," Dad said. "Believe me. Kids are writing their homework on tiny chalkboards in Haiti right now. This is a true gift for us."

My schooling is and has always been an "us" issue in the

Haltiwanger household, which explains the bow tie he wore that day as well as Ma's ironed hair and new dress when we were given access to this inner sanctum.

I was still in middle school over at MS 250 when we had first learned about the existence of the Fine Arts Technical Education Academy. MS 250 with the same off-putting sea-green walls in every classroom and metal-detecting security checkpoints that did not work, which only made passing through them more unsettling every morning. But for FATE, the elitest of the elite schools in Manhattan, "diversity" and "inclusion" have become key words, and simply spitting out another generation of world-wrecking Finance frat boys is no longer in vogue. (Don't worry, they're still alive and well.) And since these schools are looking to diversify their student body, and since I am: a.) very smart (not bragging, just true); b.) Black; c.) poor (sounds depressing that way, but strictly speaking, also true); and d.) the kid of immigrants, the admissions director literally shook my hand four times over the course of my interview. And so I was to be a FATE student: tuition, spaceship-looking building, and megawatt future all included.

Another point of pride at FATE are the extracurriculars, which are, in fact, *curricular* here and mandatory for students. From chess to basketball to fencing, you can do anything here at the highest competitive national level, but you *have* to pick one, which explains my presence on the debate team. On paper, debate was the right fit for me according to Mr. Vu, my academic adviser. "Charming and unafraid of public speaking! You'd be wasted anywhere else. It'll be a breeze for you."

At the time, he had failed to mention that the debate team's current iteration is the prized child of Greg Polan, the team captain who insists on three practices every week. We placed third in the state last year, behind The Chapin School, and Greg sees it as his mission to get us the gold trophy before the end of his tenure in another year and a half. Sophomore students can afford to have these lofty goals—we seniors can't think about much beyond the C word these days.

This explains why I'm now rushing back to FATE for yet another practice, late again due to a rush-hour train delay at Times Square. On the way in, I spot Corinne Troy, already sitting pretzel style on the bench outside the classroom. Mass of curly hair, stuffed under a pink beanie, and thick horn-rimmed glasses; it would be very easy for a boardwalk artist to turn her into a cartoon. She has the room booked right after us on Wednesdays.

"You're late," she notes without looking up from the chemistry book she is currently reading. "Again."

"Happy New Year to you too, Troy," I say, jumping over her backpack. I throw her a wink, which lands like she just smelled a fart.

"How vile," I hear behind me as I sneak into Room 402-B, twenty-seven minutes late.

I can't help it. Corinne Troy is one of those hyperfocused FATE students you just kind of have to shake your head at sometimes.

Also: she lives in my building. She and her mother moved in a few years ago. Maybe it's the fact that I've seen her in slippers and

13

a fuzzy purple bathrobe with lime-green flower petals after she locked herself out of her apartment and needed Dad to go let her in one Sunday morning, but I simply can't be afraid of her after that. Dark-skinned Black people don't tend to blush easily, but she was ten shades of red that morning—a stark contrast from the terrifying Type-A-with-extra-assignments-and-perfect-attendance-on-the-side Corinne Troy who stomps around FATE Academy.

And one last fun fact. That interview for a new dog I mentioned earlier? It's with her mom, Chantale Troy. I can't wait to see the look on Corinne's face when she finds out I'm going to be walking her adorable new pup.

I stand in the back of the mostly empty classroom, hearing a snatch of Greg's monotonous and stilted rebuttal to today's topic. Something about "Texting Spaces Being Allowed in Movie Theaters," according to the emailed schedule. Yadira is taking notes, fighting back a yawn. She's adopted a pretty drastic hairdo over the winter break, and the shaved side of her wavy black hair has externalized that intimidating part of her personality that previously didn't come out until she actually, y'know, spoke. On the stage, Yadira is a debate chimera of perfect posture, piercing eyes, and retort that always skirts the line between well read and downright condescending.

"Now, a typical LED headlamp puts out roughly five hundred to a thousand lumens. Your average smartphone can easily meet that wattage," Greg sputters.

He's panicking, even with Yadira being the only person in the room. His facts are correct, I assume, but as always, his voice is full of contradictions, stilted and frantic. To say that public speaking does not come naturally to Greg is an understatement. He is phenomenally smart—three of his essays have already been featured in small print magazines and one of them even won a statewide contest. But unfortunately for Greg, he is also the embodiment of the word "harmless": cursed with big innocent eyes and curls so bouncy you have to control yourself not to pull one to watch it boing.

"Multiplied by the average number of times people check their phones, with check ranging at less than two minutes of continuous usage, the cinematic viewing experience becomes a veritable, um, ordeal."

"All right, I'm calling it, Greggers," Yadira says, putting down her pencil and making a T with her hands. "You've officially lost me."

There are no big real-world topics at these debates. No gun control, no immigration. Nothing that could derail a YouTube comments section. We're high schoolers, after all. We tend to be given topics that audiences might discuss among themselves in the hallway after the competition.

Yay or nay: should J. K. Rowling have come down on Dumbledore's sexuality or leave the page to speak for itself? Double-dipping a chip at a party: ethical or monstrous? Rushing to the airport to declare your love: romantic or emotional coercion? I swear, they just go by TV sitcom premises. Where the rhetorical academic rigor comes in is in the soundness of the arguments, thoroughness of counterarguments, and creativity of delivery of the three-person teams.

"I was building up to my thesis," Greg says defensively, catching me out of the corner of his eye. "I'm highlighting the clear link between the luminosity of phone screens and the theater experience."

"Yes!" Yadira says, rolling her eyes. "And the strongest argument against this premise is obviously the disturbance of aggregate luminosity. That'll get us a round of applause."

Greg doesn't take notes well. And Yadira doesn't give them that well, to be completely honest. Not a fan of the soft touch, that one.

"She has a point there, Greg," I say, clearing my throat and stepping into the auditorium. "Hello, children."

"You're late, Haltiwanger!"

"Which does not negate her point, Greggers," I continue, because the best way to defuse Greg's annoying thing about punctuality is to ignore it until he forgets. "You don't want the judges to check their phones while you're actively making a point against using phones in theaters."

"Thank you!" Yadira exclaims. "But you *are* late, Henri."

"Aye, aye, captain!" I salute jokingly.

The worst thing about being on a debate team with Greg and Yadira is being on a three-person debate team with Greg and Yadira that's been on a winning streak all semester. The momentum is . . . suffocating.

"H!" comes a familiar voice as a silhouette appears in the doorway.

"Hey, Evie." I smile as Evie Hooper peeks her head into the room.

"I thought I heard your voice. What are you guys doing in here?" she asks, leaning against the door and smiling in that way she tends to do. Like the whole world is a photo shoot.

"Debate practice," I answer. "You?"

Yadira throws her hands up as though she's given up any idea that we'd get back on track for the remaining few minutes of practice.

"Film." She shrugs. "I was editing something in the lab."

Two short film competitions and an internship at Fox Studios last year. Evie may come off as a detached, white downtown girl who likes to knot her uniform blouse and defiantly wear her tie undone around her neck and her fingernails black, but she's by all accounts the next Greta Gerwig.

"So, I'm having a party Saturday," she says, stepping into the room as if no one else is around. "Will a wild H appear?"

The stereotype isn't all wrong in Evie's case: she does love to throw a rager here and there.

"Yeah, maybe I'll swing by."

"I'm not a maybe, H," she says coolly, flicking at my ear playfully. "In or out?"

"Evie!" Yadira yells out, finally out of patience. "What if we decapitate him and keep the head? All we need is his brain, but you can have his body."

Greg has been rendered silent by Evie's appearance. Girls like Evie Hooper are his Kryptonite.

Evie laughs before leaving. "See you Saturday, Halti!" she calls over one shoulder.

"Are you guys done yet?" comes another voice from the

hallway. Corinne this time. "You're seven minutes past your window!"

"Haltiwanger was late!" Yadira tries, although under the Corinne Troy glare even she tenses up like a soldier just hearing her drill sergeant storming the barracks. "And then his girlfriend walked in! We haven't even done a single round with him yet."

Let the record show that Evie Hooper is not my girlfriend.

I mean, she's not *not* my girlfriend. And she's definitely not just a friend who happens to be a girl either. It's, er, tricky.

"That is not my problem," Corinne says, arms crossed. "An unreliable teammate is something that should factor into your scheduling, not mine."

I roll my eyes at the drama. It's not that I don't feel bad about being late, but no NYC subway line is above the occasional fourteen-minute delay. And beyond that, Yadira has a personal driver who parks right in front of the school in a giant black SUV every day and a trust fund waiting for her twenty-fifth birthday, so I'm not going to lose any sleep for needing to squeeze in my dog walks after school and being late to practice.

Eventually, Yadira and Greg concede to wrapping things up, already knowing that there's no point in putting up a fight with Corinne Troy.

"Don't forget to collect the wreckage of your presence," Corinne adds, motioning to the bags of takeout in the corner while already scrubbing the dry-erase board of Greg's scribbles. Honestly, who talks like that? I swear there's a regime in this girl's future.

"Sorry, Corinne," Greg says as he scurries—actually scurries—to collect the greasy brown paper bags and bundle them into the recycling.

"What do you even do in here?" I wonder out loud, finding it all a little amusing. Her temper is so high with the stakes so objectively low: after-school debate practice in a school with dozens of empty classrooms right now.

"This room has the best projector. I rehearse my flash cards."

"You what?" Yadira asks, balling up napkins and hurriedly zipping her backpack.

"I'm a visual learner." Corinne sighs as though explaining it is a bothersome waste of vocal cords. "Seeing the material in a gigantic font makes it easier for me to retain it. Plus, it's proven that recalling material is easier when said material is studied in the same environment in which it will later be recalled. Mr. Shapiro's weekly quizzes are in this room."

"That's intense." I snort.

Corinne Troy's eyes are on me like a hawk's, which is intimidating, yes, but unfortunately for Troy, I don't tremble as easily as poor Greg.

"*Why* did you just say that?"

"Er, because it is?" I blink. "I mean, kudos to you. Shapiro's quizzes are brutal, but that is still—I don't know—an intense amount of studying."

The answer doesn't seem to lighten her mood.

"That word," she says through clenched teeth. "Why did you use that word?"

"Uh . . ."

"Intense," she snaps. "Why did you just call me that?"

"You're kidding, right?"

I hear Greg swallow a laugh, but he's already out the room, squeezing himself past Corinne, who really will not move an inch to be accommodating. Yadira follows suit, shaking her head.

I swear I don't pathologically enjoy riling people up—Greg and Yadira will get an apologetic text from me, and I will make it on time next week, come hell or high water. They'll forgive me. They always do. And I'll come through next time. I always do that too.

But torturing Corinne Troy? That might be the exception.

"See you around the Wyatt, Troy," I say, backtracking as slowly as possible and making a grand show of closing the door, enjoying every second of the glare that follows me out of the room. *Sooner than you think.*

For a while, I settled for being a mediocre dog walker. Paws were left cursorily wiped. I was a ninja: in and out. A ninja that could fit in more walks that way. A relatively well-remunerated ninja. Dad was furious with me when he learned this.

It's cost-effective, I told him. *I squeeze in more walks and make way more money!*

You don't do it for them, Henri, he said. *You do it for yourself, you hear? So you can look your clients in the eyes, shake their hands, and collect your payments proudly, knowing you're not hustling anyone.*

"Punctuality, Work Ethic, and Education" would be the words on the Haltiwanger family crest. And that's a very good thing for today's client who, I already know, won't tolerate anything less.

Mrs. Troy answers the ring to her apartment after one buzz, which lets me know that she has been expecting me.

<<Troy Residence?>>

"Yes, hi, Mrs. Troy. I'm here for the interview," I say loudly into the relic of the intercom system that still plagues the building.

<<Okay.>>

"It's Henri Haltiwanger, from Uptown Updogs."

<<Yes . . .>>

"Um, Jacques's boy from downstairs, ma'am. The super's son. We had an appointment at eight p.m.?"

<<Yes, I know. I'm just not sure why I'm conducting it through an intercom. Please come to the door.>>

And with that, communication cuts off. Yikes.

Mrs. Troy greets me at the top of the stairs of the building, outside her door on the top floor.

"Hello, Mrs. Troy." I Smile, extending a handshake that she politely returns. I clock her noticing the Uptown Updogs T-shirt.

She motions me inside. "And please call me Chantale. If you're going to be in our home, we might as well be on a first-name basis."

I occasionally help Dad with various two-person tasks

around the building, but I've never been in this unit before. A handful of floors apart, hers feels completely different, with higher ceilings, arched hallways, and framed art on nearly every wall. There are bold-colored paintings and Africana art in every other corner and the distinct smell of Earl Grey tea around the open kitchen. Something about the space feels both homey and staunchly academic. The living room end tables, I realize, are in fact stacks of neatly aligned hardcover books with a thin layer of dust. It's weird to imagine Corinne living here.

"To make a long story short, my daughter received this from her father." Chantale sighs as we come to the sight of a crate in which sits a tiny border collie mix, whose tail is batting so hard at the sight of a new person, it might take off flying inside its cage.

"Well, hi, little buddy!" I wave.

The puppy itself is pretty freaking adorable. I'm not a dog racist—all breeds are beautiful in their own right—but holy crap, is this one a cutie: black and white, with patches of marbled gray around its neck and chest.

"What's its name?"

"Palm Tree," Chantale says, rolling her eyes at the cutesiness. "I can assure you that the brown balls he produces do not smell like coconut."

"Hi, Palm Tree."

"As I said in the email," Chantale continues, immune to his charms—or mine, for that matter—"I'm often at my office this semester, and my daughter has a very rigorous academic

22

schedule, so we need some consistent help for the foreseeable fut—"

"You've got to be kidding me."

Corinne stands in the doorway, her overstuffed backpack slung over both shoulders. She gives the straps an angry tug. My smiling is sometimes genuine and involuntary.

"Hi again, Corinne." I grin. "Cute dog."

"Mom, no," she says, instantly dropping her bag to the floor, still in her FATE uniform and carrying the notebooks she had with her earlier. "This can't be the new dog walker."

"Don't be rude, Corinne," Chantale says. "They have a five-star online rating."

"Just request a different walker, then!"

"The headquarters assigns walkers based on zip codes," I quickly step in to say. "They probably wouldn't be able to find another walker that's closer than me. Same door address and all."

Corinne narrows her eyes at me. "Mom, I can find us a better dog walker in three swipes," she says, brandishing her phone.

"One that lives in the building? And has twenty-four/seven access to the super in case of emergencies, too, Corinne? This feels like a great arrangement."

"He's a high schooler," Corinne continues, undaunted. "Palm Tree deserves better than a wildly immature seventeen-year-old."

"Ageism," I whisper, which causes Chantale to smile, ever so slightly.

"Quiet, you," snaps Corinne.

"He's not wrong, Corinne. Are you advocating for discriminatory hiring practices right in my home?"

Chantale seems to be the sort of mother that enjoys rhetorical arguments over breakfast. I wonder if she was on a debate team during her high school heyday.

"I don't— Whatever. This is so boring," Corinne says, shaking her head. She walks past me, reaches into the crate, and scoops up Palm Tree with a free hand before grabbing her bag with the other. "I have application essays to finish."

She purposefully moves the eager dog's head out of the way as I move to pet him. Rude.

"Don't come into my room when you're here—that's trespassing—and there's legal precedent for prosecuting negligent dog walkers in the state of New York," she says before disappearing down one of the apartment's multiple hallways and slamming a door.

"She wants to be a lawyer," Chantale explains, sounding a little proud of her daughter at the moment. "Apologies for the tantrum. College anxiety."

"Oh, I'm familiar with it."

"Right, of course. Well, her father, my ex-husband, thought a puppy might lighten her up with college applications at the door. He's . . . a very dumb man."

I Smile and nod at the awkward conversation turn. It feels safer not to comment. Chantale retrieves a pair of silver keys from a drawer in the kitchen and slides them my way. Numbers are exchanged, security code granted, and she seems to approve of the app I use for dog walk payments. In two texts there's the first of a weekly sixty-dollar deposit into my checking account. After being on the receiving end of a handshake firmer than Dad's, my first walk is agreed to be this Friday. I'm to let myself in.

And so it begins.

THREE

According to his last text, my friend Ming is still nearby and about to make a colossal mistake. That blurry shot of hastily photographed probable contraband tells me exactly where to stop before heading home on Friday afternoon. We don't have any classes together this semester and are on wildly different schedules, but of all the FATE students, Ming Denison-Eilfing might be the only one I consider a bona fide bro, as opposed to simply a cohort.

DON'T BUY! I rapidly text as I quickstep out of FATE. I turn two street corners and up four blocks to the storefront I recognized in the photo. When I find Ming, ungloved hands against the glass, he's so mesmerized by the window display of sneakers that it's a wonder he's not getting pickpocketed right now.

"Dude!" I say, snapping my fingers in front of his hyperfocused eyes lovingly gazing at a pair of Nikes behind the glass.

"You realize these are total fakes, right?"

That seems to pull him out of his trance. He eyes me up and down like I might be a doppelganger sent to distract him from his righteous path of owning a new pair of sneakers this week.

"How do you know?" he eventually asks in a whine.

I stare at him blankly until he concedes his passive agreement with a long-suffering sigh.

"Fine, fine. Don't go Yoda on me."

If there is one thing that Ming knows that I know in this world, it's sneakers—and even he doesn't quite know the extent of it.

The walls of my room are covered in them. Well, sort of. Not actual sneakers. The walls are covered in labels I found, sketches of early drafts of limited editions from that student exhibit at the Parsons School for Fashion Design, a few printed designs from the web. I've never been able to afford many sneakers, but if you know where to look, you can find some pretty cool things around the city. Original. Designers passing through town are also always game to autograph an empty shoebox. If you flatten them into one another, the result is something that comes pretty close to a mural of sorts. I used to spend a considerable amount of time on the specialized blogs and message boards before little by little, college fare replaced most of those bookmarks on my phone.

"The SKU number is scratched out on the box, for one," I say after a closer look inside, which confirms what I'd assumed from the window.

"I always forget the SKU number," Ming eventually grumbles, falling out of love as quickly as he fell in.

"That's what they're counting on." Stock-Keeping Units. Eight characters that will tell you the full life span of a pair of shoes if you know how to read them. "Plus, check the tongue label. Those sizing labels that were designed in 2014 and these were 2012 releases. . . . Also, seventy-nine dollars? C'mon, dude. These retail for two forty online!"

"Stop," he dramatically whines, passing his hand over the rows and rows of shoeboxes like some southern dame grazing a lake during a boat ride. "You've already crushed my 'sneakerection' into dust."

"Ew. If something is too good to be true . . ." I shrug, drifting off because I'm sounding way too much like my dad right now. "How did you even know about this place?"

"What do you mean?"

"You shop in Harlem a lot?" I ask skeptically.

"I'm not a high-rise kid, Haltiwanger!" Ming says with a glare. We listlessly walk through the shop, taking in the new designs and colors of the season. Purple and green are going to be in this year. The streets of New York are going to look like the Joker's laundry basket.

"You're a little bit of a high-rise kid. One of the good ones but still."

I get a six-pack of athletic socks upside the head for the affront and can't help but laugh.

High-rise kids are what we call a certain specimen of children of Manhattan (and a few in Brooklyn too). They're that

28

breed of rich kids that rarely take the subway or even cabs because there's always a family car service waiting for them around the corner. FATE is full of them. Their buildings, expensive multi-floor high-rises, have apartments as big as any suburban home, with gyms, entertainment centers, and roof-top pools. Ming technically qualifies, living in Hudson Yards, overlooking the Hudson River with a dental surgeon as a father and a regular retired surgeon as a mother. Ming also hates being referred to as such.

He is, in truth, a high-rise kid.

"Don't pout," I say, throwing a bundle of socks at him.

"So, what are you doing tonight? Maybe hang at your place?" Ming asks.

Despite my best efforts, I can feel myself tense up. I've got-ten used to planning FATE study groups, social gatherings, and cram sessions before finals anywhere around the city but at my place, but Ming will occasionally bring it up so casually like this that it will slip right past my radar. No one from FATE has ever seen or been to my place. Not since the days of Daniel Halkias.

Daniel was probably my first friend at FATE freshman year. Halkias, Haltiwanger: that nominal connection found us stand-ing in line with each other at almost every gathering in which students were alphabetized by last names.

Pokémon, Dragon Ball Z and Super, and Fortnite: the kid was literate in every corner that filled my brain back then, and we pretty much spoke the same language right off the bat. We might have been friends all through high school if a.) Daniel and his family hadn't moved away last year, and b.) I hadn't made the mistake of inviting him over.

I begged my mom to make all the good Haitian food. But I still remember the specific way Daniel's face fell when he stepped through our door. It wasn't even a sad-face emoji; it was a brand-new release not yet distributed across all operating systems. Confused with a touch of frightened and just a hint of "Get me out of here, now!" coloring.

Something about the memory must be playing out on my face because Ming starts laughing that knowing laugh of his. "Or not."

"I've got pups to walk tonight. See you tomorrow, dude." I wave off on my way out of the store. "Those black ones are also fake, by the way! Don't you dare buy them."

"You should be an app!"

Mom cooked tonight: chicken from the Belgian corner store (recooked because, as Mom says of all white cooking, "heat is not a spice") and djon-djon rice that's been simmering in the Crock-Pot all day. She always makes sure to cook something delicious on nights before she leaves.

I decide it's as good a time as any to tell them about Palm Tree and the Troys. I normally avoid updating them on my dog routes or Uptown Updogs in general because Dad would make me shutter the site right away if he learned that I was lying to people—and probably make me reimburse every client—but the fact that Corinne goes to FATE and the Troys are our neighbors means that I have to tell my folks.

"Chantale Troy is a demanding woman," Dad muses.

"Another dog?" Ma asks, concerned. "That's a lot of commitments, Henri. Are you sure you're not overextending yourself? You're not doing it for the family pot, are you? Because we can manage without."

No, we can't. A good chunk of Haltiwanger money comes with a "we" pronoun. It's all household money. Three people, one set of bills.

I've been chipping in since I was fourteen and did grocery runs for some of the elderly tenants upstairs. I throw in a couple of hundreds from my walks and Ma and Dad aren't well off enough to ignore them. Part of it is because New York City is, simply put, hella expensive. The fact that Mom quit her job to become a firefighter trainee certainly contributed to the collective tightening of the belt, and I know she feels guilty about it.

"I promise you it's not. I need the money too, Ma," I say between bites of chicken so spicy you need to blink the tears away when you hit a pepper. "I need to pay back the credit cards on all those college applications, remember?"

Ma nods reluctantly. I applied to nine colleges total, each ranging from sixty to ninety-five dollars in application fees.

"Doesn't the daughter go to your school?"

"Corinne," Ma chastises.

That's how Dad likes to talk about the tenants and their broods. The daughter, the son, the other son. That cousin that stays with them. It's not that he can't remember the names, considering he keeps track of which light bulbs are used in which kitchen renovations. To their faces, he acknowledges the first names (especially the "call me Bill" types who love to give

31

fist bumps to the super and in return bestow us pretty good Christmas bonuses), but as soon as we're home, they revert to their nominal titles.

Ma told me his logic once. *It keeps things simple. That's how your dad likes the world. Simple.* She'd then laughed at the face I made. *Imagine dating him!*

"Are you friends with her?" Dad asks. "I can never keep track of all your friends."

"We run in different circles."

The truth is it had taken weeks last year for me to realize that the new resident of the top-floor unit was that intense girl from school.

"You know, Chantale Troy needed a contractor to do some work for her when she first moved in. I tried to get Lionel that job," Dad says to no one in particular, chewing more angrily at the mere name. "Another job he was too good for."

Ma and I share a look. It's not every dinner that that name comes up.

Lionel Haltiwanger—or Lion, as he prefers to go by—is Dad's younger brother. He lived with us for a little while when he first came here to the States, orphaned and on a student visa. It didn't take long for us to realize he and Dad are very different people. To Dad, Lionel Haltiwanger would be the eager-to-learn little brother he would shepherd toward a better life in America. In actuality, Lion was a smirking and charming young guy with aspirations of a music-producing career. He'd never seen a corner he didn't think he could cut and loved to

32

talk about the lavish parties he'd DJed for back in Haiti.

Brothers, Ma used to say when dinners got too tense and Dad looked like he didn't recognize the young man—really, only a few years past being a teenager himself—he'd brought into his house. *He's getting the hang of America*, Ma would say. *Give it some time, Jacques*. That was until Dad found little bags of not-oregano and pills of not-aspirin in Lion's corner of the room we shared with a curtain in the middle. That was five months ago, and I don't think he's even seen Dad.

Ma clears her throat and turns to me. "I can't believe you have your Columbia interview tomorrow."

"It's going to be great." Dad smiles because nothing clears the dark Lionel cloud from his face faster than planning for Columbia University.

That's why I really need to lock down this interview. I'm an A-minus student with SAT scores in the 92nd percentile after two tries—great, not exceptional—and nothing less than a glowing "O Captain! My Captain!" interview recommendation is going to get me through Columbia's gates. The informal interview with an alum had already required Mr. Vu to call in a personal favor on my behalf.

"Just be yourself, all right?" Ma says, patting my arm lovingly.

I Smile, and feel guilty. Ma deserves only the real thing.

Unfortunately there's no market value in that.

FOUR

"Diaspora" was the first SAT word I remember learning last year. "A scattered population whose origin lies in a different geographic locale." For Haitians—the Haltiwanger clan, specifically—it means to split apart and put yourself together someplace else. I'm from a branch of a tree that, at some point, gave way to five siblings. All smart, all filled with potential, all hungry for a better life elsewhere.

Dad chose New York. One sister chose Switzerland because they also spoke French there. Another sister followed her husband to New Port Richey, Florida, with a son my age that I've never met. His other brother was apparently in St. Bart's, working as a caterer, and did not keep in touch. Strange relatives, unknown cousins, and faces you don't recognize in photo albums. That's the longer, Haltiwanger-specific essay-form definition of diaspora.

The story of Jacques Haltiwanger, Haitian, forty-eight, is

in many ways the story of the Wyatt building, 86th Street and West End Avenue, which, in truth, is the only home I remember. Dad has tied together the story of our family to that of the building into such a knot that, by now, it's impossible to untie the two. I've heard every permutation of it.

The Happy one that started in 1994.

"We'd moved the Christmas before. It was my very first job in America. It was just an evening desk job. Back then, Mrs. Landau, RIP, liked the fact that I could speak French. In her mind, it added sophistication to the building that the janitor would be international. We lived in the Bronx and commuted in before this unit opened up and was offered to us."

The Sad one.

"Your mother wanted us to stay in New York City because she didn't want you to be the only little Black boy in some small town. And she wanted you to see snow. What was the point of coming to this country if you didn't show your kid snow?"

The Inspiring one.

"This is the land of Doctor King, Maya Angelou, Michelle, and Beyoncé. This is the only place in the world where those stories can happen. All those town cars passing through? They're as likely to have a Black or brown person in them these days. Back in Haiti, for me and your mother, that wasn't the case."

So here I am, on the afternoon of my Columbia interview, the only college interview that matters, deciding which family story to tell. Of all the applications I sent out this past month—all the essays, recommendation letters, SAT scores,

AP test results, and that little vial of your soul all top colleges essentially ask for—Columbia University was the only one I submitted with shaky hands, shut eyes, and Dad's hand on my shoulder. The truth is, I couldn't tell you what the school mascots of Duke, NYU, Northwestern, McGill, Brown, University of Pennsylvania, Oberlin, and City College—my backups—even look like. For me and my dad, Columbia has always been the dream—the beacon of possibility, the ticket to a better life for me and my family.

I get off at 116th Street, which opens right onto the University, and cut through the orange bricked college walk, looking around, soaking it in. I know the layout by heart already. The dorms are on the south side, surrounding Butler Library, the massive building in and out of which students in light blue hoodies are constantly pouring. Some look tired, others are buzzing with energy, but all are barreling forward with purpose.

The interview is scheduled for three thirty at the Hungarian Pastry Shop, a staple of the college community with low orange lighting. I order an overpriced cup of coffee and sit by the entrance, ten minutes ahead of our scheduled meeting time, surrounded by bearded graduate students on laptops wrapped in political stickers. Nothing about my Smile is disingenuous today. I start to read a magazine with an in-depth interview with one of Nike's oldest designers, but change my mind and quickly switch to the copy of *Catcher in the Rye* borrowed from the library, which makes for better optics, all things considered.

"Henri?"

A freckled, light-skinned Black woman with a streak of white hair tumbles into the coffee shop, bumping into the back of someone's chair on her way in and sending packs of artificial sweetener flying off the table before she apologizes profusely.

"Donielle?" I confirm, moving to help her pick them up.

"They're renaming a hurricane as we speak," she jokes.

She orders a tea, and I pick up the stirrers that get knocked by her large bag when she turns around. So, this is what a National Endowment for the Arts winner, MacArthur Fellow, and *Forbes* Top 30 under 30 playwright looks like. She's decidedly a lot less intimidating when not being handed an award in a Dior gown to uproarious applause.

After I thank her profusely for taking the time, she settles in and unwraps herself, layer after bright layer. First a scarf, followed by a coat, then a bubble jacket, then a wrap. Her arms are jiggling with bracelets, some metallic, some in painted wooden beads.

"I hope you weren't waiting long, Henri. I'm workshopping a play at the new Highline Theater House and rehearsal ran over," she says, and then snorts, laughing at her statement. "Well, ran dramatic, I should say! Two of my actors are married and came in with such bad energy this morning. I didn't know they were together when I cast them, believe you me— and short story long, the whole thing turned into group therapy for two hours. They've been having problems. Of the bedroom kind." Her voice turns into a conspiratorial whisper on that last statement, and she mimics zipping her lips shut.

"Oh, um." I didn't have a prepared segue for that vaguely inappropriate soliloquy. "Did you manage to get back on track?"

"Nope! We're well behind schedule now," she says, and then laughs again. "You're Haitian, right? I was in Port-au-Prince ten years ago for research on a project."

"My parents are Haitian immigrants, but I was born here. I think that makes me first generation, or is it second? I can never tell."

Another laugh. This one was predicted. "You're the first gen. Me too. Now take a breath."

I make a show of exhaling. She laughs again.

Truth be told, I'm nowhere as nervous as I'm making myself out to be. But performing a bit of anxiety can be an endearing quality to some adults. If nobody likes to be fawned over, a lot of people respond positively to having created butterflies in someone else's stomach. They want to calm you down.

Donielle Kempf tells me about her life growing up in Jersey City. Her multiple siblings, attending public school and then community college, graduating in six years instead of four since she had a child and needed to work the entire time. "And then I applied to the Columbia Master of Fine Arts program. It was the only place for me—I knew it in my *bones*. I could taste it. I refreshed my in-box every ten minutes for two months."

Now it's my turn to laugh. "I can relate."

She gives a wistful sigh. "Then it turned out that was only thing number five of a million more things I would go on to also really, *really* want with every fiber of my body. You never stop wanting, y'know? That's the human condition."

The Haltiwanger Hunger, indeed.

"But enough about me!" she says, throwing a glance at her phone, placed on the table, clock showing. "Henri Haltiwanger. Bright, Haitian American, child of immigrants, what else?"

I Smile.

And we're off. I tell her about the debate team, our almost-victory last year, about the opportunity of attending a school like FATE, which could have easily gone to a thousand other kids. I tell her about how I begged Mr. Vu, my academic adviser, to set up a meeting with her based on her profile because her play about the Diaspora was so incredible. That part isn't BS.

"I loved your play," I tell her emphatically. "My parents moved here from Haiti in their twenties. Their extended families are around the world now. The only relative I know is my dad's brother Lion. But they're not close."

Her eyes are on me with unprecedented intensity, as if the loud hurricane playwright of the past twenty minutes had merely been a role and now we're on to the real thing.

"So. Why Columbia?"

I had prepared for this part. I wrote an application essay answering this exact question, for Pete's sake. I go through all the reasons I had thought up in the numerous essay drafts. Columbia's Core Curriculum, which touches on Art History and Music Humanities, making sure that all the students, regardless of their majors, share some unified body of knowledge.

I list the interesting majors, the teachers, the fact that the college doesn't float above the city but is a part of it with an active alumni network of those who graduate and then stay put in New York, enriching the community.

And when I'm done, after pausing at the right parts, passionately rambling at others, and meaning it all too, Donielle Kempf is still looking at me, only now it's with a slight, almost confused frown.

That was . . . not the response I was expecting.

"Well," she eventually says. "That's all great, Henri. But . . . anyone could have told me that. Why Columbia—for *you*?"

What the fresh hell? I wasn't expecting her to be on her feet clapping—okay fine, maybe a little bit—but . . . this?

"Is there anything else I should know?" She leans forward like she's expecting something specific and . . .

I let out a nervous chuckle.

"I'm a Scorpio on the cusp of Sagittarius?"

She returns my awkward laugh before glancing at her phone again. Dumb, Henri, real dumb. My brain feels like a hallway with a bunch of locked doors I keep trying to rattle open, but nothing reveals itself.

"Seriously, Henri—why Columbia? You can get a great education in a hundred other places. Why *this* school?"

My mind spins through a hundred answers, but nothing sounds right. Because my dad wants it more than anything? Because I hear his voice lilt when he says Columbia? Because I saw his face that day they asked us to leave, and I'll never forget it?

"I . . . ," I stammer. I take a breath. "When I was younger, five or six, Dad and Ma would sometimes take me here in the summer. My mom would read a book under a tree or on the

Lowe steps while I fired up the old Game Boy 3DS. I'm not sure what Dad did. I think he just enjoyed watching the people. We couldn't go on vacation, but this campus was a little green oasis right here in the city with way fewer tourist crowds than in Central Park."

"That's beautiful," Donielle tells me.

I take a breath. Okay. Getting back on track. "It was. But it stopped when campus security started to crack down on 'urban loitering.' They didn't come out and say it, but the message was clear—we didn't belong here."

There's another SAT word: loiter. *To stand or wait around idly without apparent purpose*. Well, that encounter was all it took to give me a purpose.

"Going to Columbia has meant everything since then. My dad's a super in Manhattan, and I end up at Columbia. It's his American Dream."

The corners of her lips tick up. She narrows her eyes just the tiniest bit.

"'It's his American Dream,'" she repeats.

"I mean, that's *the* American Dream, right?"

"I'm just noting your phrase, Henri." Donielle readjusts one of her bright scarves.

"Okay." What is happening here? I just poured my soul out on the Hungarian Pastry Shop's sticky-ass floor, and she's parsing words?

"It's a beautiful dream. It really is. I'm just asking, is it *yours*? What's *your* dream, Henri?"

My mind cycles through a thousand answers. *I don't have a lot of free time; school keeps us so busy! I run my own business, not that I can tell you about that, since it's a total fraud! I draw sneaker designs in my notebook when no one's watching?* As if. "Going to Columbia is my dream."

Donielle looks at me, and if I'm not mistaken, she looks a little sad. "It's getting late. I don't want to keep you. I'm sure you have a busy day ahead of you."

"Oh . . . Um, okay."

Outside the Hungarian Pastry Shop, Donielle shakes my hand. "It was really nice meeting you, Henri. You'll end up exactly where you're supposed to be," she says. "Things have a way of working out."

I nod and start to walk away, but she opens her mouth, closes it, and then opens it again. Please, please, please say something else, I silently will her.

"You know, Columbia is big and important and lovely. . . ." She waves her hand a bit in the air as if looking for the right word. "But it's also just thirty-six acres. That's all the space it occupies, in the grand scheme of things. Thirty-six acres in the world. Do you understand what I'm trying to say?"

"I think I do." I Smile.

I emphatically do *not* know.

"Thank you for your time, Donielle. I appreciate it."

With that, she turns to walk away, leaving me to wonder only one thing.

What the hell just happened?

* * *

42

I ride the train home, barely paying attention to the podcast Ming recommended.

You'll end up exactly where you're supposed to be.

She might as well have told me that I smell like Trump University's annex. This was bad. An upside of being on the debate team is that you develop self-awareness of your oratory performance. The judges' faces might remain stoic, but you can generally tell when a point lands or when the audience is collectively shaking its head in disagreement. Donielle might have been polite, but this was, by all accounts, really bad.

Where did I go wrong?

I need to go online and check the college boards for exactly how much sway an underwhelming interview has on your overall profile.

I need to send an email to Mr. Vu and beg him to find me another local Columbia alum to interview with as soon as possible.

I need Dad to be fully passed out in front of some international soccer game because I don't think I can handle a "So, how did it go?" conversation right now.

I exit the subway and walk to the Wyatt. I've been to enough nice buildings around the city to know that our lobby is fairly unimpressive by comparison. There are no fluffy couches, artificial fireplaces, or impossibly high ceilings like in Ming's building. The Wyatt's ground floor is clean, well lit, with the left wall comprised of three rows of brass mailboxes that Dad polishes once a month.

"Jeez," I hear through my headphones as I approach our

doorstep. "What happened to you?"

Of course Corinne Troy is sitting outside my apartment. As if this day couldn't get any worse.

"I've never seen you not smiling," she notes, closing her binder and capping a yellow highlighter.

"What are you doing here?"

"We need to talk," Corinne says, gathering her study materials.

"Evening dog walks are extra." I sigh, cracking my back. "Give me ten minutes, and I'll be up to—"

"Palm Tree has been walked, peed out, fed, and is in a pillow fort on my bed right now, thank you very much." She next pulls out a phone and swiftly begins to tap and swipe.

"You really shouldn't let him sleep on your bed. It's cute when they're puppies, but that's going to be seventy pounds of conditioned behavior you'll have to undo sooner than you think."

"Noted," she says before turning her phone to face my way. It's the Uptown Updogs home page on her mobile browser.

"That's the Uptown Updogs website," I state as blankly as possible.

"No it's not," she retorts. "That's *your* website."

I freeze and look to my door, a foot away. I can hear Dad's soccer game on the TV.

"As I said . . . ," she repeats in a lower tone before heading toward the lobby, expecting me to follow. "We need to talk."

Oh, eff my freaking life to hell right now.

FIVE

oblige and follow Corinne out of the building quietly. We begin to walk in complete silence. She's either waiting for a confession on my part or, more likely, she's read some book like *The Art of War* and learned speaking first is a sign of submission. An amateur.

The walk takes us down the street and onto Broadway, bustling with passersby, and back up on West End Avenue. It is, for all intents and purposes, a dog-less dog walk. Although considering I'm tired, confused, and kind of really need to pee, I might as well be a Yorkshire terrier right now.

We return to the front of the Wyatt. I look up at the building and back to her again, raising both eyebrows.

"I know there's no Uptown Updogs!" she finally says just as we're about to begin circling the building again. She's visibly exasperated at having spoken first. "Or rather I know there's no central office in Tribeca—it's a sneaker store, according to

Google Maps. No dozens of well-trained employees either. As far as I can tell, it's just you."

I quirk an eyebrow. I need to know all that she knows before actually commenting.

"And don't try to gaslight me into 'crazy talk' either," she preempts. "I looked up the domain, which is registered under your name. That's just sloppy, frankly."

Okay, so . . . everything. She knows everything. Fantastic.

"So what?" I finally say, sighing and sitting myself down on the building stoop. "Your mom sent you to fire me and reimburse the down payment, is that it?"

The key to being a decent liar is occasionally knowing when it's best to come out clean and tell the truth. Corinne Troy looks at me with crossed arms, clearly enjoying the moment.

"No," she eventually says. "I mean, I considered it. I don't want a weird con-artist seventeen-year-old taking care of Palm Tree, but your online reviews themselves are real, as far as I can tell, and you do have dog-walking experience, fraudulent as it may be. Plus, there's no arguing the proximity."

She speaks in the same succinct intonation as her mother but with far less polish. As though she's only hearing the words for the first time as she's saying them. Must be nice to live life this unfiltered.

"Well, then, what do you want?" I finally ask.

She bats her eyelashes. "Are you not enjoying the neighborly chitchat?"

"This isn't chitchat," I state plainly. "You clearly want

46

something, so can we get to that part?"

"What happened to all that Halti charm you're always oozing around the school?"

"I had a long day, Troy." I tuck my arms into my pits and tilt my chin, ready to return to complete silence.

"That word you called me at school this week," she finally says. "Intense. Why did you choose that word?"

I can't help but let out a spastic yell and flail out my arms. Are you kidding me? *That's* my great sin here? That's what got Dora the Nosy-Ass Little Explorer all up in my business? "This again? Why are you so obsessed with two syllables?!"

Corinne takes out a piece of paper from her bag, folded into a perfect square. She adjusts her glasses once, and then another time, and then finally begins to read out loud.

"'Corinne is a gifted student and will make an excellent academic addition to the class of 2025. Corinne is smart, meticulous, and outspoken, and while her level of intensity may not serve her socially, her commitment to her academic pursuits is undeniable.'"

"What was that?" I ask.

"The recommendation letter I got from Mrs. Carroll."

Dang. I made it out of her two history classes with an A– and a B+ respectively, but even I know that Mrs. Carroll is not to be trusted. She's the kind of teacher who pulls quiz questions from optional readings and insists you print out papers in Arial 12. Not Times New Roman, not Calibri. Arial. Failure to comply will result in an entire half grade being docked on papers. The woman would excel in a dystopian world where teachers can electrocute students.

"It's not that bad of a recommendation," I lie.

"Are you kidding me? This is for Princeton! She might as well have put a red 'Do not admit: Social Pariah' sticker on my forehead."

"I'm sorry," I say after a beat. And I am, actually. Donielle's *You'll end up exactly where you're supposed to be* is burning a fresh hole in my lower cortex. Corinne seems taken aback by the apology, but I just shrug. "I get it," I tell her.

She looks at the letter again, shaking her head. "She looked me right in the eyes and said she'd be happy to write the recommendation. 'Happy to do it': those were her words."

I raise an eyebrow. "Really?"

"I mean, first she 'strongly suggested' that I consider taking a year off and traveling like some Instagram influencer or child of screenwriters, but I insisted. Maybe the fourth handwritten request was too much, but still . . . this is just mean." Corinne sits down a few steps higher than me on the stoop.

"I had a hunch too," she adds. "That's why I requested an extra sealed copy for a college I wasn't applying to, just to see what she wrote about me."

That's *brilliant*, I think but don't say. For a moment there Corinne Troy, of all people, looks truly lost. As if the letter simply doesn't compute.

"It's exhausting," I offer. "I thought the whole point of a school like FATE was to spit us into Ivy Leagues and corner offices."

48

Corinne doesn't say anything, still staring at the letter. I feel a thoroughly weird compulsion to comfort her.

"A single letter can't keep you out of college," I continue. "You know that, right? You're always on the Dean's List at school."

"But colleges like Princeton don't have to make concessions, Haltiwanger!" she snaps. "They get thirty-five thousand applicants from all over the world, every year! They'll pick some other Dean's Listed applicant with my exact grades and extracurriculars and ethnicity, even, but who also happens to be breezy, with, like, fun braids and poetry blogs. Some Black girl magic social media influencer with viral makeup tutorials will elbow me right out with a stain like this on my file."

It's dramatic, but she's also not wrong. It's established knowledge that all the effort you put into being the perfect college applicant should in turn also look effortless. The great catch-22 of Higher Education. *Be perfect and make it look easy.* Meanwhile, Corinne Troy is nothing if not intensity and effort. She folds the paper again, rubbing two fingers over every side as she does.

"Like, am I that intense?" she asks, glancing at me. "What do the other kids, y'know, say about me?"

Of course Corinne Troy does not have the largest audience of friendly acquaintances to poll on the matter. Because she is, in a word, *intense.*

"They think . . . you're fine."

"They think I'm terrifying," she says, unconvinced.

"Fine, they think you're the Loch Ness monster without the gift-shop plush toys."

Her eyes widen, and she actually shoves me. "You're such a jerk, Haltiwanger!"

"Well, look at the evidence!" I say, recovering with a chuckle and getting to my feet. "Someone refers to your studying behavior as 'intense' and your reaction a few days later is to wait outside his door with extensive blackmail material. Not exactly proving the assessment wrong."

She puts the letter away, tucking it into one of her binders. "I know. That's why I'm here. I have bad social instincts. I need . . ." She visibly swallows bile. "I'm aware that I need help. Socializing. That's where you come in."

"Where I come in?"

"Oh, don't make me say it, Haltiwanger. I need help. . . ." She rolls her eyes and then whispers the rest. "Getting . . . cooler. More chill."

"You want me to *She's All That* you?" I manage to say, hiding the smile I feel creeping on my lips.

"What's that?"

"Oh, my God," I groan. "Watch more movies. Maybe that's been the missing ingredient all along."

"Oblique pop culture references do seem to be a cornerstone of social language, actually," Corinne says, as if making a mental note.

"A.) I was kidding; b.) I'm a guy," I point out. "I don't know how to make a girl popular."

"I've mapped it out. You're the perfect gatekeeper of the senior-class social scene. You get invited to every big gathering.

You're seemingly comfortable with every subgroup. You're tagged in all the big group photos, despite not having an online presence to speak of. Everyone likes you. Or at least thinks you're likable. That's what I need!"

"You think Mrs. Carroll will see you with a group of pals in the hallway and rescind the letter she already sent to Princeton?"

"Maybe! Maybe seeing me with more kids will cause her to change her mind. It would at least let me make a better case for myself instead of storming her office and calling her a bitter, incompetent hack, which was my first impulse."

"Doubtful," I say. Then again, I really shouldn't talk, considering I'm going to raise every Hail Mary out there to get a new Columbia interview.

"I know, but I want to prove her wrong. I'm not . . ." She pauses. "I'm not what she sees me as, okay? I don't want to end high school with everyone thinking that about me."

"Just be yourself," I say. "And even if you don't end up at Princeton, I'm sure you'll end up exactly where you need to be."

The words taste hollow, but Donielle Kempf's reheated casserole of nonsense might be just the thing to get me out of this. Unfortunately, Corinne only rolls her eyes in response.

"I guess I'm not making myself clear here," she says, standing up with pursed lips. "I will blow up your little operation if you don't help me. This is New York City: people are psychotic about their dogs. Plus, nobody likes to be hustled by a private-school punk."

"I'm sorry. Are you *blackmailing* me?"

"It's your choice," she says, and we both understand she's not bluffing.

"Fine, fine, fine! Look, Evie Hooper is having a party this weekend," I concede, hands on my hips, trying to work out the speediest fix to this. "I will introduce you to some folks there. I will . . . fluff your social self, to be as graphic as possible."

Corinne smiles, looking satisfied. "Do you really think that's all it will take? Walking into a room with your thumb of approval?"

"Yup," I say with a firm nod. I walk back into the building first, and she follows suit. Our lobby isn't exactly a space for tête-à-têtes or advanced blackmail. "Take it or leave it," I say, with crossed arms, casually leaning against the mailboxes for full effect.

"*Fine*," she gives. "It's a start."

"Deal," I tell her with a nod, and wonder if this day could possibly get any worse. "See you tomorrow."

SIX

7:02 PM

Ming: **Corinne Troy? You invited Corinne Troy?**

She invited herself! I text back. **Long story. I'll fill you in.**

"Henri, for God's sake!" I hear Dad whine, actually *whine*, from the other side of the bathroom door.

"I'll be one minute!"

"You said that twenty minutes ago! It's an emergency."

"Oh, God, Dad, just come poop already. I'm doing my hair," I say, brushing against the grain with one hand and applying conditioner to the top curls with the other. "It's a delicate process. I can't just stop. Do your business, I don't care," I say, trying to open the door with my elbow to let him in.

He slams it shut right away. "N-no," he says, although he sounds like he's considering it. "Just hurry up, all right?" I hear him grumbling as he makes his way to the kitchen, pacing up and down.

"I'll be home by one a.m., tops," I say through the door, returning to the delicate operation happening around my edges. One wrong step and my curls end up looking like Sideshow Bob on uppers.

"Two a.m. is fine." Dad sighs through the door.

"What? Why?" I ask.

"You crossed a big threshold this week," Dad says through the door. "You deserve a night out."

"R-right. Thanks."

Well, shit. Look, I didn't lie, all right. Not technically. Donielle Kempf *was* a character, and I did technically elicit a lot of laughter throughout the exchange. He wanted a word-for-word recounting, and it's amazing how different *You'll end up exactly where you're supposed to be* can sound when you're telling your dad you're as good as in. Besides, I'm going to fix this—I'll talk to Vu and get another interview, and my dad will never know the difference.

"I'd better still have some hot water in there," he adds in that tone he uses to put his foot down and that never sees any actual dropping of said foot. Dad's just a big softie at heart.

Sorry, Dad: the hot water is a distant memory for another half hour.

Maybe Ma is not entirely wrong when it comes to my bathroom grooming habits—although, I take exception with the word "preening"—but there's nothing wrong with that. It's a necessity when you attend a school like FATE and occasionally frequent parties thrown by the likes of Evie Hooper.

Evie's parents live in Tribeca, and her version of "a small hangout" is usually a full-blown, unsupervised bacchanalia. Fashion *matters* there. Her friends use these parties as occasions to cut loose and break away from the purple-and-gray uniforms. Everything is branded and shiny and aims to make the impression that our FATE uniforms can't. Having money is not noticed at these parties, but *not* having it is.

After a scalding shower, I opt for a simple white T-shirt—label-less but by choice—and my big guns: my turquoise Jordans. A limited edition that somehow made it from Switzerland, where they were released, to a serendipitous fire sale at an East Village sportswear store going out of business last summer. Ming offered me three hundred dollars and his two firstborns to try to pry them from me. I only occasionally wear them to keep the magic alive, even though I would have them on all the time if I could.

I open the bathroom door.

"Finally!" My dad throws up his hands.

"Worth every second." I grin at my reflection. "Bye, Dad! Enjoy your throne!"

"Home by two a.m., Henri!" Dad growls. "I mean it!"

"Love you too, Dad!"

Ming is already waiting for me at the Chambers Street subway station, eyes on his phone and wearing a plaid shirt with rolled-up sleeves and a popped collar. He is one of those kids who just effortlessly has a closet of branded items gifted to him by his parents that he can reach into and pick from when he gets spontaneously invited to one of these.

"Hello, my pretties." He grins, greeting my shoes by actually bending down to speak softly to them as if they were babies in a stroller. "I haven't seen you in a while."

"Stop talking to my feet, dude," I say, motioning for Ming to bend his head while I un-pop his collar.

"Too much?" he asks, still letting himself be fixed.

"Entirely. We're not time-traveling to 2008."

Ming wasn't explicitly invited, but he and I come in a pair; Evie knows that by now.

"So, Corinne Troy," he asks. "How did that happen?"

I shake my head and fill Ming in on the whole blackmail saga while we trek it to Evie's building. He might not have access to our apartment, but Ming has known about Uptown Updogs since Day One. It just seemed strange not to loop him in on it. And as a good friend, he pauses only twice to catch his breath from laughing.

Corinne is waiting for us outside Evie's address.

"You came."

She sounds genuinely surprised—like someone experienced with being ditched. Her hair has been bundled up for the evening—good edges—and she's wearing an outfit that looks cool but decidedly un–Corinne Troy, thanks to the sequined shirt under her cardigan and the colorful bracelets she's wearing tonight that feel borrowed from Chantale's closet.

"Blackmail is a great way of ensuring that." I Smile.

A middle finger is the last bit of attention Corinne pays me before turning to Ming. "Is he coming with us?"

"Ming, Corinne. Corinne, Ming."

Ming smiles and waves.

"This wasn't part of the deal," Corinne protests.

"Ming was already coming with me," I say. "Besides, I'm not leaving my best friend behind to train you in the lost art of socializing. Ming's not optional."

Okay, that might be a little rude, but the ruder I am, the less likely she'll want to do this again. I'm not doing this every weekend.

"Whatever." She glares with crossed arms, throwing another look at Ming. "Just please don't get in the way."

"I reserve the right to get in the way." He smiles back, easy and casual, because that's more or less Ming's only speed. "I like your outfit, by the way."

"I . . . Thank you?" She stares like she's not sure if it's a real compliment or not, but with Ming, it's always a real compliment. The guy is walking Earnestness.

The doorman lets us up, and clearly, we're not the first teens he's seeing tonight. Otherwise, two Black kids and an Asian kid in a building like this might have given him more pause than the quick glance up from his phone we're granted before being nodded toward the elevator lobby.

Evie Hooper lives in the penthouse, naturally. From what I can gather, her dad didn't invent a very famous music-recognizing app, but he does have a sizable chunk of shares in the company. I've been here only twice before and am always a bit in awe of how Evie's hallway is the literal size of our entire apartment, with a stylish, polished concrete floor. An odorless smoke is rising from somewhere inside the home, which is pulsating with music the moment we walk in. Who has a smoke machine on hand?

This isn't the sort of party where people take photos of where everything goes to put it back in place before the parents get home. Evie's parents are aware of their daughter's thriving social life and support it fully, down to her dad's alcohol cabinets—literal cabinets, kept unlocked and replenished every time they're emptied. I think their parenting style amounts to "better under our nine-million-dollar roof than outside of it."

"We have a Haltiwanger!" Evie shouts, jumping out of nowhere and kissing me hello on the cheek. She smells like really nice perfume and her brown hair has been meticulously made messy for the night.

"I promised I'd show!" I laugh, feeling Corinne and Ming watching us.

"Please," Evie says with a smirk. "You said you'd try to come. No one has ever actually gotten a promise of attendance from Henri Haltiwanger."

"Hi." I Smile. This one says, "I'm totally confident in your multimillion-dollar palace in the sky."

"Hi," she answers, still hanging on my shoulder.

"They have great sexual chemistry," I hear Corinne comment to Ming in a whisper that carries. If that didn't catch

Evie's attention, Ming's laugh certainly does.

"Oh! Corinne. Oh, my God, hi!" she says, blinking away the confusion as soon as it begins to set in.

"Henri invited me," Corinne says, sounding uncertain for the first time. "Is that, um, okay?"

"Of course, sweetie! I'm so glad you're here!" Evie smiles, moving on to effortlessly kiss Ming and Corinne on both cheeks. Four kisses in the blink of an eye.

It's amazing sometimes to watch Evie operate. I'm decent with people when I need to be, but Evie is a genuine people person. If you ask her, she'll give you the party line that she's "a mess," but everything she does looks like she's not even trying. She's just naturally likable and flirty and fun. It's easy for kids who are less popular, or less rich, to dislike the rich white girl from afar, but up close, it's clear that anyone who actively dislikes Evie probably also hates birthday cake and underwear fresh out of the dryer.

"Find me later, okay?" Evie says as she is waving to someone across the crowded space. And with that, she disappears into a trio of shrieking girls with beers in hand.

I turn back to Corinne after making sure Evie is out of hearing range.

"Okay, quick note, right off the bat," I say. "Can you not comment on my sexual chemistry with people? That'd be downright nifty."

"Well, it was borderline inappropriate," she instead comments, causing Ming to laugh again.

"What happened to you not having time to date?" Corinne follows up, and really, who is this feral person the gods have cursed me with?

"They don't date," Ming chimes in, because suddenly he and Corinne are best friends.

"Just sweaty hookups here and there."

"The analysis of my private life isn't part of our deal, Troy!"

She does the blinking thing again. "Sorry."

Just then Damon and Nick, two tenth graders, approach us, and Corinne straightens her back, clearly expecting to be introduced. When that doesn't work, the quick kick to my tibia does the trick.

"You guys know Corinne, right?" I say, smiling through the pain.

"Sure, hi," Nick says, and there's a note in his voice that's just an inch too close to sleaze.

"You're in my Advanced Calculus elective," Damon notes, more conversationally. "You talk a lot."

"By design. Statistically, women don't talk in arithmetic fields," Corinne quickly retorts. "I make an effort not to fall prey to that trend."

The only person having a good time right now seems to be Ming, shaking his head with giggles.

"Right. So, Cori, what do you like to do around town?" Nick tries.

"Corinne."

"Um, what?" Nick asks.

"What do you mean 'what'? My name is Corinne, not Cori."

Nick and Damon both smile tightly to each other and disappear back into the crowd a few moments later. My phone immediately buzzes, and it's Nick texting me a string of emojis that amounts to *Yikes, dude.*

Soon, Ming recognizes a passing friend from his coding boot camp, and the two trade shoulder bumps and part ways with us. It makes sense; he didn't sign up for the Corinne tutorial, after all.

"Godspeed, young Padawan," he says, clasping her shoulder before heading off. "Please feel free to embarrass Halti as much as possible!"

"You know, the whole point of parties is to mingle," I say as we watch Ming go.

"I didn't want to spend any more time talking to those two morons. Find us some other people."

"Life is going to be full of very short parties if you only talk to the people you like," I reply. "You know, it's okay not to enjoy stuff like this. It's not for everyone. There's nothing wrong with wanting to go home. Mrs. Carroll is an ass." I smile the Smile of I Understand Your Pain.

She looks at me for a moment, processing my intentions like a freaking replicant from *Blade Runner.*

"Uptown Updogs!" she exclaims loudly, sounding like an infomercial. "'A trusted team of well-trained professionals for your furry family—'"

"Okay, okay, okay," I groan. It was worth a try. "New plan: Cori!"

"Cori?"

"Yes. Just tonight, you're not Corinne Troy"—kraken of FATE Academy—"you're *Cori*. Cori is chill. If you bump into Cori and spill her drink, she will laugh and let you get her a new one instead of . . ." I trail off.

"Asking them if their family has inbred so much that 'walking' and 'standing' are no longer a given of the gene pool?"

"Exactly!" I say. "Cori doesn't even have access to that unhinged level of psychosis. Trust me, Cori will have at least forty new followers on social media after the end of the night."

She opens her mouth to counter the thought.

"If Corinne stops getting in her way," I complete.

In essence, it's the same thing as being Henri, Halti, H, Double H. People have different expectations of you. It's often a lot easier to simply adjust to these expectations instead of being yourself. Give or take one renowned Columbia playwright.

"Fine," she relents, after scoping the premises one more time. "This had better work, Uptown Updogs."

For you and me both, sister, I think. Otherwise, it's very possible that I'll be a pariah by association after one party with Corinne Troy.

SEVEN

A s the evening goes on, "Cori" actually, mercifully, starts to find her footing. After getting her a nonalcoholic drink (because the last thing this party needs is a sloshed Cori Troy) and introducing her to a group of kids complaining about Mrs. Carroll's last exam, I let her mingle on her own, keeping an eye on things from across the room.

Ming is somewhere upstairs by now. However much he may rant about feeling like he doesn't belong at these things, at the end of the night, I'll always find him chatting up a couple of people with genuine interest about their favorite TV show or album or the last YouTube wormhole they fell into. The number of girls who have a crush on him around FATE is nowhere near as insignificant as he likes to believe.

For my part, I end up chatting with Abdel and Gary, two seniors from my Shakespeare class. It is a party, after all. Somehow, we find ourselves discussing everyone's favorite and least favorite topics.

"I'm so nervous," Abdel mentions after reciting some great fact he recently learned about Stanford's artistic endowment. "If I don't get in, I'm just going to take a year off and reapply next year. I already told my dad. Like, that makes more sense than spending four years at a college I hate."

Gary and I sip our beers and nod in pretend sympathy.

"What about you, HH?" Abdel says loudly over the music, which has kicked into old loud pop from the 2000s.

"Columbia, baby!"

"Early admission?"

"Nope. Spinning the wheel of regular admission."

"God," a voice comes out of nowhere, throwing an arm around me. Unlike Hooper, this one is not remotely welcomed.

"Hey, Marv." I Smile. This is the smile of thinly veiled disgust.

"Haltiwan-ker." He grins, playing with my ear, enjoying the discomfort. "Please tell me you guys aren't actually talking about colleges too," he bemoans.

Marvyn Callan. There's just something about this kid. Never have I met someone whose creepiness seems so rehearsed. It's like he was engineered and grown in test-tube conditions to get under my skin. His normally blond hair is dyed forest green tonight because, sure, why not? He's always already smiling by the time he makes eye contact with you, leaving this vague impression that he's been watching you and chuckling to himself since before you saw him. What does not endear him to me is that he's a Harvard and Columbia legacy who never fails to bring it up as though it were an unfortunate skin condition he's been living with since infancy. Not to put the cart before the horse, but I predict deep depression if I end up living in the Callan Building dorms.

I then make the mistake of glancing at Corinne.

"Ooh, she's cute," he comments, following my eyes to Corinne across the room. "You're watching her like a hawk too. You must be smitten. Evie will be heartbroken."

His friendship with Evie is just a fact of life of FATE Academy. Unlike those of us who lucked into FATE a few years ago, the two of them have been attending the best kindergarten, elementary, and middle schools of Manhattan together for most of their lives. The city is full of rich kids with that same our-parents-summer-together connection.

"Knock yourself out," I say. I've seen Marvyn slapped across the face twice before, and I can't think of a better person to make it three for three than Corinne, should he try his chauvinist crap on her. "Now, if you guys will excuse me, a profound piss beckons." With a pat to Marvyn's shoulder, I disentangle from the group, effortlessly sliding him into my former spot. Gary is already talking about the dorms at Stanford, but Abdel glares at me for having substituted myself with Marvyn Callan, king of douche. Sorry, dude.

"Can I ask?" Evie says, startling me after I come out of the bathroom. "What's with the Big Brother/Little Sister act with Corinne Troy?"

I walk her puppy, and she's blackmailing me with outing my

less-than-completely-honest dog-walking venture.

"She lives in my building."

Hooper throws another look toward Corinne's corner of the party, where "Cori" is moving her arms animatedly, explaining something to a girl that actually seems interested. Probably a refresher on the Pythagorean theorem.

"She's treating my party like a petting zoo, H." Evie laughs.

"I'm sorry."

Evie takes another sip of her drink, signaling that it's still my turn to speak. The upper hand always defaults to Evie Hooper. Especially when she has home court advantage.

"I should have asked before just inviting her," I apologize because, really, I should have.

"That's okay." She eventually smiles. "Want to go upstairs?"

"Sure." I smile effortlessly, because Evie is very pretty and making out with her, as we occasionally do at these things, is always very fun.

I take it back. Making out with Evie on her California king bed, which may just be the most comfortable thing I've ever bounced up and down on, is not just fun: it's the bee's knees.

The bee's whole legs dancing the Charleston, frankly.

She hasn't bothered to turn on the lights, and the only brightness in the room is her alarm clock, the 11:52 p.m. in the corner, and the hue of a party streams in through the door crack.

"Why are you bouncing so much?" Evie laughs in the dark

when she joins me on her bed, which shifts slightly under her weight.

"It's a very bouncy bed!"

"You're ridiculous, H."

We're both whispering, and the party noises downstairs are reduced into strangely comforting background noise.

Evie suddenly stops our kissing.

"Is everything okay?" I ask. "Did I misread, um, this?"

It's not our first time hooking up, but there have been plenty of parties where we do nothing more than wave to each other from across the room too.

"No misreading," she says. "Um, do you have a condom?"

Oh.

Before I can answer, the door of her room swings wide open, bathing us both in entirely unsolicited, retina-scalding light.

I leap off Evie so fast, her hair gets a blowout. I expect a father with a baseball bat, but of course, it's Corinne, standing at the door looking at us with complete shock. It's as though she's computing years of anatomy books, trying to figure out how to solve the puzzle in front of her right now.

"Can I help you?!" I yelp, tightening my belt buckle, even though it hasn't even been unbuckled yet.

"Oh, my God! I'm so sorry! I was looking for Henri!"

"You found him." Evie sighs, dropping her head back on the pillow, staring at her ceiling.

"Knocking is nice!" I add. "*Cori* knocks, for the record!"

"I'm sorry!" Corinne yelps, hand still frozen on the doorknob, but her brow is now furrowed like she's clocking a chemical reaction in a classroom lab and the frog suddenly starts to gasp back into life. "Were you two having sex?"

"Get out!"

"Okay, okay! Jeez," Corinne says, excusing herself to the hallway roughly three minutes too late. "Resume your coitus!"

Corinne, Cori, CT, CeeCee, Riri—whatever name this door-swinging personality has, she is decidedly my least favorite now.

"Sorry again!" comes from the hallway.

"It's okay, babe," Evie calls after her with that easy laugh, even though there's a clear hint of annoyance to her voice. She claps twice and the room floods with light. Fancy.

I turn back to Evie now leaning against her nightstand, a pillow clasped against her body, staring back at me with raised eyebrows.

"I'll see you at school, H," Evie says, shaking her head and signaling that it's time for me to join Corinne outside. "And, er, maybe wrap up the field trip?"

"Right. On it."

I close her door as gently as possible and imagine the end of this evening if I somehow hadn't found myself chained to a Troy boulder.

I text a quick **SORRY** to Evie, which goes unanswered. Next, Corinne and I pull Ming out of a college-abyss chat with Abdel, making up some lie about Ming being my ride home. The three of us head for the nearest subway stop. When I ignore her,

Corinne, of course, details the entire trauma to Ming, who is utterly delighted.

"I can't believe I missed that to hear about Abdel's travel plans! Next time, please film it," he says, cackling so loud a woman with grocery bags glares at us from a few rows back. "A video of Haltiwanger with his pants down could crash a few internet servers."

"Jesus, who raised you?"

"A very nice Jewish couple." Ming smiles, getting up at 34th Street. "Thanks for an eventful night, Cori. We definitely have to do it again."

Corinne seems to have something to say and stands up after Ming as the subway doors open.

"Um . . ."

"Yes?"

"Thanks for letting me come along."

Ming looks at me and then smiles at her. "Of course. Next time, I'll stick with you in case you walk into Henri emergency trimming his nose hair in the guest bathroom or something."

One time, and it was a false alarm. Did I mention I hate Ming?

"He's very nice. I really am sorry," Corinne says as she sits down and the train starts moving again. "I've apologized seventeen times. Ballpark figure: how many more until you say something?"

"It's fine." I sigh. "You had no way of knowing." She really does seem remorseful.

"So, is Evie Hooper your girlfriend?" Corinne asks, which

prompts me to take out my phone. I'm certainly not having this conversation now.

"We're not discussing it."

"Fair enough. God, it's not just social life–wise, is it?" she continues. "I'm stunted on every level."

"You're not stunted." I sigh. "It's perfectly natural to be, y'know . . . curious."

Corinne's eyebrows seem to take great offense at that. "I meant in terms of personal experience. I know what sex is!" she says. "I can draw and label the human reproductive system from memory."

"Not quite the same."

"Not to mention the amount of porn I stream is almost fraternity house level."

I almost choke, wishing Ming was still around to bear witness to Corinne Troy casually mentioning the volume of porn she consumes.

"It's always ethically made, and I only look for female directors, thank you very much," she says, crossing her arms. "Now who's the prude?"

Who *is* this girl?

We transfer to the 1 train and get off at the 79th Street station. The stores are mostly locked at this time of the night, but the signage is bright. I realize now that I've never technically walked home with a classmate before.

"So," I ask as we walk. "How's your mom handling the dog?"

"I think she likes him more than me," Corinne admits. "Neither of us are dog people. And between the books, the bound thesis printouts from grad students, and the dog supplies, we're starting to run out of space. I've checked the city restrictions online. We're getting close to the fire hazard status."

"Your mom's a teacher, right?" I ask.

"Columbia," Corinne answers distractedly, checking something on her phone. "Well, she was until last year. She's Dean of the English department now."

I become very aware of my face, controlling every muscle of it as best as I can. If there's an eye twitch, Corinne doesn't register it. How did I not stumble across Chantale Troy's name during all those nights spent browsing the Columbia website?

Holy crap.

"Look!" Corinne says, snapping me out of it as we turn the corner to the Wyatt street entrance. "Forty-eight followers now! I had, like, thirty-two this morning. I guess I was tagged in a photo."

"Congratulations."

"I know you have, like, fifteen hundred, but this is still cool," she grumbles.

Corinne smiles and pockets her phone. Two minutes ago I might have added that these numbers are utterly meaningless, and most important, followers are not friends, but seeing how happy Corinne is, everything feels different somehow. I guess it's not every day someone who lives on the top floor looks at my life with envy.

"It *is* cool," I acknowledge. "People liking you is a good feeling, regardless of the scale."

We reach our building. Corinne is faster on the draw to get her lobby key out since, I realize, she's been walking with her keys between her fingers like Wolverine since we got off the bus. Ma does the same thing: NYC late-night walking safety 101.

"Evie isn't my girlfriend," I answer her, finally. "We just—I don't know—fool around sometimes. It's a thing," I continue, coughing awkwardly at the topic. "An understanding if you will."

"Just hormones and an understanding?" Corinne nods pensively.

"Something like that." I shrug, suddenly feeling like a case study.

"So, have you had sex bef—"

I quickly raise a hand. "Nope, stop. Again: reading the room is going to be essential to your journey."

She shrugs and extends an arm at me. "Well," she says. "Our deal is done. Congratulations. You're off the hook."

I take the handshake with some apprehension. "Really? You're not going to . . . blackmail me into bringing you to every event and helping you become prom queen in a few months or something?"

"I'm not an asshole, Henri," she says, actually sounding offended. "I would never do that."

"I have no way of knowing that. Blackmail is kind of a rough first impression, Corinne."

"We've been in the same school for, like, three years and living in the same building for one. It wasn't our first impression," she retorts. "It was just the first one you noticed."

She would be deadly in a debate setting.

"Look, I gave you my word. Besides, you're great with Palm Tree and my mom doesn't actively hate you, so as far as I'm concerned, Uptown Updogs is just another thirsty high school kid overpricing a basic service to people who can afford it."

Uh. That's not inaccurate.

"Well, good night," she says. "And, y'know, thanks for everything."

"Sure."

If questioned at gunpoint, dangling over a vat of acid, I might have to admit that Corinne Troy is—can be—kind of cool. Even the whole blackmailing thing had a certain hustle behind it you kind of had to admire.

"That was an . . . interesting night, Cori."

And actually: it was.

EIGHT

Like most of FATE staff and faculty, Mr. Vu is a man of many specialized talents. Guidance counselor. Peer adviser. Walking college encyclopedia. He can recite the most up-to-date Ivy League admissions statistics by heart but also knows which varsity recruiters will be present at any given state competition. He's been known to put a handful of FATE athletes on the Olympics path for a variety of sports and two years ago, the class valedictorian apparently tearfully thanked him during her graduation speech for making all her dreams come true. She's at MIT now.

"Thanks for squeezing me in," I say, sitting down and still pawing the empty cup of coffee I forgot to throw out.

"Eleven emails in one week, I believe." He smiles as he lifts his trash basket at me and nods to the cup. "You kids drink so much caffeine. Do you have any idea what you're doing to your nervous system?"

"It's what powers us through that eleventh email."

"Those ridiculous metabolisms of yours." He sighs. "You'll miss it."

You could call him out of shape, but he makes up for it with great posture.

He clicks his very loud computer mouse, and his eyes dart from left to right as he scans the screen, humming every few moments. I don't have to lean forward and sneak a peek to know he's reading my file.

"Give it to me straight, Mr. Vu," I urge, getting antsy.

"Your chances for Columbia without Ms. Kempf's recommendation," he says, quoting my last email back to me.

"Yes, sir."

"Well, it's not just the recommendation, Henri," he says after a moment. "Your grades could be better."

"I'm on the Honor List!"

He clicks his tongue, to temper my enthusiasm. "Not the Dean's List."

In its never-ending quest to give as many trophies and congratulatory awards as possible, FATE has both an Honor List, which refers to the top 15 percent of the student body in terms of grade point averages, and a Dean's List, which refers to the top 5 percent of every class, both displayed on an LED screen at the top of the Achievement Library's entrance.

I've made Dean's List twice in the past two years but am always on the Honor List. Corinne is a staple of the Dean's List.

"Look, you're a very good student, Henri," Mr. Vu says. "I

don't mean to diminish your accomplishments. You're every-thing we want in a student here at FATE. But you asked for my honest assessment about Columbia."

"So, one interview and, what, my chances are shot? There's no leeway? That's draconian!"

"It's the cream of the Ivy League crop, these days." He sighs. "Phenomenal academic offerings here in the cultural capital of the world. That has a lot of appeal for international students, as you can imagine. This also means that Columbia doesn't need to make concessions. I mean, except for their football team."

I groan and fall back into my chair, letting myself embrace the drama of the moment. There's something oddly soothing about Mr. Vu's ceiling. If I didn't know better, I would swear he had it painted a slightly warmer, creamier shade than the stark white of his walls.

"I see this every year," he comments, out of sight. "Amazing students put all their dreams and hopes in a single college, for whatever reason, and crumble when it falls out of reach."

I don't ask the question, but he must sense my stiffening like a corpse.

"Please don't make that face," he says, avoiding eye contact. He sounds downright in pain at the prospect of my bursting into tears in his office right now. Not that the impulse isn't there. "I, erm, I don't have the right pedagogical skills to deal with students when they make that face."

Last year, when Erica Mayfield and Jim Wardell were having their umpteenth and historically most vicious breakup to date right outside his office, Mr. Vu was spotted backtracking into the men's restroom with his lunchtime salad bowl and staying there for the remainder of the hour instead of stepping into the teenage melodrama that pulsates FATE's hallways each day.

"I'm fine, Mr. Vu," I manage to muster. "But I can't promise you not to start crying if you give me a pep talk to get excited about my safety schools right now."

He pages through my files. "And why are these safeties? You have so many other great options, Henri. GPA 3.77, ninety-third percentile SAT score. You're all but a shoo-in for the University of Pennsylvania, McGill, and Duke, most likely. These are phenomenal colleges. Why do you want only this school so very badly?"

Because it's all I've ever wanted. Because it's all my dad's ever wanted for me. Because nothing would make him prouder than wearing Columbia blue and telling everyone his son is an Ivy Leaguer.

"Did you get into your dream college, Mr. Vu?"

"I did, actually," His normally borderline concave chest puffs up a bit at the memory. "Harvard, class of 2008."

"Could anyone have convinced you not to make it a big deal back when you were on this side of things?"

He gently puts his monitor to sleep and returns his full focus to me, pursing his lips in sympathy. "Fair enough. I'm sorry I can't be the bearer of better news."

I sigh. "Could you just try to line up another Columbia interview for me? Please?"

"I'll see what I can do. In the meantime, though, try to trust the process. Consider your other options. No need to put all your eggs in one basket."

"Okay," I say.

But there's only ever been one basket for me.

After school, I take the train down to River Terrace, all the way downtown, to visit my uncle Lion. Back when Lion lived with us, he was the person I always turned to when I needed advice. It's been a while since I've seen him, but Mr. Vu put me in a real funk, and if anyone can shake me out of it, it's him.

I get off the subway and head for the modern, tall, glass high-rise building where Lion works as a doorman. It's not my favorite part of the city, to be honest. The foot traffic is heavier than I like. Not quite Times Square–tourists bad, but the entire area facing the Hudson River has been turned into a giant outdoor mall.

When I reach the building, I stay on the sidewalk carpeted with a monogrammed "River Heights" at its center and watch as Lion chats with a tenant: an elderly woman who seems to be handing him a piece of paper and conveying very specific instructions to be carried out. There are no dogs in sight, but she looks like a Pomeranian owner.

I wait for her to exit the building, holding the door open with a "Ma'am" and a Smile before making my way in. I'm there to distract the staff during work hours, after all. I should be polite.

"Well, well," he says with a grin upon seeing me. "Hi, nephew."

"Hey, Lion," I say, stepping out of the way as a UPS delivery guy arrives, headphones in. He has Lionel quickly sign an electric pad before handing him the package. Lion collects the envelope and gives the UPS delivery guy a signature Lion Smile as a tip. It's a good Smile. I should know; I modeled mine after his years ago.

Up close, the curly, unmanaged hair he had the last time I saw him, when he'd just started this job, is now in a clean cut with immaculate fades that admittedly looks a lot more at home across the marble counter. If I didn't know better, I would think that this is a doorman who takes pride in his job.

At twenty-four, Lionel is technically my uncle, although *cousin* might be a better label, considering how close in age we are. Especially compared to him and Dad, who is literally twice Lionel's age.

Dad was one of the first of his family to leave Haiti, and my grandparents had four more children after he left, of which Lionel was the last, before they both passed away, months apart. Dad didn't go back for the funerals, since we didn't learn about the deaths until weeks after. Haltiwangers are like balloons released into the air that way: you'll never get them all back into the same grasp again.

"It's been a minute," he adds.

"Yeah, sorry, dude," I say. "I've been busy. College applications, dog walks, and y'know . . ."

"And your dad." He chuckles, leaning forward into the counter.

"And my dad. I gotta say, I'm surprised you're still working here," I say, looking around. We texted and emailed a bit after Lion moved out, but three weeks was his limit at the various temp jobs he would find around the city, crashing with new friends I didn't know.

"I didn't think I would be either." He smirks. "But, eh . . . it has its perks."

He smiles and waves to a young tenant with a stroller coming out of the elevators. She's wearing both headphones and sunglasses, which she clearly has no intention to remove any time soon. I roll my eyes as Lion blatantly checks her out.

"Do you live nearby?" I ask.

He snorts. "Four trains and one bus, if you want to call that 'nearby.' But it's all good: benefits are on the horizon, and I'd be an idiot to leave before Christmas bonuses."

He looks around from the slightly elevated ground on his side of the counter, making sure there's no one within earshot.

"The cheapest unit in this building we're standing in? Sixty-four hundred dollars a month. It's tiny too. Like, can you imagine?"

I nod. After so much time at FATE, I very much can.

"Makes me want to set the whole thing on fire some days, to be honest."

"Please don't."

Lion rolls his eyes in a way that makes him look even

younger than he actually is. "I'm kidding. Such a mini Jacques, I swear. Why are you here? Did you suddenly miss your favorite uncle-cousin?"

I shrug. "Just, y'know, checking in."

"Right. I'm happy to chitchat, but my services aren't free, nephew," he says. He points to the stack of blue-arrowed cardboard boxes behind him, clearly indicating for me to help him.

Another older doorman in a similar vest arrives, headphones in, and trades a fist bump with Lion. There's a hint of a tattoo across his wrinkled knuckles.

"Cover the desk for a minute, will ya?" Lion instructs. "I just got some uptown help for these boxes." He grabs the first half, leaving the second for me, and we start from the second floor up to the thirty-eighth, dropping the small packages here and there. I easily fall into the role of assistant, tilting packages and padded yellow envelopes against doors. The true definition of residential comfort is apparently never touching your own mailbox.

"How's life at that fancy school of yours?" Lion asks.

As we work, I catch Lion up on Donielle Kempf and my awful interview and how I'm pretty sure my chances of getting into Columbia are over.

"And on top of everything else I was just blackmailed into taking this girl to a party. . . ."

He laughs with his entire body just like he used to when watching old episodes of *The Boondocks* in our living room.

"Wait, really?"

"Yes, really."

"How?"

I tell him about Corinne. "She's just really . . . something." I find myself laughing again, thinking about her "ethical porn." "She's definitely unlike anyone else at that school. And she's got this super overbearing mother who's a Columbia dean and—"

"Whoa, hang on," he says, interrupting me with a furious headshake. "Her mom's a Columbia dean?"

"Yeah," I say.

"Well, there you go! The solution to all your problems, nephew."

He nods at me as if expecting me to understand what he's getting at, which I don't. Lion eventually stops nodding in favor of a sharp sigh.

"All right: let me tell you a story. There's this lady on the fifteenth floor here. International real estate money. She lives here two weeks every other month and is, like, fully racist," he explains. "Expects you to drop a pile of packages and sprint to hold the door for her and still gets annoyed at having to put up with you being the one to do it. She's on the building's board too, which means she can get you fired for no reason if you catch her in a foul enough mood."

"I'm sorry," I say. "That sucks."

He shakes his head again. "No, no, no: this isn't a tale of woe, nephew. Listen. So, my man DeAngelo, who works night shifts, is moving to Colorado next week. His last day was last week, and I paid him fifty dollars to accidentally spill coffee on her on his way out."

"Jeez, Lion!"

"It was a cold brew, hush. But it still stained like crazy. The point is, right in front of her I made a show of losing my temper at De for the disrespect." Lion laughs to himself at the memory as we wait for the elevator down, done with the packages. "I mean, I really let him have it. Anyway, afterward, I profusely apologized to her. On behalf of the building staff but also personally, of course."

He widens his eye and adopts a straitlaced version of his own voice that sounds like it was born and bred somewhere in Connecticut.

"Sorry, ma'am! I apologize, ma'am! You'll never see him in this building again!"

Accents have never been a problem for Lion.

"She's still racist, though?" I say.

"Definitely, but now I'm one of the good ones." His voice drips with acid on the last two words. "I get good tips, and someone in a high place knows my name if I were to, y'know . . ."

"Misbehave?"

He shrugs in that mischievous way of his that makes you want to laugh along. Even before he got his first American ID, there was never a bar Lion couldn't walk straight into after two minutes of chitchat with a bouncer.

"Can I ask you something?" I ask, stepping into the fully mirrored elevator crowded with an infinite number of synchronized images of us staring back.

"Ask me something."

Lionel has a way of making even his vaguest suggestion

sound like the only logical course of action, especially when he's the primary beneficiary. It's how I ended up doing his laundry for him at least five times while he lived with us. He'd make a truly terrifying insurance salesman if he put his mind to it.

"Is being a bad influence on me your way of getting back at my dad for kicking you out?" Lionel presses for the lobby. We don't say anything until the elevator stops again, and Lion puts a hand on my forearm, forcing eye contact.

"I don't hate your dad, Henri," Lion says, sounding genuine. "He and I are brothers. Family. We just work better apart. Not to play the age card, but it'll make sense someday. In the meantime, that girl . . . you should spend some time with her. Sometimes, the only way to climb out is to realize that there are some people you can, y'know . . ."

"Use as steps?"

He rolls his shoulder. "Okay, maybe not the best, whatever, metaphor or simile or shit, but you know what I mean."

Metaphor, I think but don't say. "I don't know what my dad would say about hustling a classmate."

"Oh, bullshit. You absolutely know what your dad would say." He chuckles, settling back behind the counter. "And yet you're here talking to me."

I think about the hunger Dad always talks about. You *need* that hunger in this world. Heck, this entire city is a weird ant farm that proves that fact every single day. Who makes the food, standing on their feet all day for less than the legal minimum wage (because "go home if you don't like it"); who delivers the food, biking it across icy sidewalks in thirty-degree weather; and who collects it at the door without tipping because the sashimi was three minutes late. Whenever I ride the subway past "116th Street, Columbia University," I don't want to find myself with a sinking feeling in my stomach, thinking what could have been.

But.

There's Haltiwanger Hunger, and then there's eating your friends alive like a weird quicksandy swamp. And somewhere between Corinne blackmailing me and saying good night to her on the steps of the Wyatt last night, she somehow fell into the friend category.

On the ride home, I get a video from Lion. It's a New York I never see. A few seconds in, I realize that it's the view from the rooftop of River Heights, filmed through Lion's grainy phone. Even with the poor resolution, it's absolutely stunning.

NINE

"**C**heck your phone," I say, sidling up to Corinne, causing her to jolt like a possum.

She frowns, looking suspicious, but her face immediately lightens up when she sees the photos of Palm Tree I took this morning.

"I figured you'd want to see him at full cuteness. He's always the hit of the park."

"That's adorable, thanks!"

I see her save the photos on her phone, but she stops smiling as soon as she runs out of photos and casts me another glance. "Did you want something else?"

"You're very suspicious of people," I note.

Afua and Isabelle, two friends of Evie, nod at me as they walk past. I wave back. There's nothing conspicuous about it, but something about their shared smile makes me think that I should follow up with Evie.

"As per your recommendation," Corinne says, "I've now seen enough movies to know that one of the most popular guys in school being nice to me out of nowhere sounds some pigs' blood alarm."

"I'm not the most popular guy in school," I scoff, leaning against the lockers. "Am I?"

She bites back a comment and settles for giving me a side-eye equivalent of a *Bitch, please*.

"I'm not being self-deprecating. I'm like number seven. Tops. There's Oliver, Abdel, Marvyn . . . John-Paul . . ."

"You keep track?" she asks.

"Obviously."

She laughs, shaking her head.

"If you're worried about me blowing your cover, I'm not going to," she finally says. "I told you: you've fulfilled our con-tract. You have nothing to worry about."

"I know." And actually, I do know—but the chance to tease Corinne Troy weirdly got me out of bed this morning.

Truth be told, I've been spending more and more time with Corinne Troy.

I like spending time with Corinne Troy.

I like Corinne Troy?

No, too much. But we live in the same building and attend the same school; in hindsight, it's almost strange that I did not notice her more before. It's not just when picking up Palm Tree for his morning bathroom walks. I find myself noticing her pink hat everywhere these days. That pink hat of hers stands out quite sharply in the wave of students pouring out of the school at the end of the day and even occasionally on the subway ride home too.

I also have to admit that Corinne is . . . a pretty surprising human being as a whole. There is something about her that is dangerously unpredictable. You think you've got her completely figured out, accidentally launching her into a diatribe about the uglier, brushed-over parts of American history—which seems to be a particular area of interest of hers—and suddenly, she'll be up on her feet and holding the subway doors open with both elbows to give turned-about tourists time to hop back on the train after they realize they've gotten off at the wrong stop. And when a Finance Bro in a fleece vest and EarPods scoffs loudly at the wasted seconds, she'll throw him that silencing and distinctively Troy glare of hers. "The trick is to let them fear you might have razors in your hair and be ready to go absolutely off on them," she whispers when she plops back into her seat, resuming a point about the Elaine, Arkansas, Massacre of 1919. I wonder how many simultaneous tabs she keeps open in her brain. It's hard not to look forward to whatever she blurts out next.

"Okay, so . . . did you want something in particular?" Corinne now says, proving my point exactly.

"Not really," I say.

"Well . . ." She slams her locker shut. "Want to grab lunch?"

"You're asking me to lunch?" I repeat.

She nods as if processing. "Lunch," she repeats. "Popular

kids do eat, do they not? Or is eating not cool?"

I laugh. "Lunch is cool. There's a halal cart one avenue block away. You can practice your new social skills by trying not to kill someone that stands in line in front of you for twenty minutes and still doesn't know what to order when they get to the counter."

We walk through the streets of New York, spotting a few people from school here and there. FATE's cafeteria is more of a social space than anything. No one except freshmen actually eats there—especially not on Mondays, when classes end at two to make up for the fact that they run until five on Wednesdays. With tens of thousands of eating establishments in Manhattan alone, you don't stand in line for a tray of de-congealed mac and cheese unless you really love it.

"I swear," she continues, still on the same breath since exiting FATE. "The incompetence of the administration is only dwarfed by the incompetence of the student body sometimes."

She stops and blinks a few times as we settle in line at the halal cart. It seems to be a thing that she does a lot. "Um, how did we get on this topic?"

"I asked how your week has been so far. That was about twelve months ago."

"Stop making fun of me."

"I can't." I shrug. "It's too fun. Are you still fighting off the *intense* label?"

"Yes. Peyton Kelly? This girl from Lawrenceville I met at

Evie's party has a YouTube channel where she interviews people and cooks with them. She invited me to do it. I was thinking about it. Something nonacademic to put on my resume or something. If she doesn't pigs' blood me."

I can't help but laugh. "I feel like you have some trauma with farm lifeblood in a past life. No one is going to purchase blood and manipulate it just because they hate you. You're cool. Peyton is cool. Or at least she was the few times we talked. You should absolutely do it."

"I don't even know if Princeton is going to factor it in. My application is not selling a social media presence. It might confuse things more than anything."

"Well, don't include it in your application, then."

"They research applicants," she exclaims. "I have it under good authority that, when they're unsure about someone, they will go the extra step of a good search engine. And what if they put in 'state-legislation enthusiast candidate Corinne Troy' and . . . and get some YouTube nonsense?"

"Corinne," I say. "Do you want to do it?"

"Yes," she says after some self-reflection, looking at the halal plate she collects from the cart. We park ourselves on two cinder blocks near the Columbus Circle entrance to Central Park.

"Then that's all there is to it. Just do something you enjoy. Forget college applications," I say. "It's exhausting being so many things at once sometimes."

"I call it the O-Generation," Corinne mutters.

"O-Generation?"

"Y'know," she says with a mouthful of rice. "The children of Oprah and Obama."

I instantly understand what she means. Being Black at a school like FATE comes with a certain burden sometimes. The constant notion to prove yourself as truly exceptional to shake off the *affirmative action* cloud floating over your head, that un-fun and constant fear that other people think you're only where you are because of lowered expectations.

"Holy crap, this is good," Corinne exclaims after another voracious bite.

"Told ya."

"You have the afternoon off too, right? Were you headed home?" Corinne offers. "Or we can stutter the subway trains? I'll hop in first, and you can take the train right after me."

"Let's go home." I chuckle, shaking my head, and wonder for the thousandth time: Who *is* this girl?

TEN

The store Ming and I are set to check out together falls more under the category of *flea market* than *store*, but I need the distraction from refreshing Columbia's portal or catching myself flipping through their course catalog with a yearning sigh like it's an old issue of *Playboy*.

The stars line up, and my Wednesday-afternoon English class gets canceled, so Ming and I spontaneously ride the N train to Fort Hamilton Parkway, halfway to Coney Island. Three hours is plenty enough time to go and then make it back to FATE in time for debate practice with Greg and Yadira.

The ride ebbs and flows, filling up with riders at key stops and emptying again just as quickly. I pull out my tablet and work on an essay that's due before week's end while Ming flips through an old sneaker magazine he fished out of my locker, whistling every few pages at the styles that were once predicted to be in vogue in October 2003. It's more than just sneakers, today; his entire mood could be qualified as *giddy*. The boy is literally tapping his foot.

"Ming," I say after my umpteenth typo on the tablet dangling off my lap. "It feels like you're about to break out dancing."

"Sorry," he says, and then bursts out laughing for no reason.

"Are you on drugs?" I exhale. "Is it fun?"

"Sorry, sorry! It's just . . . ," he stammers. "I, um, so I had my interview with Peking University last night, right? At like two a.m. over webcam, since it had to be scheduled on their time with their adviser for international students. Anyway, I rambled a bunch, didn't even use the talking points I had prepared, ran overtime—my mom was giving me the neck chop in the doorway—but at the end, he said, 'Peking University would be lucky to have you, and we hope you consider us'!"

He changes his affectation for the last statement, implying it to be a verbatim quote.

"Dude! That's amazing!" I say with a nudge of his knee. "And you didn't want to tell me because . . . ?"

He winces, throwing a look out the window to the underground innards of the city. "I just know how stressed out you've been about, y'know, Columbia and stuff. I didn't want to rub it in your face or anything. I mean, it's not Columbia but . . ."

As the train comes to a stop, I close the tablet and give Ming a back pat that nearly knocks him off his seat. "Ming, that's stupid. You got in! Your dream school! That's unquestionably a good thing!"

I had told Ming about my disastrous interview with Donielle, and while part of me is sad knowing that Ming's college future is so secure while mine is so not, of course I'm also happy for my friend.

"Well, not yet. Not officially."

"Trust me, I've read all the forums and message boards from collegeconfidential.com to Reddit. 'We hope you'll consider us' is code for 'Prepare for jet lag when you land at the nearest airport.' That's truly awesome, dude!"

"I finally get to see the homeland." Ming smiles before going on to give me every detail of his Peking University freshman year master plan, which involves him spending as much time as he can in Mandarin electives to absorb as much of the language as quickly as possible.

"This little Chinese lady on the subway stopped me the other day. You could tell she needed directions. I look the part, and I couldn't understand a word she was telling me. I think she thought I was faking it in order not to help out. Like, it's my mother tongue, technically," he adds. "It's weird that I don't speak it."

The space, which amounts to half a warehouse with barricaded stained windows, is cramped but well laid out and tends to feature a lot of web-savvy retailers with boldly advertised handles prompting passersby to check out their social media and online stores. Even the flea markets are getting gentrified. Every kiosk belongs to a specific hobby. There is one for knitters, another for old-school, refurbished video game consoles and cartridges. Ming and I pass a new station that seems to traffic in only specialized editions of Scrabble. There appear to be no other board games, only different editions of Scrabble. It's kind of cool how so many people in the city have a single, soul-consuming passion that very often looks nothing like the rest of their lives.

Today, a crowd of aspiring fashionistas is surrounding the display of rolls of fabrics and hanging feather boas managed by "Tara Newone," a drag performer in full wig and makeup. They appear to be having a half-off sale and people are, very unwisely, getting rowdy. Tara also has a reputation for body-slamming anyone stupid enough to try to pocket something from the kiosk while under the misguided impression someone in heels won't give chase. It's a heck of a show.

"I get it." I nod, keeping my hands in my pockets and looking at the selection of sneakers at KICKS UNLIMITED, our destination, without touching it. Just because you're a sneaker aficionado doesn't mean you enjoy touching strangers' used footwear.

"Your mom must be a mess."

"She's seeing her therapist twice a week this month." Ming sighs, checking the stitching of a decent Jordan high-top with a sole that's unfortunately too worn out to warrant the scrutiny. Hazards of secondhand life. "But Dad keeps assuring me that it's not about me."

As far as I can tell, Ming's parents have always been open about his adoption, but his mom is also probably apoplectic about her only son moving across the planet.

"She hugged me four times this morning," Ming says. "She even brought up buying us a condo in Beijing. It's . . . a lot."

Halfway through our third bin, I get a text from Mrs. Berjaoui, one of my clients, and finally notice the three missed calls in my voice mail from her.

"Uptown Updogs," I say as soon as she answers the returned call.

"Finally!"

"Sorry about that, Mrs. Berjaoui. I was on a walk. It's company policy not to take calls."

"I'm sorry, Henri. I have the Uptown Updogs email but just realized that the only phone number I have is yours."

"Oh, that's strange. I'll get you the number."

Crap, do I need to invest in a separate phone number now?

"Another time! This is a bit of an emergency, I'm afraid," she says, sounding frazzled. "That's why I was trying to get to the company directly. I know you have a packed schedule as a student and all, but I need a dog walker ASAP."

Apparently, her husband is traveling for the week and one of her more deservedly incompetent coworkers has just been fired, and somewhere in the shuffle of meetings and extra work that landed on her desk, she ran out of the apartment this morning completely forgetting that her reminder to walk the dog was falling onto the ears of exactly no one.

"Please," Mrs. Berjaoui says in the foreground of ringing phones. "Can you ask them to send a walker? Wasn't that one of their emergency services in the pamphlet?"

In my defense, it sounded good at the time. The sort of little something extra that might send apprehensive dog owners over the hump. I didn't plan on it becoming a factor, with a bonus debate practice in two hours while in another borough with Ming.

"I know you have the key, but maybe you can coordinate with them or something? I'll pay double. I just can't get out of here until at least nine tonight, and I hate to think of Buddy alone for all that time."

Me too.

"I'll, er, I'll make a call to the head office," I say. "They'll email you to confirm."

"Great! Oh, my God, thank you!"

She hangs up before I can sign off.

"Emergency dog run," I tell Ming. "I need to hop on the Express back to Manhattan to walk a retriever before he destroys an entire apartment."

"Cool." Ming shrugs without missing a beat, flicking another shoe into the bin. "I'll come with. This is a dead end, and it's either that or Googling sneaker stores in Beijing, and there will be plenty of time for that in the summer."

He truly is a good friend. We ride the train back in comfortable silence, and Ming spends the time browsing through sneakers on his phone. Trains are always slower when experienced than as mapped out by satellites on your phone. It's looking more and more like I won't be able to make it to debate club again. Gulp.

"What would you have done if class hadn't gotten canceled

today and you'd received that call?"

Good question.

"Skipped class probably?"

"You might be spinning a few too many plates, dude," Ming says with some concern in his voice.

"It's starting to feel that way." I sigh. "But it's only a few more months, right?" I mimic removing a graduation cap and throwing it in the air.

Ming shakes his head but says nothing. We both know I'm right.

One frozen train line and a good fifty minutes later, Ming and I finally make it to the Berjaouis' completely trashed living room and instantly spot the acrid yellow pee stain in the corner as well as the under-the-sink trash bag that's somehow been excavated all over the kitchen floor. The culprit is as obvious as he is adorable, two paws up at my knee and whining in happiness at another presence in the home.

"You absolute little monster," I say, smiling.

Ming plays with Buddy with the enthusiasm of a dog person who does not have regular access to a dog of his own while I proceed to clean up the mess. I sometimes do the math in my head: if dogs age seven times as fast as humans, one hour alone amounts to more than half a day of absolute solitude. Nothing to do with yourself except build up pee, poo, and the confusion that your human is nowhere near you and might never come back and that *alone* might be your new status quo.

We head out of the Berjaouis' building after a long walk

with Buddy to tire him out, and I send photos of him to Mrs. Berjaoui. In return, I receive a string of grateful teary-eyed emojis. Uptown Updogs isn't going to lose its five-star rating today, at least. Although the same can't be said for me once Greg is done with me.

"Greg is going to kill me," I say with a groan after realizing that it's too late to even attempt to make it to debate practice.

"Greg is probably going to kill you, yes," Ming posits calmly. I sigh.

"Thanks for coming to walk Buddy," I try when we reach the subway entrance he has to take back to his place. "And congratulations on Beijing. Really. That's great."

He tips his cap and smiles, bright and open as usual, before disappearing underground. I could take a subway too but decide to walk home instead. I don't want to stand still right now, even if it's inside a train going forty miles per hour. I hate the feeling, and it seems to be present at every corner of my life these days. There's a giant black cloud building up over my head.

Columbia University feels out of reach and blurring a bit more each day. Only Duke, Northwestern, and McGill have extended me interviews, and all three are completely out of geographical reach. I have no interest in getting paddled pledging a fraternity in North Carolina, Northwestern's financial aid isn't looking promising at all in my case, and sure, McGill has a very good design program but is design really something to study in college anyway? There's something about it that sounds so . . . unserious. What would my dad say? Besides,

I don't have a Canadian bone in my body, *eh*. It's all inching uncomfortably close, that great college abyss.

On the way, my phone receives a gigantic gray text message from "Greg P" that heavily features the words "punctuality," "commitment," and "disappointing." Ming's right. Too many plates. And recently, it feels like they're starting to shatter on the floor around me.

ELEVEN

t's not that Corinne Troy is around more, because I know she's always been there, on the margins—that blurred hand always up in the front row of every class and her back tight and proud when other students snicker at her lengthy answers. It's just that now she draws the eye. She's been un-blurred somehow.

Others seem to take notice as well. When I spot her at her locker, she's with two other students who seem also to delight in her bluntness. The three of them are chatting animatedly together. She no longer seems as awkward as she was the night of Evie's party.

The bell for next period rings, and the other two students, whose names I don't remember, excuse themselves with a small wave and a "Bye, Cori!"

I sneak next to her and dramatically slam my head back into her locker, kind of hoping to startle her, which doesn't work.

"I need you to assess me," I declare as dramatically as possible, eyes to the ceiling as students around us start to quickstep to their respective classes. Luckily for me, we're just working on our independent senior projects in my Bio class. Dr. Shapandar is working on her second PhD, and rigorous attendance has fallen through the cracks in the process. As long as assignments are turned in on time at the end of the week, students can stroll into the lab whenever they want.

Corinne eyes me up and down and tilts her head. "Run-of-the-mill overextended teen, possible anxiety; one part insecurity, two parts narcissistic tendencies masked as charming extroversion," she says calmly before turning back to her locker to collect books for her next class.

I almost choke on a breath. "Jesus Christ!"

"What? You asked!"

"I meant, like, academically!" I sputter. "Like, my college chances! Not for you to dissect my personality and insult me. Also, everyone is a narcissist." I can't help but defend myself. "Every pair of eyeballs processes the world in the first person."

"A little sensitive today, are we? I wasn't insulting you," she says as we start to walk together in the emptied-out halls. "We all have our issues. It's good to be aware of them. So . . . colleges?"

"I know I won't hear anything until the end of March at the earliest, but I'm still one good recommendation away from being as competitive as I need to be for Columbia."

"Well, what does Vu say?"

I can't contain my eye roll on this one. "Be patient, trust the process, words, words, words."

Corinne throws me a look but says nothing, instructing me that it's still my turn.

"I still haven't heard back from any of my top choices. No forward motion, no nothing. I feel like I'm wasting valuable time spinning my thumbs. So I figured I'd ask you to—I don't know—assess my chances? I was going to ask you not to hold back, but, er, maybe hold back a little?"

"I'm not a Magic 8 Ball, Henri," she says. "I would need your grades, essays, and recommendation letters to give you my assessment if that's what you're asking. And even then, it would just be an opinion."

She's not wrong. Why did I want her reassurance so badly?

This might have been a phenomenally bad idea. Someone waves at us and I automatically wave back before realizing they're waving to Corinne and not me. She frowns suspiciously but returns the wave as we keep on walking.

"Cori has certainly gotten popular," I note.

"I have no idea who that was," she mumbles. "I need to memorize those flash cards."

"Those what now?"

She grins and reaches into her backpack, pulling out a stack of color-sorted rainbow flash cards. She dexterously begins to flip through them as we walk.

"Dear God, woman."

"That was . . . Ah, yes: Ornell. I met him at Evie's party.

He has very strong feelings about the anime Naruto. Also kept staring at my chest but not, like, in an obvious way. I gave him bonus social points for that."

"This is dark, Corinne," I say, watching the cards and catching glimpses of names I recognize in that tiny handwriting.

"Well! You're the one that said I had to express interest in other people's interests!" she says, clutching the cards like they suddenly hold nuclear codes I might try to pry from her. She looks around at the students passing by us and lowers her voice. "Look, a lot of people have very vapid interests that I can't remember off the top of my head. Like, the girl from my locker just now, Eloise? She's perfectly nice, but Eloise likes drawings of penguins. Nothing else, just penguins. How am I supposed to remember that?"

I can't help but laugh, which does not seem to alleviate her mood.

"Is it that weird? It's weird, isn't it?"

Her logic is sound, and if there's one thing I've learned about Corinne, it's that she doesn't mean ill.

"It . . . seems like a result-driven solution to a well-thought-out problem," I say as diplomatically as possible.

She frowns. "You're making fun of me again, aren't you?"

"I'm not making fun of you." I smile. "What does my card say?"

She smiles back and quickly flips through the deck. "Henri Haltiwanger: Senior. Dogs, con-man tendencies, sneakers."

"I mean, that's the gist of it," I concede.

We end up walking to the other building, where Corinne's next class is. Her special brand of neurotic has a way of getting me to stop paying attention to the clock.

"You two again," a voice comments behind us. "I didn't know you were such close friends."

Evie and a now shaved-head Marvyn approach us, also seemingly heading for Corinne's classroom.

"Hey, Evie." I smile before turning to Marvyn, fake Smile on full display. He extends a fist bump that inexplicably feels like a monarch who expects his ring to be kissed. "Hey, Marv!"

"I haven't seen you around, H." Evie smiles at me. There's an edge to her voice too. A certain *I should have*, given that the last time we talked a prophylactic was discussed.

"Sorry. I've been swamped. Y'know, college stuff," I say, which, to be fair, is completely true.

"Thank God for gap years," Evie says, wincing in sympathy.

"And you're assuming they're just friends, E," Marvyn says, still bored by any college talk. "We could be looking at love-birds."

I can't quite contain the eye roll on this one. Did I mention that I really do not care for Marvyn? His playbook is as generic as it is effective. Corinne nearly has a heart attack.

"What! N-no, absolutely not," she exclaims, playing right into his hand like a novice. "We just live in the same building."

"Where *do* you live, Haltiwanger?" Marvyn asks.

"Upper West Side. Near Lincoln Center," I quickly say. "Near" is a word with a lot of breadth. By all accounts, Brooklyn is near. Massachusetts is near too, technically. Corinne looks at me but, thank God, doesn't add anything.

"Oh, I didn't know that." Evie blinks. "Well, Marvyn here is having a pool party Saturday. You two should come. It will be a blast."

"Shouldn't I be in charge of the guest list to my own party, E?"

"I don't see why." Evie smirks at him, earning her a shoulder bump. Urgh.

"We'll be there," Corinne says, nodding furiously. "Sounds super fun."

Super fun?

They both duck into the classroom while Corinne lingers for an additional moment and leans into me to whisper.

She looks into the classroom where the teacher is and back to me. "What time should we leave? And do I, like, bring my bathing suit or wear it? Or—oh! Is it skinny-dipping—"

"Jesus, Corinne, no." I shake my head. "And nah, I don't think this one's for me."

"No! You have to come."

"Why?" I ask, raising a deliberate eyebrow, even though I already suspect I know the answer. Corinne navigating one of these parties is still not an altogether natural image.

"You're a . . . safe zone from me getting too into my head about these things. I—I want to make a good impression."

She turns and watches Evie and Marvyn talking. But there's something about the way she's staring at Marvyn. It's almost as if . . .

"Corinne, do you like Marvyn?"

She responds with seven eye blinks, which tells me that I have to remember to play poker against her at some point, and also strangely makes my stomach do a weird flip.

"Ewww." I make sure to stretch the word as long as it goes.

"What! I find him . . . interesting," she says, glancing into the classroom nervously.

"I promise you he's not."

Something about the entire prospect feels strangely vexing. I could have set her up with a better guy around school had she asked.

"I mean, it's okay if you want to slum it, but let's not pretend you're reaching for the sleaze bucket with Marvyn."

Corinne rolls her eyes. "Fine. I find him hot as hell. It's problematic, but I've had very vivid dreams of sucking his face. If you come, I'll help you figure out the whole college thing."

"The whole college thing?" She makes it sound so easy, like an outfit to be assembled together from a pile of clothes on a bed.

"I promise!" She looks back into the classroom. "Pinkie swear!" And she actually extends a pinkie my way, the strange girl.

"Fine, fine. Let's keep the quid pro quo blackmail going, I guess." I sigh as I hook her pinkie. It's the most childish thing ever, but it also feels like a serious covenant coming from someone like Corinne, who took a book out in kindergarten when other kids started pulling ponytails and only looked up a few weeks ago when it dawned on her that she was, perhaps, a bit intense.

"This is ridiculous," I say.

"No, it's not. Pinkie swears are philosophically no different than most G8 resolutions."

I shake.

"Also," she finally adds, chewing her lip with hesitance. "The Wyatt is a good building."

"Okay," I say, pretending not to understand what she's referring to.

"You just seemed—I don't know—kind of weird about that just now? I'm just saying, there wouldn't be any assumptions about your family if people knew your address. I live there too."

"Okay," I say again, because what else do you say when someone calls you out? She's not wrong. But I'm also not about to discuss it with her.

"So, you'll come with me to Marvyn's?" she asks hopefully. "So I can get my freak on?"

"Again," I say, making sure to make eye contact first. "Ew."

Forget Corinne being way out of Marvyn's league by every metric imaginable; it's borderline a sin against nature. Like . . . like pairing a weird breed of worm that only grows in the diseased pouches of kangaroos and an adorable, superintelligent Baby Yoda with a pink hat who's already tapped into the Force.

"You know you're too good for that guy, right? I'll come as long as we're all on the same page there."

Corinne blinks twice and then gives me a surprised smile.

"Henri—that might be the nicest thing you've ever said to me."

"Without blackmail too."

She rolls her eyes.

"Look, I'm aware of Marvyn's more agro tendencies, all right? I am. But the heart wants what it wants. And I want that ass."

She says it with such a shocking amount of yearning in her voice that I can't help a snort. She really is ridiculous sometimes. We won't even get started on her taste.

"Ugh," I manage. "I can only confirm I'll attend if you stop right there, right now."

"Deal." She smiles. "See you later!"

And with that, she disappears into the classroom, making her way to the last empty seat at the front of the class.

TWELVE

Marvyn lives right in the middle of Union Square downtown. It's far from a residential area, always buzzing and crowded with tourists, but he and his parents spend most weekends in Westchester. No one under the age of forty should use the term "pied-à-terre," but true to form, Marvyn does so liberally.

As far as I can tell, the entirety of the top floor of this building belongs to Marvyn's family. All three units. One is his grandparents', one is his parents', and the other, a recently refurbished one, belongs to his older sister and her husband. Marvyn gave us a tour at the last party of his that I attended.

Although the temperature is dipping fast, it's still sunny enough that the prospect of shedding hoodies for an indoor pool bash has appeal for a lot of FATE kids. The place is surprisingly packed. In addition to the usual suspects, there are also the water polo team members, some of their Dwight School counterparts, and some Spence girls. All seniors. It makes sense; we're all dealing with the looming trauma of graduation. Any weekend is a good excuse for a party, and any party is a good opportunity to create a memory. There's something new ahead, of course, but life as we all know it is in countdown mode.

Ming and I leave our stuff in a circular room with high walls and crowded built-in bookshelves that go up to the ceiling, at the center of which is a single circular couch. One of the handful of living rooms Marvyn's place has and that is already filled with piles of coats and bags because, again, winter. Corinne texted that she was squeezing in an extra-credit problem set and would meet us here.

"Haltiwan-ker!" I hear as soon as we step out of the elevator, and we follow the wet footprints to the rooftop area. "Welcome to my abode, man!" Marvyn shouts with an arm wave, holding court by the lounging area with a ridiculous two-beer hat and an open Hawaiian shirt.

"Hey, Marvyn!" I grin back. He instantly leans into one of his friends' ears and whispers something, eyes right on me, and they giggle in unison. All right, then, asshole.

I take off my shirt in one swift motion and give Marvyn an earnest smile. All right, fine; it's a downright smirk. Sue me. Did I do an extra set of pull-ups on the scaffolding right before we got here? Yes. Was that silly? Yes. Was it also worth it? Yes. Yes, it was.

He looks away, and I swear I can spot him sucking in his stomach.

Ming snorts behind me, materializing two beers out of nowhere and handing me one. "Does that feel good, Halti? Body-shaming your classmate like that?"

"You know what? It does," I say, knocking my bottle against his. "To pettiness."

Any weirdness from that day at the flea market seems to have dissipated, or maybe even only been in my head. It's been a crowded field lately.

"Sometimes I want to trade bodies with you," he says. "Like, if we both pee in the Bethesda fountain and hope for a body switch?" He flicks my midsection. "Like, dang . . . Seriously, how many sit-ups have you done this past week? A million?"

"I simply have no idea what you're talking about," I say.

By the time we find Cori standing near the refreshments, looking perplexed at her red Solo cup, Ming and I have already taken one group photo and been part of two live videos. She's wearing a one-piece under a jean jacket, heart-shaped sunglasses, and judging from the bulging pockets, I'd bet there are two paperback novels on her. She's not as exposed as most of the other kids, but she's not standing out either, which is just another way of fitting in.

"It's supposed to smell that way," Ming explains as we join her. "Marvyn bought like fourteen cases of the old, battery-acid-level-caffeinated Four Loko out of Jersey before it went off market. Completely different from the current sparkling water that's on the shelves now. It won't make you hurl later, but it does taste like the sort of thing that would make you hurl later."

"Not to mention they expired years ago," I add.

Corinne looks down at her cup, shuts her eyes, and then chugs it.

"Dang," Ming comments.

"*Carpe Vinum*," she says. "'Seize the wine,' if I'm remembering my Latin elective." She checks her watch. "Is this considered 'fashionably late,' or are you just always late, Haltiwanger?"

"He's always late," Ming answers before I can mutter a comeback. "Halti 101: always factor in a fifteen-minute buffer. It's annoying as hell at first, but eventually, it becomes part of his charm."

Corinne smiles, and I can tell that a bullet point has just been added to the flash card in Corinne's head.

"I don't like the two of you becoming friends," I stipulate. "It does not suit my lifestyle, like, at all."

Corinne suddenly raises her sunglasses over her head, framing her wall of curls as she narrows her eyes at me, making no effort to hide the fact that she is brazenly eyeballing my torso. She takes an uncomfortably close step forward. Well, not uncomfortable but sudden, very sudden.

"Um . . . Can I help you?"

"Are you wearing baby oil?" she asks.

It takes a good five minutes for Ming to physically stop laughing. After a brutal cross-examination and only partial exoneration—I have dry chest skin; it's absolutely a thing—the three of us settle in by the pool. It's probably not the most active way to navigate a Marvyn party, but hanging out with

113

Ming and Cori, our legs plopped into the artificially warmed water, is pleasant and easy. I wonder if this is what the water near those sandy beaches from postcards feels like.

The pool empties out and then fills up again around us as a good hour passes while we laugh and comment on the various poolside behaviors of our classmates. Corinne has to be physically stopped from loudly pointing out Derek Shaal's boner in the water.

"That, right there, that's definitely a tumescence! Look! Look!" she whispers loudly enough for a few people to hear and glance poor Derek's way.

"I'm absolutely not looking," I say, eyes on my drink. "These things, er, happen. Give the guy a moment."

"It's the humane thing to do," Ming agrees, looking at the water solemnly.

"Boy behavior is fascinating," Corinne says, shaking her head but reluctantly looking away while Derek slinks out of the pool as discreetly as he can.

At some point, someone shouts out the two magic words "Mario Kart!" and Ming all but somersaults away with a "Lata, suckas!" and almost slides directly into two passing girls.

"We might never see him again," I say as we watch him readjust the potted plant he just knocked aside.

"You can go too if you want," Corinne says. "You don't have to babysit me."

"Pass. I've lost enough races to Princess Peach for a lifetime, thank you very much." That speed boost–catching wench.

Corinne's eyes are locked on Marvyn getting ready to

attempt a backflip into the pool. He's instructing Danny O'Brien on exactly how to capture the cinematic moment on his phone.

"So, what's the endgame here?" I ask, snapping her out of it.

"W-what do you mean?" she asks after clearing her throat.

"Well, you've been a real social butterfly lately. Think Mrs. Carroll is ready to amend her recommendation from 'intense' to 'mellow'?"

Corinne smiles, shyly at first and then giddily. "She already did!"

She leans in conspiratorially. "I couldn't just tell her I had read her letter, right? So, I just stopped by her offices after class and started talking about how I felt disconnected from my peers and was worried about the social side of college."

She makes it sound like a performance, but there's definitely a kernel of truth in her voice.

"She said she noticed, gave me a bunch of pamphlet-y advice, and encouraged me to get out of my shell.

"A few days later, I sent her an email with nine photo attachments of me *hanging out with my peers* and profusely thanking her for making me stop and smell the calla lilies. She was so happy I had taken her advice that she sent me a draft of the new recommendation letter she was sending Princeton on my behalf."

"Congrats, Troy!" I say, holding up a hand for a high five. "See? You gotta play the game! Cursing her out wouldn't have gotten you closer to Princeton."

"Guess not," she continues, lining up our hands and returning the gesture with minimal force as if touching a palm scanner from an old sci-fi movie.

"Why didn't you say sooner?"

She's not making eye contact anymore.

"Well, I don't know! Because . . ."

"Not to be dramatic, but if you say it was because you didn't want to make me feel bad about my own college stuff, I will, sincerely, set myself on fire here and now."

Between this and Ming, I'm tired of being seen by my friends as so breakable. As if the fact that my future is dead on arrival is an unspoken truth traveling the pipes and tunnels of Manhattan.

"Fair enough," she says. "Sorry. Yeah, it's looking good for Princeton. Fingers crossed."

"I'm crossing them for you, for whatever it's worth."

I actually am. A universe where Corinne Troy matriculates at Princeton sounds very fair.

"While you're at it," she says, turning back to Marvyn, "please put those societal hacks of yours to good use by getting me 'Nine Minutes in Heaven' with that."

I am mentally throwing up in my mouth. "It's 'Seven Minutes.'"

"I'm going to need nine for what I have in mind," Corinne says absentmindedly, and it almost sounds like a purr. Good God.

Marvyn suddenly lets out a sharp laugh as he films one of his friends pushing someone into the water and then turns the camera around to himself to give it a signature grin.

"You could do better, but a deal's a deal, I suppose. The key to winning the attention of our dear host is a two-to-one Laughter/Ego split."

Corinne seems confused. I break down the recipe.

"Laugh at the first two things he says, and then, on the third thing, ask him a leading question about himself. Do you work out? What was the last country you visited? Were you always this funny? And then laugh twice again. Laugh, laugh, ego. Rinse and repeat until he can't stop thinking about you . . . because he thinks you're always thinking about him. Ta-da."

I'm not making this up. I've seen Marvyn slide an arm around many permutations of this exact breakdown.

"That's so problematic," Corinne notes after a disgusted beat. "On so many levels."

"If you're expecting Roxane Gay discourse from Callan you're in for a very long courting."

"Well, I'm not doing *that*," she says. "Out of the question." She looks over to Marvyn, who just cannonballed into the water, purposefully splashing someone's phone and cackling when he swims out again.

"Okay," Corinne says, despite the sight. "I'm going in. I'll improvise."

"You can't be serious!"

"Oh, *Corinne* would be on the train home right now, but *Cori* . . ." She shrugs. "Cori finds sleazy to be a bit of a turn-on, but she's not turning into a *thot* either."

Princeton doesn't stand a chance.

She stands up, looks down at me, makes as if to say

something, and then simply shakes her head.

"What?"

"I was going to ask if you're going to be okay on your own, y'know, at a party, but that's a ridiculous question, isn't it?"

I lean back on the reclining lounge chair, arms linked under my head. "Maybe the dumbest statement ever uttered. Go catch yourself an asshole, *Cori*. I'll manage."

"You still smell like baby oil!" she whisper-shouts after taking off her jacket and jumping into the water herself—a cannonball that's forceful enough to splash Marvyn and get him to turn back.

"Sorry, I was aiming for your phone!" Corinne laughs and swims away to the other end of the pool, with Marvyn following after her. It's expertly played on her part; Marvyn looks like a puppy learning how to swim, chasing an invisible treat with his snout barely out of the water. I watch as he reaches her, and she in return flips her hair, purposefully not focusing on him as he starts to talk. Just like that, Corinne transforms into Cori before my very eyes. She pinches her lips with disinterest at an inaudible thing Marvyn's stupid face mouths but eventually gives him a laugh that feels like a thin and very long needle slowly puncturing my chest.

I would take comfort in the fact that it's a fake "Cori" laugh, except that from my side of the pool her snorty giggle sounds exactly like the one I'm used to, which feels much, much worse.

THIRTEEN

"Okay, I have to ask: what is going on with you and this girl?"

Evie steps into the empty kitchen, startling me while I'm pouring myself a glass of tap water; New York City has the best in America. Her feet leave a row of prints on the ceramic and right now, damn it if her red-white-and-blue bikini may be the most patriotic thing since the Alamo.

She glances my way and notices the abs and shirtlessness, which makes all those crunches and pull-ups suddenly worth it.

"I told you; she's my neighbor." Evie is too sharp to insult with "I have no idea who you're talking about" coyness.

"H, come on," she says, opening Marvyn's fridge like it's her own and pulling out a glass bottle of expensive fizzy water. "It's more than a zip code. You've taken an interest in Corinne Troy of all people."

"I'm not dating her, if that's what you're asking."

"Well, I know that." She snorts between sips.

"She's helping me with college. Her mom is a dean at Columbia," I tell her, but coming out of my lips, it sounds wrong. Nothing I said is a lie, but it feels like one. That's not why I'm hanging out with Corinne . . . Is it? Corinne is funny, Corinne is smart, Corinne's mom is a dean at Columbia. Why does that third thing never completely leave my brain?

Hooper gives a nod of understanding, slow and wide, before taking another long sip. "That makes a lot more sense."

"Why?"

"You don't take an interest in people. I mean, not really." She doesn't sound angry, per se, but there's a sharpness to the comment.

"It's really not like that," I recover, managing a casual Smile, leaning into the marble counter. "She's into your boy Marvyn anyway."

"Hm."

"What?"

"She appears to have a type. Although, I probably shouldn't talk." She grins, leaning into the side of the counter to kiss me. "Off the record."

Evie kisses me again. I'm trying to focus on her, on this moment, but I can't keep the image of Corinne and Marvyn out of my head.

"He's not going to get pervy on her, right? Marvyn."

"What? No!" She frowns, sounding genuinely offended. "He's not like that. I wouldn't be friends with him if he was, H!"

120

Good. That's good. I could shut up, then. I really could. I know that shutting up would be the best way to continue the make out here but . . .

"Sorry, I didn't mean to offend," I say. "She's just, y'know, not very experienced with this crowd, that's all."

It's Evie's turn to stop the kiss. "This crowd?"

"You know," I say, twisting my hand in the air, trying to find the right words to mercifully lighten the mood. "Rich kids with unlocked cabinets looking for thrills that might, y'know, take advantage of her."

She tosses her hair behind her shoulder in a way that normally only happens in slow motion around the hallways, and it feels like a force field has been activated. "Well, no offense but if Corinne is interested in opportunists, I think she can scratch that itch without leaving her building lobby."

The comment feels like a quick shiv between the ribs, delivered without a hint of acid in her voice.

"Ouch," I say.

"You . . ." She exhales as if to calm down. "You never answer my texts. You fall off the face of the earth at the drop of a hat except at these parties. I have to catch you running around school to even invite you to a party. You've never even tried asking me out on an actual date."

I feel totally blindsided. "I thought this was what you wanted," I say, back stiff and hand on the counter. "I thought you didn't want anything serious."

Evie looks at me like she's slowly realizing I'm the dumbest guy on the entire planet and then slowly shakes her head. "No, H. That's what *you* wanted. You never even bothered to ask what I want."

She places the half-empty glass bottle on the counter and walks out of the kitchen without another word.

On the way out, I catch a glimpse of Corinne and Marvyn on one of the couches in one of the lounging rooms. She's next to him and wrapped in a towel, holding her head up with one hand with her legs pulled up under her. She appears to be having a good time until they spot me.

"Leaving already, man?" Marvyn says.

"Yeah, I'm going to bounce. I'm not feeling great," I say. I'm pretty shook after my conversation with Evie. "Thanks for inviting me, though. Had a great time."

"Of course, any time."

Marvyn and I Smile at each other and in another reality, very close to this one, it's clear we're both extending middle fingers at each other.

"Hey, hey, Henri, wait!" I hear Corinne behind me a few moments later. I've already dressed and packed up my stuff. "You're leaving without Ming?"

Just then a room down the hallway, one of the many hallways, erupts in shouting and laughter, and I recognize the signature cackle accompanied by the cartoonish sound of Princess Peach knocking someone off the track.

"He's having a good time. No need to ruin that. I'll text him later. I just, er, can't be here right now."

"Well, give me a second. I'll be right back," she says. "Don't . . . leave without me, okay? I know where you live."

It's selfish, but I want to take her up on it, and actually *selfishness* goes hand-in-hand with the callous sociopath I apparently am.

"You don't have to leave because I'm leaving," I say when she comes back.

"I'm very aware of that, thank you very much," Corinne says, stuffing her signature pink hat back onto her hair, damp from the pool and drying frizzy already. "I'm bored, and I miss my dog. Let's go."

Corinne and I stand near the door on an at-capacity train, keeping our balance in silence, eight local stops back to our respective homes a few floors apart. In the corner is a pack of college students. A kid is playing YouTube videos on his phone without headphones, legs spread out over two seats. A worker in heavy work boots crumples up his brown paper bag and slides it under his seat. Brazenly. Or at least the opposite of discreetly.

Everything about the city annoys me at the moment.

A nearby guy looks our way as Corinne takes off her hat, pulls out a towel from her big bag, and begins to furiously rub her still-damp hair.

"What? I'm happy to leave with you since you're obviously upset, but it's getting colder by the day, and I'm not catching pneumonia for you."

"I didn't say anything."

She resumes staring at me in a way that unsettles me at a molecular level. "So," she eventually blurts out. "To be clear, I'm inquiring about your emotional health and not gossiping, but what happened with Evie? Did you guys break up?"

"We were never dating!" I answer, maybe a smidge too emotional for public transport. "I just . . . I thought we were one thing, but we were another. I guess? I honestly had no idea she wanted things to be more serious between us."

"For someone so good with people, you're also pretty thick."

It doesn't sound as brutal of an analysis coming from her.

"But I believe you would never hurt someone on purpose," she continues. "You just happen to hurt people on accident."

"Thanks, I guess." I sigh. "So, how did things go with Marvyn? He seemed enthralled on that couch."

Corinne leans against the railing for support as the train jolts to an uneasy stop. "He's very boring and kept calling me 'babe.'"

"Ha!" I laugh. "I hope you told him so."

"I did! The more I called him boring to his face, the more interested he seemed. He kept saying he liked my flirting style."

"I'm not one of those people who go around saying, 'I told you so,'" I remark. "That would be petty."

She rolls her eyes. "I don't know how you do it. Spend time with people you don't actually like. I would go nuts."

"I do like Evie, you know. . . . I wasn't using her or anything."

"I know," she says matter-of-factly but without any harshness.

"I guess I thought *she* was using *me*, which frankly would have been the best thing for everyone involved. I'm just not, y'know, the dating type. I've never even had a 'girlfriend.'" I mime exaggerated quotation marks around the last word because the notion truly is ridiculous.

"Why not?"

I shrug. "Who has the time? Besides, it's too late anyway, right? We're seniors. Next year, we're going to be in college. Everything about this year, FATE, it all feels . . . I don't know . . ."

"Temporary," Corinne completes, staring ahead as we ride.

And that's the perfect word for it, isn't it?

"So, if you've never had a girlfriend, then are you still a virgin?" she posits, way too loudly, after another long stretch of silence.

My eyes widen at her sheer volume. The young Black guy sitting to our left chuckles openly after glancing my way.

"I already told you," I whisper. "I'm not discussing that."

"Guys are so strange." She laughs. "You'll text and talk about the filthiest things imaginable, openly, loudly, in the middle of the school library, but heaven forbid you answer a direct question about your practical sex life."

Still, she doesn't push the topic further. The rest of the ride falls into a comfortable silence. The train empties at Times Square station as people pour out to catch the express train across the platform, but Corinne and I stay put instinctively, settling for two now-empty seats instead of rushing to save, at most, three minutes of travel time.

"I'm sorry I'm not very good company right now," I say after a beat.

She looks at me, perplexed as she puts her earbuds in. "I'm not a master of it myself, but you really should try to think less about what people think of you."

It's not dismissive or rude, and before I can reply, she hits Pause on whatever she was listening to, rips a single disinfectant wipe from her bag, removes and thoroughly cleans one of her earbuds, and offers the earbud to me, shining clean like a fancy hotel bathroom sink.

"NPR," she says, and I take it.

Eventually the train pulls into our station, and we walk out together, shoulder to shoulder. It's not just proximity but also a weird form of familiarity I'm not entirely used to. We walk all the way to the Wyatt in tandem, shoulders occasionally bumping, both implicitly knowing the path.

"You're sure Ming won't mind that we ditched him?" Corinne asks by the mailboxes as I hand her the earbud back, wondering when we'd transitioned to jazz.

And as if on cue, I receive a selfie of a grinning Ming in front of Marvyn's flat-screen. On the monitor is a gleaming Mario Kart trophy, and in the background, Colleen Patrick is caught midshout in defeat with a controller in hand.

Caption: *YEAH U 2 BETTER RUN B4 THE NEXT CULL-ING!*

"Ming Denison-Eilfing, ladies and gentlemen."

Corinne laughs at the photo and takes two steps onto the staircase so she's standing a bit taller than me.

"Well, thanks for coming along," she says, currently distracted by her reflection in the glass door lobby, gently tapping at the poof of her wet hair now dried back with even more volume than ever before.

"Of course," I say, shuffling my feet. "And I wanted to say . . ."

"Yes?"

Her entire attention is on me again, which does not make it easier to keep talking, but we are dangerously close to friends now and . . . if anyone deserves a photo finish to their high school experience, it's Corinne.

"I wanted to say that if you really like Marvyn, well, he'd be a lucky guy." I sigh. "And I have it under good authority he's not that bad, and you, y'know, deserve the big high school romance as much as anyone else in that school?"

"I see." She blinks. "Do I, Henri?"

There's a smile dancing on her lips that feels off right now. As though it's at me rather than with me.

"Er . . . Yes?"

"And are you sure you don't want to run it past the village elders before giving me such blanket permission?"

"Okay, no! I didn't mean it that w—"

Corinne starts up the stairs, now bopping her head vigorously.

"No, no, no. No takebacksies. I have the golden ticket now:

127

permission from another dude! I mean, wow. I get to date? A real-life boy of my own choosing? I must tell Mother at once."

Thankfully, she doesn't seem that mad, chuckling between bursts of her soliloquy.

Okay, that wasn't what I was trying to say. What was I trying to say? I stand there, chewing on the inside of my cheek to keep from trying to defend my statement and sink farther into the floor.

"So, um, I'll see you tomorrow to walk Palm Tree, then?" I shout after her, fidgeting with my door keys.

Her head peeks back down over the stairwell, looking serious all over again. "Oooh! I just remembered."

"What?"

"He touched my shoulder . . . while we were both in the water—and in our underclothing," she says, hand on her chest. "God, I hope I'm pregnant. Fingers crossed, Haltiwanger!"

Her cackle echoes all the way up to her own doorstep, and I'm left to try to remember a time when I was actually good at talking to girls. What was it, third grade? I was awesome at it in the third grade.

FOURTEEN

"Halti!" Greg yells, snapping me back to the reality of him and Yadira both staring at me expectantly.

"Um . . . I'm sorry, what?"

"You only have ninety seconds for rebuttals," he dramatically states, his voice echoing outside the empty classroom. "You're welcome to start at any time now."

I try to focus on the debate topic, but it's almost impossible to concentrate today. I keep replaying Saturday night's exchange with Corinne, trying to make sense of my reaction. She totally threw me off, and I had no idea what to say. Me. How is that possible? I've always got the right words.

But something about Corinne disarms me. And the most surprising thing is, I don't mind it. I actually kind of like it.

I actually kind of like . . . her.

No, that's crazy. I do not have feelings for Corinne Troy.

But then why am I still thinking about her?

Plus, there's the Marvyn of it all. Does she still have feelings for that butt, inhaling his own farts in the back of his town car? Not that I'm biased or anything.

"Right! Well, Yadira makes a very fine point, but what we have to do here, when considering this, uh . . . matter, is look at the social ramifications of such a policy. . . ."

However long I babble next, the remaining seconds of my rebuttal manage to feel extraordinarily long. Once I'm done, Greg is visibly unhappy with my performance, and I can tell from Yadira's pursed lips that she agrees with him.

"That was . . . hollow," she finally says, taking it upon herself to speak first. "You spoke for ninety seconds and didn't say anything, Halti. Sorry."

Greg is far less diplomatic.

"It was nonsense is what it was!" he exclaims with raised arms. "You sounded like an evil politician trying to sound moderate."

He's been even more high-strung than usual today. It makes sense: this weekend marks the semifinals of the New York City debate circuit, and we're up against St. Celeste. Somewhere along the way, I must have slipped into a time vortex because I swear this round of the competition was still two months away, last time I checked my calendar. With the college stress migraines, it's admittedly been bumped down my list of priorities.

"There's a reason all those people are always grabbing babies and kissing them to distract from what they're actually saying, Henri," Greg continues, clearly on a roll. "Unfortunately, we don't get props against St. Celeste this weekend."

I sigh and lean into the podium, balls already fully busted. "Give me a break here, Greg."

"I think what Greg is saying, Halti, is that if you're going to make an emotional appeal, there has to be an earnestness to it, right?" Yadira tries. "You're usually better about BSing that part, that's all."

Greg nods so furiously his neck might break, which I wouldn't altogether mind right now, to be honest.

"Yes! Thank you. There's a human component missing, Halti." He exhales. "That matters a lot more in these final rounds. Right now, you're coming off like a sleazy comptroller with slicked-back hair and mob connections."

"Where's this creativity when you're on the stage, Greg?" I snap back, because, really. "Because shaking the entire time isn't projecting. FYI."

"All right, boys. Put your dicks away; the smell is terrible," Yadira chimes in.

"I don't need this today," I grumble, slipping my blazer back on and collecting my bag. "We're done for today anyway, right? I'll see you guys later."

"You can't get by on charm alone, dude!" I hear Greg shout as I head out of the classroom and resist the impulse to throw a middle finger behind me.

Luckily, Ming is there after debate practice to talk me down from the ledge. Or, at least, to lend an ear to the myriad ways in which I would personally go about killing Greg Polan.

"Maiming is the way to go," I say, biting into an apple from the East Hall lunchroom machine like it's Greg's ankle and I'm a pit bull mix. "Also evisceration. And don't you forget skinning."

"Wouldn't dream of it." Ming smiles, filling a cup of black coffee from the machine. He hands it to me as he taps his credit card. Both the coffee and the presumably limitless credit card look appealing this morning.

"Oh, no, it's oka—"

He interrupts me with a performative eye roll. "You look tired as shit this morning. It's coffee, not a mortgage. Don't get weird on me again, and just take it, Haltiwanger."

I used to get a bit weird about benefiting too much from the (as far as I can tell) unlimited credit card Ming's parents have given him instead of an allowance. I kept diligent track of the amounts incurred whenever he grabbed me coffee or lunch or gum from the bodega or MetroCard swipes in the subway when my card was empty.

At some point paying him back these small amounts in quarters and crumpled bills, often days after the fact, became its own weird conversation until last year in which I was drunkenly told, *Dude, there's no receipt or tab. Trust me. So find your chill about money stuff!*

In hindsight, it might have been the one time Ming ever snapped at me.

"Thanks," I say, after a sip of the coffee. He pours himself one too. And then I take two more sips after that. FATE admittedly has really good coffee. I've never bothered to look into it, but it's probably made from those expensive coffee beans that first pass through a civet's intestinal tract before being collected from the creature's poop and retailing for an absurd amount. "Where was I?"

"Maiming?"

"Oh, yes," I continue, feeling like I just hit a bonus, caffeinated life. "Well, the maiming is essential, obviously. Oh, and all that stuff? The maiming and the eviscerating? It's all happening to Greg's flayed body."

Ming smiles as we walk through the hallways, nodding to people here and there. "Here." He pulls a rolled-up magazine out of his messenger and hands it to me. It's the latest issue of *Pavement*, a biannual designer shoe wear magazine filled with jaw-dropping photos.

"New collection. Let the beautiful, pretty sneakers calm you down from wanting to go House Bolton on Greg Polan."

But $18.99 for a magazine is a luxury I can never quite convince myself I need when passing by a bookstore row of periodicals. "I won't be distracted. The full order is to skin him, *then* eviscerate, *then* maim the limbs," I say distractedly, thumbing through the pages as we walk. "Clip nails, remove the skin, remove entrails, and— Ooh, pweetty."

Ming laughs and then fades into the background of the universe as I take in the new styles and bold colors currently flowing in from Detroit.

They're purely aesthetic, mind you. Almost none of these could be worn without severely damaging someone's spine, but high-fashion sneakers trickle down to the marketplace. The main brands will borrow a color here, an angle or pattern there, and pretty soon, we'll be spotting them all across the subway.

I fall into pattern behind Ming and might just follow him off the edge of a cliff, my eyes glued to the *Pavement*, if he didn't suddenly yell out words that deserve a trigger warning.

"Hey, there's Cori. Cori! Cori!"

I quickly duck behind the nearest pillar before I even realize what I'm doing. Am I seriously hiding like some kind of second grader? Jeez—what is wrong with me these days?

By the time Ming backtracks my way, he looks like he's fully ready to institutionalize me. "Um, dude?"

"What?" I cough. "Nothing. All good here. What's up with you shouting her name like that? Preschool basics: Indoor Voices inside, Ming."

"You're hiding behind a pillar, you sitcom!"

He looks back toward Corinne—what I assume to be Corinne—like a very slow detective. Thank God, the bundle of hair at a water bottle fountain doesn't appear to have spotted us.

"I've never seen you hide from a girl before. Or anyone, for that matter. Hell, I've seen you talk yourself out of detention. While chewing gum."

Ming is right: something about Corinne has been playing with my source code.

"Wait, Halti. . . ." Ming stops walking. He looks at me with deep concern. "Do you like Cori?"

"I don't *like* anyone," I scoff. Ask Evie Hooper.

"Quit dodging the question," Ming says knowingly. "Do you, like, want to go there?"

I feel myself swallowing painfully. "I legitimately . . . don't know. She's interesting."

And cute. And weird. God, what the hell?

"You do! You like Corinne Troy," Ming says, practically jumping up and down in excitement.

I sigh. "Would that just be the weirdest thing? If I did?" I genuinely ask.

Ming sighs and joins me behind the pillar, taking a long smug sip of his coffee. We both stand there, sipping our synthetic cups, backs tight against the concrete. To people walking by, it might look like two bros simply chilling, one of them not being on the verge of a personal breakdown.

"I mean, you've hung out with her too. She's fun, right?"

"She's fun," he agrees after a moment. "And as far as I can tell—"

"What? Authentic? Fun? Bluntly honest?"

He just stares at me. "I was just going to say a cool chick, but wow, by all means: keep going. You've got it bad, dude."

"I might have it bad." I groan, letting myself dramatically fall into his shoulder. We resume walking once the road is clear. "But she's into Marvyn." Maybe?

Ming scoffs. "Marvyn's appeal is just off-brand Haltiwanger appeal."

"What?"

"He's the Popsi to your Pepsi, dude. That's why you two have all this tension. Everyone knows that."

Ming has long since been one of the only people with whom personal space stopped being an issue. A side effect of having spent so much time together, I guess.

"You're free now, right?" Ming asks, patting my back sympathetically. "Let's deal with your drama in the tradition of every stylish New Yorker that's come before us and go get our shoe on. Cab ride's on me."

"Can't. I have an appointment with Mr. Vu," I say, handing back the magazine and nodding to the glass office right ahead of us. He emailed last week to say he had an update for me, and I'm hoping it's good news about a new Columbia interview.

As if on cue, the door opens, and Mr. Vu peeks his head out and looks down at his watch.

Does everyone always expect me to be late?

"Oh!" He smiles, spotting us. "Hello, Henri, Ming. Congratulations on Peking."

Ming pretends to pat down his hair smugly. "Oh, that? I'd almost forgotten."

Mr. Vu rolls his eyes and turns to me. "Well, shall we, Henri?"

His voice is soft and calm as always but maybe a bit exhausted. The bench outside his office is always crowded with anxious seniors at this time of the year, and now that I'm a senior, I get why.

"Let's shall!" I Smile.

"Get this man to Columbia, Mr. Vu!" Ming yells, pinching my shoulder before waving us off.

FIFTEEN

"Take a seat," Mr. Vu says, motioning to the chair across from his desk.

"So, were you able to line up another interview for me?" I ask eagerly.

"I'm sorry, no," he says, and my face drops. "I did, however, take the liberty of reaching out to Ms. Kempf, to ask for a bit of insight on your meeting. I knew it was bothering you, and I thought you might like to know where she was coming from."

And maybe it's all the caffeine in my veins, but I can't contain an audible "pfft" at this one.

"She loved meeting you. She agrees with me that you're as smart and special as any other student here but . . ."

"But . . ."

"She says she doesn't think you want Columbia for the right reasons," Mr. Vu says. "Perhaps she is being dramatic, as those in her line of work can be. But nonetheless . . . I'll leave it at that to avoid further misquoting her."

I've been freaking dreaming about Columbia since I was five years old. What more could I have said?

"Well, good to know legacy Marvyn Callan won't have any competition from me, and the world can continue spinning on its axis." I'm sure he'll get the girl too, I almost add.

When I say nothing again for a beat too long, Vu's innate push to fill awkward silences kicks in again, this time surpassing his professionalism.

"Marvyn's grades are excellent, as are his extracurriculars. You may not like his disposition, but his interview column in the paper was picked up by *The New Yorker* last year. From a purely academic standpoint, he's a great student."

"Oh, he's a shining beacon of FATE excellence, for sure."

He frowns at that. Another thing about the FATE faculty? They are very loyal to their employer. Their retreat photos always look like an eerie summer camp where everyone sincerely loves one another.

"Do you believe we don't assess our students fairly?"

I don't answer. I don't have a Smile for this answer.

"Marvyn has a tutor, two tutors, actually," I say before I can stop myself. "He has only three classes this semester because he did that Paris Immersion program last summer, which counts for six credits."

Price tag: eight thousand dollars for two weeks.

"I don't know if he has a part-time job on the side, but my money would be on no. Meanwhile, I was up at five forty-five this morning to pick up dog poop, and it categorically wasn't to write an essay about it. Oh, and his big interview that won the student paper its award last year? The one with the Lincoln Center's creative director? Did you read it? That's his uncle! It took place at their family cabin!"

Marvyn also buys his problem sets off previous seniors who graduated, but I don't say that part because being a snitch right now won't get me any closer to Columbia.

"I know I'm as smart as anyone here, Mr. Vu." I sigh, suddenly very tired. "That's . . . That doesn't make it any better. Every banner in this school tells people they can be whatever they set their minds to, and it's just . . . Well, it's a lie, isn't it?"

He's looking at me with a mix of sympathy and outright pity that feels like a cup of gasoline on a lit match in my belly.

"I mean, you should just tell us scholarship students who get into FATE that this is all make-believe, and that as soon as the ties and blazers are off, what matters is the same thing that's ever mattered: who you know and how much dough your parents have."

"Henri, I understand yo—"

"I'll see you later, Mr. Vu," I say, tumbling out of his office.

The rest of the day is spent in a funk. I don't have a Smile, smile, or smile™ left in me for anyone in the halls of the Fine Arts Technical Education Academy. And when you're not smiling in a school like FATE, everyone thinks you're sad, upset, or, worse, angry. This alone is, in fact, sad, upsetting, and angering. I spend lunch and my following free period completing my midday walks, careful to take a well-known path through which I know for sure I won't run into anyone from school. The dogs help my mood because dogs were designed by a benevolent universe to help with moods. But after stuffing my Uptown Updogs hoodie into my backpack, it's back to the purple and navy humdrum. The last two periods of class that follow drag on particularly slowly.

After taking care of my evening dog walks, I swing back to FATE after hours to finish a Biology lab assignment that's worth 30 percent of the final grade. Tiny little monsters, those things. On the way out that evening, exhausted and ready to crash, I spot Corinne again, seated alone at the center of an empty seminar classroom, staring at the projector. Right: her weird slides-studying thing.

I watch her for a moment, her gaze focused and her lips inaudibly repeating the content of each slide before clicking on to the next one. I discreetly walk away before I'm noticed, or so I thought.

"Halti? Halti!"

I choose to keep walking, pretending not to have heard her until a text arrives on my phone a few seconds later: **YOU CAN'T BE SERIOUS?**

After assessing all my reply options, I backtrack toward the darkened classroom. Corinne has twisted around in her seat and is waiting, phone in hand, looking very much like the textbook definition of "intense," especially under the projector's lights.

"You're seriously avoiding me?" she says. "What, am I back to being a social pariah?"

"No! I just didn't see you!" I lie.

"Bull," she says flatly. "I saw you and Ming earlier."

There's an earnestness to her intensity today. She's staring at me, genuinely thinking she's done something wrong. It's strangely destabilizing.

"I've just been in my head a bit," I say.

"Oh." The slideshow seems to have been paused. "Is it Evie?"

I shake my head to say no.

"College?"

I shake my head to say yes.

And just like that, I find myself turning on the lights and joining her in the empty room. We both sit pretzel style on top of desks, across from each other, as I unpack the meeting with Mr. Vu in a single continuous vomit that she seems to follow completely, blinking at every new chunk I drop at her feet.

"Uh," she asks when I finally exhale. "Okay: so that was just a long way of saying that Columbia is a long shot for you. How very dramatic. What are your safeties?"

For some reason, her matter-of-fact tone is easier to answer than Mr. Vu's sympathetic one.

She fishes a bag of chips out of her bag, opens it, and tilts it my way. Kale chips, of course.

"Let's see. Brown, Duke, U Penn, McGill, Oberlin, and City College here as my backup. NYU's financial aid is horrible, so that wasn't worth the application fee."

She doesn't make too much of the financial aid slip, thank God, and reaches into her bag again. "Well, if you hadn't avoided me all week, I could have given this to you earlier.

Here." She hands me a heavy, purple three-ring binder. Every college worth the name seems to be indexed in here. "I'm tired of carrying it around school. It's a loan, and I expect it returned in pristine condition."

"T-thank you. Jeez. I thought Mr. Vu was prepared."

"Oh, he's a very good resource, but I went for a more comprehensive take. Websites, testimonies, studies, research, and FATE alum experiences," she says, flicking the labeled sheet separators as she flips through the binder. "But what's important here is that there are other colleges beyond the Ivies. They just don't have the centuries of patriarchal branding."

The founder and CEO of Uptown Updogs knows the value of good marketing.

"What about McGill?" she offers. "It's very affordable."

"Canada," I answer flatly, which earns me a raised eyebrow.

"They have airports up there now, I hear," she deadpans.

"Look, I only applied because Mr. Vu got me a waiver for the application fee. And they have a pretty cool design program," I say, absentmindedly flipping through the binder.

"Design? What, like, architecture?"

"No, more like patterns and textiles and stuff. A bit of fashion."

Corinne gives me a look meaning for me to go on.

I sigh and fish out my phone.

"Cute," she comments, and I realize that she's referring to my current wallpaper, which is, appropriately enough, a vintage newspaper ad scan of two rottweiler puppies pulling on the laces of a sleek, black-and-white Slam Jam x Nike Blazer sneaker, Class 1977. I always loved that photo.

I pull up my web browser and take us through a few 3D sneaker mock-ups of up-and-coming designers who came out of McGill's program and added brief backstories of what led me to bookmark them in the first place. Luckily, I've never closed a single browser tab since getting this phone. It's pretty evident that Corinne never gave sneakers a second thought, but somehow she doesn't make me feel dumb or hoodratty for sharing this stuff. She doesn't laugh or frown, or bring up the factory conditions in which the big American designers keep their workers in other countries. She just listens with a knitted brow, occasionally asking me to scroll back and explain a term I don't realize I'm dropping without context.

"Halti . . . ," she eventually says, looking up at me, genuinely confused.

"Okay, okay!" I preempt. "I know what you're thinking. I'll concede that last pair was definitely inspired by Crocs, but I low-key think that Crocs look kind of edgy? I mean, design-wise they're even a little sexy, y'know?"

She blinks furiously again.

"I'm . . . going to need college-level psych classes to be equipped to address that one," she says. "Next question: why didn't you think to bring any of this up in your Columbia interview? Your eyes light up when you talk about this stuff!"

Oh. That.

I shrug. I had briefly considered it, but design, especially sneakers, always felt a bit silly and . . . unpolished. Especially next to kids with violin and opera on their resumes. I hadn't even told Ma or Dad about the program and mostly applied to McGill to see if the few sketches I submitted would pass muster. There was never any other light in the room beyond Columbia University, but there was no harm in flicking on a night-light in the corner.

"I don't know. Seemed dumb. Especially for Ivy League."

"I don't think it's dumb at all. It's definitely unique to you. . . . This might be what Donielle Kempf was talking about, you know. She wasn't seeing this side of you."

Maybe Corinne's right. Then again, maybe not. Gambling with Columbia like that wasn't something I was prepared to do. Donielle Kempf was a renowned playwright, after all; how would sneakers have ranked against *zee theater*?

"It's nice to think that being honest about my passion and dreams and whatever would have worked, but in my experience, most people already have a clear idea of what they want to hear from you from the moment they see you," I say, pausing to huff against my phone's screen and wiping it against my sleeve to clean a smudge. "It's not fair. You can fight against it, I guess, but to me, it's best to just go along with it and coat the whole thing in a smile."

I turn to her and give her the full Prince Charming Smile that she's effectively immune to at this point, and she expectedly rolls her eyes.

"That has to be exhausting," she notes before giving me a light shove. "Also cut that out. It's so creepy!"

"*You* don't talk a lot about Princeton," I say in maybe the least smooth topic change in recorded history, leaning toward her to return the shoulder bump. "If I'm freaking out about Columbia, I would imagine you would be thinking about Princeton twenty-four/seven."

Corinne picks at her nail, and her perfect pretzel posture wobbles a bit. "I'm trying very hard not to think about it too much, to be honest. I can't control what happens now," she finally says. "I gave myself an ulcer, an actual medical ulcer, during the SATs. I got seven recommendation letters and opened all of them. I blackmailed someone because of a bad recommendation letter," she adds, giving me a pointed look and shaking her head. "I'm putting it out to the universe now. There's nothing more I can do. I did my best. And if it's not enough, then Princeton wasn't for me, y'know?"

Did you *do your best?* I hear, in Dad's voice. I shake the thought away.

"Or I'm just waiting for the actual rejection letter before burning this city to the ground with the fire of a thousand dragons. We'll see," she continues.

I snort. That seems like a very plausible course of action.

"What's wrong?" she asks.

"You know those intolerable kids who get into, like, every Ivy League college? And then someone interviews them, and they trend online and are always so obnoxiously smug and earnest at the same time?"

Her eye roll confirms that she does. Anyone who has ever even Googled the requirements for a top college has come across those smug little bastards laying out their admission letters on the kitchen table for the local news anchor while their parents beam in the corner.

"I really thought I was going to be one of them," I say.

The thing with being good at lying to others is that you end up being pretty great at lying to yourself too.

"Don't be too hard on yourself, Haltiwanger. Like I said, it's the great promise of the O-Generation," Corinne says. "Either you're exceptional or a nobody. No permission to be anything in between. It's bullshit."

It may be the first time I've heard Corinne Troy curse out loud. It's pretty hot.

"It's getting late," she says as she begins to gather her things. "I'm meeting my mom at the IFC Center for this retrospective."

We've been at it for close to a full hour already, I realize. Time tends to dissipate with Corinne.

"Are you headed home?" she asks, coat on and books in hand. "Want to walk out together?"

I think of home. Of our tiny apartment, my tinier bedroom—and Dad with all his hopes and dreams for me in the next room. Suddenly the prospect of going through the Binder of Colleges That Are Not Columbia feels slightly nauseating. Security keeps the school open until nine for students anyway.

"I think I'll give this a read here," I say. "Better lighting and I don't feel like going home just yet."

She nods. "Just remember, you have plenty of options if Columbia doesn't pan out. Although I'm very serious about the state of that binder. I can't even imagine how people just go around lending out their books. Troglodytes."

I laugh. No one makes me laugh like Corinne.

"Hey, Corinne?"

I can't believe I'm about to ask this. "You and Marvyn? Is that . . . that a thing?"

Corinne raises an eyebrow. She's frowning at me, specifically my forehead. Is she actually watching me *sweat*? "Nah," she finally concedes. "I'm kind of into someone else."

She smiles. Or maybe it's a smirk. Since when does Corinne smirk like that?

"Lights on or off?" she asks by the door, beanie on.

I silently raise the binder with a raised eyebrow, which seems to rattle her confidence.

"Right. Reading. Um, good night, then! Happy reading."

I chuckle. "Good night," I call after her, then open my binder and slide into a seat. I shake myself awake and dive into an objective assessment of pristine institutions.

The lights suddenly turn off as Corinne disappears into the hallway.

"Hey!" I say.

"Things don't always work out the way you want, Haltiwanger!" she shouts. "Get off your butt, and do something about it."

I let myself sit in the dark for a moment and think that, if nothing else, at least this clusterfuck of a senior year has had one good surprise—even if she's been upstairs all this time.

SIXTEEN

Today's debate semifinals are to be at St. Celeste. Intrastate New York debates tend to rotate schools depending on availability and to keep some sense of fairness to the proceedings. Every one of the competing schools (Trinity, Regis, FATE, St. Celeste, Brearley, Horace Mann, Collegiate) is therefore theoretically available to host a meet at the drop of a hat.

If two teams are competing against each other, one of the two will host the other in a display of decorum and sportsmanship that looks great in school pamphlets and websites. It's a weird bit of logistics, but I imagine that Slytherin and Gryffindor kids still often have to pose together and smile extra bright in Hogwarts brochures to show that the pesky Potter-era animosity is indeed ancient history.

So far, the early qualification rounds have taken our three-person team to Horace Mann in the Bronx, to Trinity's new campus annex, Brearley on the East Side, and now St. Celeste. FATE still hasn't hosted a competition, which means the finals could be there if we can score another win today. If.

Located across Central Park, firmly anchored on the East Side of Manhattan, the St. Celeste School is the visual opposite of FATE's sleek, sci-fi sanctuary aesthetic. Things are all red bricks and French windows around here.

It's not that there's really a rivalry between the elite schools of New York City; it's just that the St. Celeste kids tend to, by and large, think they're better than everyone else. Or at least that's how it feels. Their school was founded in the 1900s, and they, in turn, find us FATE kids to be upstarts without the pedigree of the true elite, no matter what our endowment might be. (Equal to theirs, for the record.)

I arrive early, courtesy of two alarms and quick, efficient dog runs around the building that did not go into overtime. Just as I'm about to text Yadira, she steps out of a town car across East 89th Street, in front of the St. Celeste gates.

She joins me on the sidewalk, coffee mug in the crook of her elbow, and looks around before removing one of her earbuds. "I freaking hate St. Celeste kids."

"Good morning to you too, darling." I grin. "Didn't you date a St. Celeste girl last ye—?"

The glare I receive tells me it's best not to broach the topic.

"Never mind. Different Yadira. Alternate universe Yadira. That Yadira has an eye patch and a Gatling gun."

There's a bit of a crowd outside St. Celeste today, which

probably means we're in for a packed audience. Our FATE uniform colors aren't the kind typically spotted outside the school, making us stand in sharp contrast with the weekend sea of strollers and carefree toddlers that make up the Upper East Side. Uniforms are mandatory for debate rounds. You proudly represent your school. Again, Quidditchian logic.

"Where's Greg?" I ask. "Should we text him?"

"No need," Yadira says, fidgeting with her tie. "My money is on he's already measuring the stage—or on all fours in front of a toilet."

"Ah! The rest of the Fine Arts Technical Education team, I assume!" a balding man with gray sides and sunken eyes says as he approaches us, taking in the uniforms. "Welcome, welcome! My name is Mr. Garrison. I teach history here at St. Celeste and oversee the debate team, among a few others."

FATE Academy has committees and subcommittees for nearly every facet of student life, but as few teaching coaches as possible for its extracurricular activities. There is no adult to intervene with us when Yadira, Greg, or I step out of line or eschew our commitment. Teaching us to manage our schedules as well as each other is a big part of the school's extracurricular philosophy. Did I mention that we're a very woke school?

"Hi, sir. You look, er, familiar," I say, blinking a few times and thinking back to the nights I spent binging *South Park* reruns on Comedy Central's website while my parents were sleeping.

"I get that a lot from you kids."

He confirms our IDs and leads the way toward a side

entrance, expecting us to follow. The unfamiliar hallways are buzzing with energy.

"Your teammate is already inside," Mr. Garrison says. "He was feeling a little queasy earlier. We got him some soda."

"Told ya," Yadira whispers.

"And are your parents in attendance?" Mr. Garrison asks. "They must be excited."

"My parents are working," I say, taking in the gray photos of rows and rows of white guys in white-guy haircuts that eventually fade into color photos and a probably mandated sort of diversity as we step into the eighties and nineties.

"My dad doesn't close his bathrobe for *semi*finals," Yadira says, armor up already and emphasizing the "semi" just enough to sound like this is nothing but an administrative box to be checked. "Charm" and "Anti-Charm" is what Greg called us when we first met.

"Oh, th-that's a shame. Well, our audience is pretty much packed today. Parents here are very involved. I hope it won't be too nerve-racking for you kids alone up there."

Yadira and I share an eye roll. "We'll manage."

It's always amazing how competitive teachers and faculty get about debates, no matter how hard they try not to. There are stories of teachers and parents getting into arguments and collar grabs before and after debates—and even one or two during the actual debates.

Having the home-field advantage for the St. Celeste team mostly translates to an audience that's completely on their side:

parents and debate enthusiasts that will politely clap when the visiting team makes a decent point but erupt in pointed and rapturous cheers when one of their own wins a rebuttal.

We reach an open room filled with rows of vanity mirrors and racks of zipped garment bags. Costumes. St. Celeste's theater department, no doubt.

"Here you go! I'll come to collect you guys when it's time to go on stage. In the meantime, enjoy the snacks. Bathrooms are right down the hall," Mr. Garrison says with a dismissive wave, and okay, but he really does look *exactly* like the *South Park* character.

"You guys are late!" Greg exclaims, jumping off the couch, uniform already wrinkled. He is even paler than usual, and there's a crumpled brown paper bag he might have just been breathing into.

I wasn't kidding when I said that public speaking wasn't his forte. The day of every debate plays out exactly like this: like someone about to confront their fear of snakes by spending ninety minutes in a pit of anacondas. There's something admirable about it, I think but don't say because Greg is also a major pain in the rear a good 40 percent of the time.

"We're almost an hour early, dude," Yadira says, settling on the opposite corner of the couch. "Halti is here looking like a six-foot-two-inch snack. I'm as pleasant and curse free as I can possibly be." She raises her mug. "This is decaffeinated tea, for God's sake. So please, don't start."

"I'm sorry, I'm sorry! I just—I want to win," Greg says,

making it sound like a yoga affirmation. "We're so close to the finish line. I just want it, y'know? I want a big win."

I do know.

"Greg, isn't there something you want to tell Halti?" Yadira says, somehow urgently and disinterested all at once.

"Right, Halti, um . . . ," Greg begins. "I meant to apologize about last rehearsal. I was a little too extra the other day at practice. Um, sorry."

It's Yadira talking, clearly, but it's still weird for a guy like Greg to apologize. About anything. Really, ever.

"Are we good?"

"We're good." I Smile and give him a fist bump. It's safe to say that neither of us will name their firstborn after the other, but Greg's a good teammate.

"So," I say, moving past the awkwardness as Yadira smirks smugly. "Did you have a chance to meet them before that guy quarantined you in here?" I ask. "Our distinguished competition?"

"Briefly." Greg sighs. "They're probably creeping right outside. They've been walking by the door, chatting and laughing way too loud for it not to be some kind of mind game to try to psych me out."

I open the door and catch a clear look at our opponents, a yard down the hallway: the St. Celeste counterparts to Greg, Yadira, and me are three guys in navy blazers and red ties. They look like an a cappella group.

They catch my eye, and the tall guy with a mess of freckles

and close-cropped hair nods me a *'Sup*. There's a vague Marvyn Callan energy to him.

"Creeps," Yadira says, returning to listlessly swiping her phone with an arm behind her head.

Another one sends us a big wave, smiling, and his Smile™ is much worse than mine.

I return the gesture, adding a thumbs-up for good measure, which causes one of them to snort. If Greg and I were sharing summer camp cabins with these little clichés, we might wake up to them beating us both with bags of oranges.

"Should we—I don't know—try to retaliate?" Greg asks. The paper bag is back in action, blowing like a respirator between every other word. "I could make myself throw up on one of them on that stage."

"Nah, that wouldn't be very sportsmanlike," I say after gently closing the door.

"That's how the Trinity team got disqualified two years ago, remember?" Yadira points out.

"Then what do you suggest?"

"Well," I start, "I don't know about you guys, but I would settle for their complete and total humiliation in front of their own school."

Greg and Yadira both look at me like the words aren't coming out of my face correctly.

"Is this a 'Go, team!' pep talk, Halti?" Yadira asks. "From you?"

"No, no. No 'Go, team' on this end," I say. "We're not those singing pricks from *Glee*. More of a 'Let's screw them to the bottom of hell.' I just don't like these guys. We're smarter, prettier, and way more prepared than they are! So let's beat them so hard they experience mild trauma whenever they even step on the Upper West Side."

Yadira snorts. "Fine by me. But just out of curiosity: how pretty are you inside your own head?"

"Beyoncé could write an album covering the topic," I answer very seriously.

She bursts out laughing, and I even manage to get a little smile out of Greg.

"Well, hear, hear!" she says, sitting up, rubbing her hands together. "Let's rock this moldy bitch."

Credit where credit is due, the St. Celeste debate team is very prepared today.

They came in third last year, which is by all accounts a failure at this level. Parents that spend fifty thousand dollars a year on their kid's competitive education don't do it for a tiny bronze trophy. This year, they have the bombastic confidence of handsome young white men of good families, which is to say infinite.

The first round is on Greg. The prompts are pulled out of a glass bowl today. "An argument for gentrification."

It's the sort of devil's-advocating prompt that they love to spring up at competitions. How quickly can debaters think? How cogently can they make their argument? How many inches to your side can you bring the audience?

Greg's smart. That's a complete given. He limits the scope of the argument to small businesses and the increase in lifestyle that comes with gentrified neighborhoods. He's visibly shaking the entire time, and there are a few throat-clears and yawns in the audience, but he stays focused and takes us through his flawless, monotonous arguments.

Just when I think he's running out of steam with a good fifty seconds left on the monitor, he brings up the example of neighborhoods falling into disarray without "the benefit of gentrification." It's brazen and easily refutable in writing, but there's no way for the St. Celeste boys to come at such a broad argument without rhetorically unraveling themselves. Two of the three judges seated in the front row take dispassionate notes.

The second round is me. Which is objectively the better color: blue or red?

Silly rounds are my jam. I go all personality on this one, starting with a comment about how our competition didn't have to make that choice in designing their uniform. It's the sort of cheeky self-awareness that works well in jolting the audience.

I go for the comedic angle and passionately commit to red as though the alternative of blue was a grotesque offense to my very being.

"It is the most inoffensive color in the spectrum of the human eye for a reason, people. There are studies that I won't cite here because they are so numerous and definitely real that confirm beyond a shadow of scientific doubt that the color blue is in fact the favorite color of your most boring coworker. . . . Shannon in HR loves it!"

A few chuckles start to pepper the room. For four minutes, two hundred forty seconds, I obliquely and then directly talk about the blandness of people who proudly declare blue to be their favorite color.

"They're the same people who call fall 'their season.' Love Labradors, and put their interests down as being 'music' and 'laughter.' Be honest. Have you— Has anyone in this audience ever had a conversation with one of these people where you didn't want to claw yourself out of your own skin? Be honest."

More laughter. It's nonsense, but the only people actively frowning are the St. Celeste boys, unhappy with the temperature of the room no longer leaning their way, which is just how I like it.

"And if you were offended by this statement because you love your Labrador, 'Lucy,' and think music and laughter are gosh darn neat, then I suggest you go stare at an robin's-egg blue wall to regain your composure."

In the end, I clock three laughs, one snort, and an aborted round of applause that's quieted down by the judge. They have no idea what I just said—which rhetorically amounts to nothing—but loved hearing it.

The Haltiwanger method. St. Celeste's own silly round ("music or silence?") is treated too seriously to be entertaining, and one judge actually checks his watch.

Finally, Yadira takes the rebuttals, and unfortunately for

the St. Celeste team, she is an expert at noting logical fallacies as though they were typos being proofread. She's ruthless at casually bringing up the ceteris paribus of the lengthy socioeconomic argument made by the guy who proposed eliminating moving walkways from airports to champion cardiovascular health.

Yadira is all poised and stern on this one, which makes up for her slip in decorum. "A truly ridiculous argument that inaccurately assumes equal physical capabilities for all human beings that frequent airports."

She sounds a little embarrassed for them. She finishes her round with an acknowledgment of their tu quoque approach to rhetorical debate (appeal to hypocrisy), which circumvents the arguments in favor of moral outrage. It is just a chef's kiss of derision that causes the ears of one of them to go bright red.

In the end, it's a slaughter. An elegant slaughter filled with rebuttals, but the downside of all the St. Celeste guys sounding exactly alike is that they get the same exact grade after their performances, and the judges concede us the win with a total of twenty-eight points over St. Celeste's twenty-four.

The applause is as expected: unhappy but polite. Mr. Garrison is tight-lipped as our team members all gather to the front of the auditorium to take a photo together. I grin and throw an arm around Greg and place myself in front of the bargain-bin Marvyn as Greg beams with the trophy in hand. His satisfied smile betrays weary eyes, like tonight will be the first time he has a good night's sleep in weeks.

"Admit it," I say, kissing him wetly on the cheek and

watching him recoil. "You're going to miss me next year!"

"I'll definitely have difficulty finding a replacement next year," he concedes, wiping his cheek but smiling.

The crowd disperses quickly after, and pretty soon it's just the three of us at the center of this unfamiliar auditorium. It makes sense that they wouldn't want to entertain the conquerors too long. Yadira scans the premises, phone in hand, and darts up the stairs when she spots her prey.

"What are you doing?" Greg asks as she quicksteps after the St. Celeste guys scurrying out through the back.

"I'm going to go take a selfie with them. Fellas? Oh, fellas!" she shouts, and it sounds like a poacher wanting to preserve the memory of herself crouching next to her slain prey.

Greg and I head out on our own, knowing we won't see her before Monday. Let the record show that, win or lose, Yadira is always terrifying.

"Do you need a ride home? My car is picking me up around the corner."

"Nah, I'm good." I smile. "It's a nice day, I'm just going to walk through the park. Burn off this victorious energy. Thanks, though!"

He nods, but I can still feel his gaze burning the side of my head as we walk.

"Dude, I'm not going to try to take the trophy home." I laugh. "It's yours until the FATE Powers That Be lock it behind glass, man."

"It's not that. It's just . . . do you have any idea what a gift that is? Not having your stomach fill with bile when you're in front of a crowd like that? You would have spent an hour up there, huh?"

"You're only being so nice to me because we won. You would be destroying me right now if we'd lost."

It's still nice to hear.

"Well, obviously," he scoffs as we step out of the strange school, catching the eyes of a few people lingering in the courtyard discussing our performance.

Greg's chest puffs a bit at the attention, and he turns my way one last time before sliding into the back seat of his car. "But I mean it, Henri. It's, y'know, a rare gift."

On the walk home, I can't help but think about Greg's words. He's right. I've been so in my head lately that I might have forgotten that I am normally good at this stuff.

I text a quick selfie of myself throwing a victory sign to Dad and Ma and to Ming. I consider sending it to Lion but change my mind. I doubt he has much use for the extracurriculars of a privileged high schooler.

But there's one person I want to share the news with more than anyone. I pull up Corinne's name in my phone.

WE WON! I won't be strangled to death by my teammates!

I know, I caught the stream. You're an expert bullshitter. :)

I prefer pre-congressman. Was streamed? Where?

FATE's website. Peak viewership: 538. Three times more than the fencing matches.

For a moment she looks like she's texting a lengthy reply. The ellipsis on her side of the conversation blinks for a good ninety seconds. Not that I'm counting.

Sorry I didn't make it, finally comes through, simple and succinct.

No worries. I wasn't expecting you to.

Oh. Cool, then.

Not that I wouldn't have wanted you there or anything. That would have been fine.

Cool.

Ming wasn't even there. I'm just saying there was no wide-scale invite that you weren't included in. Plz don't say cool again.

Coolio.

It's my turn to take a very long time to craft Corinne a simple message. I type and retype it again and again, trying to formulate a clear explanation, but in the end I choose to use her own words.

It would have been more fun with you there, though.

It takes twenty-seven seconds that feel much, much longer, but Corinne's reply eventually comes:

It's nowhere close to matching my own.

SEVENTEEN

Today is another Corinne day on my calendar. I don't quite know when I began marking these as "Corinne" days instead of "Palm Tree" days, but my Sunday walks with the pup now feel like strolls with Corinne that just happen to feature a cute border collie mix. It feels strange to think that blackmail was technically the start of something that I now feel like I've been doing forever, even though it's been only a few weeks. I imagine this is how childhood friends feel walking together, talking animatedly without a clear thesis in mind, throwing multiple conversational balls into the air, all at once, and picking them up whenever feels natural. Sometimes days later. I've been looking forward to these walks more and more.

"So, did you give any more thought to McGill?" she says as soon as she spots me waiting in the lobby, fast-forwarding past the hello, chitchat, and any other topic. Her usual pink beanie has been replaced by a wool-knit seasonal version of the same thing, this one a hotter shade of pink.

"Good morning to you, too," I say as I hold the door and Palm Tree darts out, snout already to the ground and pulling Corinne behind him.

The February air provides the right chill as we step onto the busy weekend sidewalk. The city is orange today, beaming with an almost abnormal amount of sunlight. The fruit in stands on Amsterdam Avenue all looks juicy and fruit bowl ready.

"Try steadying your hold on the leash, so he's not wavering so much," I note.

She follows the instruction and turns back to me as soon as Palm Tree steadies. "So, you want to interview for McGill: yes or no?"

"Man, small talk is not your forte, huh?"

"I don't believe in it as a lifestyle choice, no."

I sigh and answer her question. "Maybe."

If I'm being honest, I have been thinking about McGill more and more. Since pulling up those designs for Corinne, I've been finding myself revisiting them on my own. In bed, on the subway, or at the dog park. The designers in question have all graduated from McGill by now and are a bit all over, all in different facets of the industry. None of them appears hungry or destitute on their social media pages. One of them just did a show in Atlanta, and another one is making waves in the Japanese menswear scene, which looks bonkers with styles and designs that won't hit the United States for another few seasons at least. It's pretty clear: it all started with McGill.

"Well, for the record, I think it's a great idea."

"You do?"

"McGill is a fantastic school. A lot of people go up to Canada for college these days. It's way cheaper, for one. And for two, their curriculum is very competitive. It's an international experience at a fraction of the price."

We fall into step easily on Riverside Park's cracked pavement, led by Palm Tree, who darts left and right at every new winter smell that the city provides. The brightness of the sun, the touches of Valentine's Day decor on the stoops, and the easily fashionable hipsters in striking scarves and jackets seem to brighten the colors. It's one of those days where everyone could probably take an amazing photo without much effort.

"They did invite me to interview a while back." One of the many emails I'd opened and discarded, refreshing for a new notice from Columbia instead.

"Why haven't you agreed to see them?"

I stop and think. Because I didn't want Columbia to think I was too serious about other colleges? Colleges are conscious, telepathic organisms, and the second I stop actively wanting to attend CU is the second the CU hive-mind turns its back on me?

I don't say that part out loud because, in hindsight, it wasn't the sharpest logic out there. Instead, I give a hapless shrug.

"I'm not sure I would fit in Canada, eh? Although lumberjacks are insanely ripped but at what cost?"

"Oh, stop it. My aunt lives in Montreal. It's an amazing city."

I shrug. "They have good programs. But I don't want to give up on Columbia yet." I throw my head back in a way that causes Palm Tree to tilt his.

"That's ridiculous. Interviewing for another college doesn't mean you've given up on—"

"I know, I know," I say, rudely interrupting because I have no idea how we ended up in this conversation and part of me already wants out. "I know it's not logical, Troy, but accepting a non-Columbia universe feels like I'm letting my dad down. Giving up on the great Haltiwanger Hunger."

"The what now?"

As soon as we enter the dog run, Palm Tree and a young, dark, almost red golden retriever slam into each other's necks and take off for what will undoubtedly be the time of their lives. It's going to be a heartbreak to separate them in a few minutes. It always is.

"It's what my dad calls it," I finally explain as we settle on a bench to watch them. I spot Gigi on the opposite end of the dog run, headphones in and two huskies vying for the roped tennis ball dangling from her belt. She waves at me from afar, and I return it with a nod.

"The Great Hunger that got his Grampa from some little shack in Gonaives, like the backwoods of Haiti, to Port-au-Prince, the capital of Haiti, to New Jersey, to the Bronx, and now Manhattan. I think he looks at me and sees a penthouse next. With a wall of framed Ivy League diplomas."

Corinne listens, eyes on the dogs, without saying anything.

Despite our both being the O-Generation—a concept I have to admit rings terribly true the more I think about it—Corinne isn't an immigrant. Or the child of immigrants. It's a distinction that's mostly irrelevant except in moments like these, where it could easily place us on two different wavelengths. There's no Haitian in her, no Jamaican, no Puerto Rican. Her Blackness is American, born and raised. Stolen and enslaved, technically, but still, it's rooted here. She never aspired to be here from another shore elsewhere. She might not understand.

"If I give up on Columbia, then . . . I don't know."

"Then it's like you're no longer Haltiwanger Hungry?"

"Something like that." My logic is stupid on the face of it, but somehow I feel no judgment emanating from Corinne.

"Look," she eventually says. "Take it from someone whose last birthday gift from her dad was an eighteen-karat white-gold diamond bracelet he then begged me to mail him back because it was accidentally sent to me by his assistant when he meant it for his girlfriend . . ."

Yikes.

". . . and then a dog to make up for that fiasco—months before I go off to college. Parents don't always know best."

Yikeser.

Although the image of Corinne opening her mail to find a diamond bracelet in there, rolling her eyes, and tossing it aside before returning to her reading is very easy to imagine.

"Whatever happens at Princeton for me," she continues. "I know I'm not going to be exactly the daughter Gilbert pictures.

Or Chantale for that matter. From now on, we get to shape ourselves. Isn't that the point of college?"

An exhausted Palm Tree waddles back toward us, tongue out and panting. His eyes fill with puppy recognition at the sight of Corinne, and he eagerly sniffs her hand as she takes out a bottle of water and collapsible bowl from my doggy bag.

"Look at this. Corinne Troy: dog person. Who would have guessed?"

"I'll miss the little inconvenience next year," she says, smiling as she watches Palm Tree take massive gulps of water.

"It's a good reason to visit home."

"I hope he remembers me. I bet you I'll drop my bags at the door, the first weekend back home, and Palm Tree here will be renamed Pumpernickel and elegantly licking African herbal tea in a corner."

We gather Palm Tree's supplies along with a very, very tired pup and head home to the Wyatt.

"My mom mentioned you the other night, by the way," she says as we walk, much slower without Palm Tree pulling us forward.

"Your mom?"

The one who is a dean at Columbia University, I think, always a little too quickly.

"Well, she noticed Palm Tree is still alive and getting bigger, and the other night, she mentioned how he was much better behaved than before. So, yes, you came up. She wanted my opinion on the walker behind the results."

Did my heart just skip a beat because Columbia University gatekeeper Chantale Troy asked about me, or is it the idea that someone out there has the unrestricted access to Corinne's real opinion of me?

"Well?" I manage, keeping my cool, at least vocally. "What did you say?"

"I was honest in my assessment." She smiles, clearly reveling in keeping her cards close to the vest.

"But she wouldn't stop gushing about how punctual you've been. She thinks you're an 'upstanding young man' and the only person that has made the whole dog situation, as she puts it, 'bearable.' Congratulations: you have a fan."

Lion's directive to look at the opportunity in front of me floats through my mind. This is probably the most direct chance I'll have of steering Chantale toward a recommendation of some kind. But it just feels . . . weird. Wrong.

"Cool."

She throws me a strange look. "Cool?"

"I mean, hurray for satisfied customers." I shrug, focusing on Palm Tree. "Besides, this little dude is my real boss, technically."

Corinne smiles and acquiesces. "Well, that's true."

"Have a good nap, buddy," I say, scratching Palm Tree's chin goodbye once we get to the lobby of the building. Corinne smiles and makes it all of three steps up before stopping and turning back to me with sudden urgency.

"By the way, do you have a valid passport?" she asks.

"Uh, yeah, of course," I answer. Child of immigrants, after all. I'm pretty sure Dad and Ma applied for it before I could crawl. Not that I remember ever using it.

"Good," she says. "It's irresponsible not to have one."

She makes it up the stairs, the puppy still asleep, and then stops and turns back again.

"You'll be great, Halti. Wherever you end up."

I smile. "Thanks, Corinne."

She disappears up the stairs, her steps rhythmically click-clacking all the way to the top floor of the building. It suddenly dawns on me that there is a lot more to lose here than just a client and polite lobby smiles.

Ming is on a trip to Vermont with his mom this weekend, whatever that means. The selfie he sends me has Ms. Denison-Eifling hugging her son tightly by the neck in a purposeful grasp that borders on the overly attached. To say nothing of the matching scarves the two are wearing. She is still processing Ming's international future.

There are also texts and private messages flying about multiple parties around Manhattan tonight. Abdel, Dorian and his crew, and Celia Donavan too. I'm not in the mood for any of them. "HH" is a performance I just don't have the bandwidth for right now.

I power through an English essay that's due on Tuesday and fall asleep on the living room sofa to some *Rick and Morty*, still wearing my Uptown Updogs T-shirt. At some point, Ma must have put a blanket around me. I either vaguely remember her passing through the space in a hurry to change before going back to the station or dreamt the whole thing.

When I wake up later that evening and yet again refresh my in-box, I notice a new, unfamiliar entry: an Amtrak train ticket to Montreal forwarded by a Corinne Troy.

Don't be weird about it, reads the email. *I'll ask my mom to dock your pay to make up for it. Corinne*

I quickly dial her number.

"Meet in the lobby at 8:23 a.m. sharp. Do not forget your passport," she says without so much as a hello.

"Corinne, no."

"I was patient and listened to your argument today," she says. "It's complete nonsense. Your interviewing for McGill in no way affects your Columbia chances. So you're interviewing for McGill. It's so simple, it's barely worth discussing."

"I don't want your pity," I say sharply because, while I'm happy for her Princetonian future, I do not want to be a charity case.

"Look, my aunt already agreed to it." She sighs, sounding bored by the minutiae of even discussing this. "I was supposed to visit her for spring break, so I just moved it by a few weeks and asked if I could bring a friend along. She has plenty of space, and we'll be back Wednesday. I checked the website, and McGill interviews are typically slotted early in the week. They have a very transparent system."

"Corinne, it's not that—"

"Oh, my God, this is so dull. Yes, it is that simple, and no, it's not pity. Are you telling me your parents will object to you traveling north for a college interview of all things?"

"Well, no, they wouldn't but—"

"I'll see you in the lobby at 8:23 a.m. sharp. I've budgeted for travel time to Penn Station. And remember: passport."

It's insane, but something about Corinne's confidence is almost contagious.

It's impulsive, but I put up a quick *Dear Uptown Updogs Customers* message on the website, edit a truncated version for my seven clients scheduled for the next two days, and loop in Gigi from the dog run, who is more than thrilled for the opportunity to poach some of my clients by filling in for me. I arrange to leave the keys for her. In a few phone calls, my schedule is cleared until Wednesday. So much for customer loyalty.

"Yo, Dad!" I shout after it's all taken care of. "Can I borrow your rolly luggage?"

"Sure. Why?" he shouts back from the bathroom, mouth audibly foamy and full of toothbrush.

"Er . . . How would you feel about your only son hopping the border for a couple days?"

EIGHTEEN

The train comes to a stop twenty minutes ahead of our expected arrival time, which is still a good ten hours and fifteen minutes after leaving Penn Station this morning. Seven p.m. and Montreal is already dark, and my muscles feel sore from the swallowed day of travel.

I barely have time to wake up from my post–US-Canada border nap to find Corinne already looming over me, bag under her arm.

"Are the gendarmes searching the train?" I ask, midyawn. "Why are you in such a hurry?"

"I've been sitting for ten hours. I could run a marathon," she says, dragging me to the front of the train. She seems committed to our being the first ones out. "Aunt Terry is meeting us a few blocks away. She didn't want to pay for parking."

"Slow down, will you?" I shout out in the brouhaha of tourists and cross-country travelers pouring out of the Amtrak 69 train and into Montreal, still carrying that New York quickstep in their walk.

I don't know what I was expecting, but so far, the population of Montreal isn't all that different from New York's. No Mounties to speak of yet. Visually, the ethnic breakdown of the crowd definitely tips in favor of white people, but there are still plenty of shades and shapes and ethnicities to be found.

The crowd may even skew a little younger—according to Wikipedia, there are eleven colleges and universities in the Greater Montreal area. As a whole, though, Montrealers are just as fashionable as New Yorkers.

"Keep up, Haltiwanger!"

As we make our way out of the Gare Centrale station, Corinne defaults to tour-guiding mode. Her style is a mix of casual factoids, circumstantial ones, and familial details about Aunt Terry, all delivered at a brisk pace while we weave through the crowd, under English and French train announcements. If I didn't know better, I would say she even seems a little nervous.

"Montreal is fully bilingual."

"McGill's campus is actually within walking distance; we'll come back tomorrow."

"Poutine is honestly kind of disgusting, but you can't in good conscience leave Montreal without trying it."

"Terry is a baker. She has a shop on St-Laurent. It's pretty famous."

"Aunt Terry is nothing like Mom; unless they're standing right next to each other, you almost wouldn't know they're twins."

"Wait, wait, wait—your mom is a twin? A real one?"

Corinne finally comes to a halt as we stand on the escalator, and she laughs a little.

"You're in a new city . . . in a new country, mind you, and the fact that my mom is a twin is what's blowing your mind?"

Sure, Canada is all well and good, but twins have always fascinated me. Another wrinkle of siblinghood to observe from the outside as an only child.

"Well, this wouldn't be happening now if you'd let us sit together on the train, Troy. That was the perfect time for factoids like these."

Corinne shrugs. She had insisted that we sit on two different ends of the wagon because "the impulse to chitchat" would have distracted from the work she needed to get out of the way. We met for a brief lunch in the dining car, after which she returned to her seat to study with headphones in.

I have to admit that, this way, the ten hours of travel time were at least productive. Now I won't have to think about a backlog of problem sets during this interview.

"Do you have, like, a cousin you share a telepathic connection with?" I can't help but follow up as Corinne leads us down onto foreign streets with echoes of French in the background. "That's so cool. Like, if they stub their toe in Canada, do you feel a twinge in New York? Do you look like them?"

"No cousins. Aunt Terry doesn't have any kids. She and Mom are . . . Well, you'll see," Corinne says, with a note of dread.

"C-c-cold!" I yelp out as a wave of chill hits my bones, right through the bubble jacket and long-sleeve T underneath. Unlike New York, which has been snowless, Canada has solid banks of white coiled along the sides of every street. Some dirty, some clean, with lines of boot holes stepping into them. Every step feels gritty from the salt that's been put on every inch of the sidewalk to help with the visible patches of ice.

"It's Canada." Corinne laughs, making a move to tighten my scarf but then moving her hands to the straps of her backpack. "Even if you go by the broadest stereotype, the cold would be at the top of the list."

"I, um, didn't expect the temperature to go down by this much since we were traveling by train and not, y'know, plane. Like, how many weather patterns could we have crossed?"

She stops in the middle of the sidewalk and looks at me with a brow so furrowed it may never unwrinkle.

"Thank God you're pretty because that's sincerely the dumbest thing I ever heard. Just smile a lot during the interview or something."

I'm about to excavate as much material as I can from that stray compliment when a singsongy voice beckons to us.

"Riri! I'd recognize that hat anywhere," a fluffy purple faux-fur coat says, waving at us from across the street. "There she is!"

"Hi, Auntie," Corinne says—sighs, really—letting herself be hugged tightly by a mauve blur of a woman I assume to be Theresa Bien-Aimée, the decidedly mismatched twin to the elegant and stoic Chantale Bien-Aimée Troy.

175

"Thanks for hosting us last minute. Mom says she really appreciates it."

"Oh, stop that!" the woman says, pulling away only to cup Corinne's cheeks, seemingly immune to Corinne's invisible force field of personal space. "Look at you! All woman-sized."

Up close, it's a bit uncanny: Terry's features look exactly like Chantale's. The same sharp eyes and chin, inherited by Corinne too, but this version is from an altogether different time line: one of shaved heads, dangling earrings, and blue lipstick. Nothing she's wearing matches, which somehow totally works.

I imagine all the tea and rye toast that Chantale spent a lifetime eating while working on dissertations were replaced by muffins topped with butter, cupcakes, and donuts for this larger-than-life version of Chantale, emanating joy with every fiber of her being.

"Hi, Ms. Bien-Aimée." I Smile, removing my glove and extending a frostbitten hand toward her to introduce myself formally. "My name is Henri Haltiwanger. Thank you so much for hosting me."

She vigorously shakes my hand and pulls me in, tilting my chin down with a gloved hand and grinning into my eyes.

If only all women in this family were so easily charmed.

"Now, Henri, first things first: were you always this handsome?"

"No, ma'am," I say, following her lead, wiggling my eyebrows at Corinne for good measure before getting into the front seat. "But that Monkey's Paw had one last finger on it, and I made the most of it."

She lets out a sharp cackle from the driver's seat, craning her neck to pull us out of the parking spot and into the mild traffic of Montreal, Quebec.

Corinne's smack to the back of my head is so lightning quick that I would need slow motion to prove it in a court of law.

Of course, Aunt Terry lives over her bakery. The building in question is a two-story structure by a small park. The forest-green roof looks black at this time of the night, especially covered in a layer of snow.

"'The Good Twin,'" I read aloud. The name is in cursive, and at the side is a sketch of Terry, complete with a shaved head and round gold ear hoops, holding a pie with cartoon flavor lines drawn over it like it was baked for the express purpose of luring in Wile E. Coyote.

"Mom was not amused to learn the name when we drove up for the grand opening," Corinne comments.

Judging by Terry's hint of a smile, I'm going to guess that that was partly the point. Having a sibling that close must be a hell of a thing.

The store is closed when we pull into the parking lot, but there's an orange hue coming from behind the glass front window. It's easy to imagine Terry humming at the ovens in the wee morning hours.

We take the second door right next to the bakery's entrance and climb a narrow set of carpeted stairs that lead up to a rather large apartment with yellow-painted walls and frames all around, knickknacks on every shelf. The air smells of tea, just like at the Troys' but a different, spicier flavor, maybe.

"Bienvenue! Welcome! *Mi casa es su casa*. Look at that; three languages right there! They might have room for me at Princeton, huh, Riri?"

She laughs at her own joke. It's both corny and the laugh a little infectious, and Corinne shakes her head as she removes her scarf and lets herself fall into a couch. She is fully at home here, whereas I find myself lurking, taking it all in.

There's an American flag magnet on the fridge that reminds me of Ma's Haitian flag-patterned oven mitt. A touch of home in the room that sustains the house.

"I told you we were only going to be here for less than forty-eight hours," Corinne says, stealing a glance at me when she thinks I'm not looking. "I told you not to make a fuss for us." She points with her socked toe to the kitchen table filled with tinfoil-covered trays. "This qualifies as a fuss."

"Calm down, Mini Chantale." Terry waves her off, checking the oven. "Half of this stuff is for a food fair at the end of the week. Henri, sweetie: stop standing by the door like a butler. You're stressing me out. There's no grand tour; make yourself at home. Go have a poo or something."

By the time the three of us settle in for dinner in the living room and the coffee table is packed with tray after tray of food—roasted carrots, mac and cheese, and rosemary turkey fresh from the oven, all dishes that Aunt Terry waves off as being whipped up in a few minutes—it's clear that Terry is the sort of person you believe when she says something like "Make yourself at home." We end up watching French-Canadian news about America's upcoming elections.

"You people sure know how to take the fun out of a country that has Las Vegas, Miami, and New York City." Terry sighs, and neither Corinne nor I can exactly argue with that. "So, Henri: is McGill your dream school, as you kids put it?"

"And exactly what's wrong with dream schools?" Corinne says. Terry doesn't seem to mind her niece's eye roll, laughing along with it.

"Let's just say that my dreams never involved a syllabus when I was your age," she says. "And your mom used to roll her eyes at me that same way when I said that."

"It's not my dream school, exactly. That would be Columbia but um . . ."

I'm not getting a lot of catcalls from that construction site, I think.

"It's good to have options, Auntie," Corinne chimes in, as if sensing my butt cheeks clenching at the topic.

"But McGill's a really good school," I find myself saying. "They have an amazing design program."

Corinne raises an eyebrow at me.

"Yeah, I heard something about that from one of the girls at my Zumba. Well, I'm sure you'll nail it, babe." Terry pats my shoulder.

I Smile and she smiles, seemingly happy with the answer. Here's a-hoping, Aunt Terry.

"I was a little afraid when you said you were coming— unannounced, no less. Last time, she rearranged the seating downstairs because it was 'suboptimal,'" Terry says. "Your boyfriend has mellowed you out, Riri."

"You can keep making all your jokes, but we're still not dating, Auntie," Corinne corrects. Was that a snort?

"And why not?" Terry asks. "Look at him. Handsome young man with a future. You could do worse. Ask your mom."

"I am really handsome." I grin with teeth fenced with mac and cheese.

"Ugh," Corinne says before turning back to her aunt, legs folded under her. "He's a hussy, for one," she adds.

"Excuse me?" Is that what she really thinks of me?

Auntie Terry raises both eyebrows at me as if awaiting rebuttal, and for a moment, I feel like I'm presenting a dissertation to Chantale Troy.

"I—I don't— I'm not a hussy! Is this because of Evie?"

"And Charlotte . . . And Jayna-Mae . . ."

Charlotte was my partner in a play who fully stuck her tongue into my mouth when Juliet was supposed to be comatose. And J-M was only a few Shake Shack dates sophomore year, back when I thought I would have time to date. The text she'd sent me after being left waiting outside the movies had been very, very long. A lot of exclamation points that climaxed with a *DELETE MY NUMBER, FCKBOI*. But that was a lifetime ago!

"You have a reputation around FATE, that's all," Corinne says, chewing very deliberately. "There's a shocking list in the third-floor girls' bathroom stalls."

I would ask for a follow-up, but Corinne is smirking in a way that makes me want to refuse her the satisfaction with every fiber of my being.

Terry is ready to issue her verdict. "Well, Henri," she says after literally smacking my hand away when I try to help clear the plates. "I've made up the couch in the study for you. Dating or not, I'm not having Chantale call me to ask why she sent her daughter up here for two days and ended up a grandmother."

"Auntie, for the love of God, you have got to stop," Corinne says.

"I don't have to do a damn thing except stay Black, pay my taxes, and die, honey." She cackles all the way to the kitchen with that one, arms full of empty plates.

Later, when Terry has gone off to shower, after doing all the dishes, Corinne and I set out to straighten up the kitchen and living room area—if for nothing else than to make up for the fact that this woman worked all day, cooked all afternoon, picked us up from the station in Montreal's definition of downtown traffic, and even insisted on doing the dishes, all in the middle of the workweek.

After changing out of our travel clothes, Corinne and I put away the dishes as best we can figure out. It's a nice feeling, caring for this comfortable, colorful home with Corinne Troy.

I want to say something, maybe "Thank you for bringing me here" or "Thank you for being here" or even "Thank you for being you. I'm really glad we're doing this together, and I like you a stupid amount." Instead, I just say:

"What if McGill turns me down too?"

"It won't," she says, taking wide sweeps of the kitchen floor. "It's going to go great, Halti. Just be yourself."

"People love saying that." I sigh. "That's like screaming at someone having a panic attack not to panic. What if I don't know what that means?"

She pulls herself from the wall and steps into the study, flopping herself on the makeshift bed, bouncing a few times, completely comfortable. Not just in this home, I realize, but also in her skin. Being Corinne Troy is not a performance to Corinne Troy.

"Okay, okay: no platitudes. I hate getting those myself," she says. "Real advice, though? Stop trying to imagine what the other person wants to hear; that's actively dumb. Plus, they're likely to be Canadians. Their brains are harder to read what with all the politeness protocols happening up here."

That's what I had done with Donielle Kempf, wasn't it? Maybe this time it might serve me to be a little more like Corinne Troy: speak first, think later, and live with the consequences. There's a certain courage in that.

"So," I say.

"So," she repeats, raising her eyebrows, almost defiantly, but does not move otherwise.

"Hussy?!"

She chuckles lightly, balancing on her knees like a toddler.

"I knew that got into your head."

"Is that really how you see me?" I try to sound casual about it, but I can't say the word hasn't been bugging me since I heard it.

She throws me a look as though she's considering all the bullet points associated with the term and assessing whether or not I meet them. *Hus·sy / ˈhə·sē / Impudent, immoral, loose person.*

"No," she eventually admits. "For one thing, it's a very gendered term. 'Tart' is more gender-neutral, maybe? But not by much."

"Corinne . . ."

"You'd be more of a player or womanizer or a philanderer or a roué, even. How come all the guy terms for 'hussy' sound so distinguished? That's some patriarchal bull right there."

"Corinne!" I repeat, though I can feel a smile creeping on my lips, matching hers.

"Okay, okay, I'm kidding! Find your chill, Haltiwanger."

"I'll squeeze that into my calendar of hussy appointments."

"You're not a hussy. You're . . . aware of your charms, yes, but I don't think you're immoral, and you mean well. As far as I can tell."

I catch a glimpse of myself in Corinne's eyes and suddenly feel stuck in place, realizing how physically close we are right now—physically close and on something that by definition amounts to a bed. Whatever I was going to say next dies in a choke halfway out my throat. I'm torn between wanting to duck away from this sudden makeshift intimacy and also lean into it all at once and to hell with all the second-guessing. And unless I'm completely insane, Corinne might be leaning forward too, eyes darting back and forth across my face like she's also looking for a clue that she's misreading this. Maybe neither of us are, and this is where all those weird feelings and false starts were always meant to land. In Canada, on Aunt Terry's couch.

"Master of the house, doling out the charm."

We both startle back at the booming male voice that suddenly overfills the room, and I knock my head into the wall, leaping away from Corinne as she lets out a curse under her breath.

"Ready with a handshake and an open palm. . . ."

"What the hell is that?" I say, looking around for this singing, gravelly male voice that sounds like it's coming from the very walls of the room.

"*Les Misérables*, original London cast recording." Corinne sighs knowingly, falling back into the couch and staring blankly at the low ceiling.

"Definitely not some Barry White, huh?" I say, forcing a laugh, heart still in my throat.

"Terry loves a good musical. I guess she finally installed the digital sound system my mom got her for Christmas. I can't believe I was the one who suggested it."

"It was a wonderful gift, baby girl!" Terry's voice shouts from her room, a few doors down.

I rub a frustrated hand across my face, realizing that there's probably not an inch of this deceptively teched-out apartment that Aunt Terry can't see from her phone. As if on cue, the volume goes up under us.

"Food beyond compare, Food beyond belief, Mix it in a mincer and pretend it's beef."

"Okay, I'm going to my room now, Auntie!" Corinne shouts

into the air because there is really no recovering the mood once entrails get in the mix in surround sound.

"Sounds like a fine plan, babe," Terry answers back, decidedly pleased with herself.

"*Kidney of a horse, liver of a cat, Filling up the sausages with this and that.*"

"It's getting late, anyway," Corinne says, now on her feet with half a room between us.

"Look, Corinne, I'm sorry if that wasn't—"

"G'night, Henri!"

And just like that, she is already out of the room, which is back to an eerie silence. I fall flat onto the pillow and can't help but let out a weary laugh. At what, I'm not sure. The weight of North American travels, maybe; of being in Cana-freaking-da, in this strange doppelganger's home, with Corinne a door away; of having a McGill interview on the docket in less than eleven hours. Or maybe it's just not knowing which of these facts is currently making me the most nervous.

NINETEEN

McGill University is a relatively small campus up on a hill in downtown Montreal, not too far from yesterday's train station. Aunt Terry drops me off at the bottom gates, since she doesn't have a pass to drive onto the campus. The new Design School building is located up Rue University, at the corner of Pine Avenue West, an appropriately bilingual corner of the map. It's a bit of a walk, which makes the fact that I'm early a good thing. The last I saw of Corinne this morning, she was a very still bundle of covers through the crack of her door. Not that I was trying to catch a glimpse of her before leaving for good luck or anything.

"Babe, I have to cover the morning shift at the bakery," Terry says, checking her watch. "But Corinne knows her way around town, so I'll make sure to tell her where to meet you, okay?"

"Thanks for everything, Terry. I really appreciate it."

"Your parents raised you right. So polite! And so handsome

in that suit!" she squeals. "Dazzle 'em, you hear?" she orders as she pulls away.

Dazzle. Right.

Everything about McGill's campus feels aged to just the right age, like the architectural equivalent of expensive wine. Unlike FATE, which sometimes feels like some Manhattan spaceship, most of the buildings are bricked, coated in frosted snow, with rusty staircases. There are just enough modern steel-and-glass constructs peppered throughout to also see why the school is the academic beacon of Montreal. The cold (because there's no denying it—it's a hell of a sting to the face) makes everything feel crisp and new.

After slipping down two separate ice patches in my weather-inappropriate Jordans, I forgo my pride and hold on to a sidewalk railing the whole way up the hill, even if it means getting outpaced by two white-haired men who probably got tenure a century ago.

I manage to make it to the Design School, spine intact and pride devastated. Room 608, where I arrive a good twenty minutes early, is bustling with activity and about forty people in various stages of phone swiping at the moment. I most definitely miscalculated on the attire front.

"Excuse me: is this the waiting room for the Design School interviews?" I whisper to the nearest person by the door, a white university employee with a shaved head in his late thirties. The man nods. He's sitting away from the pack and wearing a crisp suit and silk scarf far too expensive for an aspiring college student.

"And have they started to call names yet?"

"Not yet."

"I'm Henri Haltiwanger. H-A-L. Haltiwanger."

"Good for you, Henri Haltiwanger."

A moment passes between us and the man frowns.

"Screw me," he groans. "You think I work here, don't you?"

"Er . . . No, of course not."

"I'm not that old!"

"Oh, no . . . I just assumed since you're, y'know, wearing a suit," I say, having not yet converted my Smiles to Canadian currency.

"So are you, kid!" he sputters. "Off-the-rack but still."

He nevertheless removes his bag from the seat next to his, which I take as a reluctant invitation. He introduces himself as Steve, and his handshake is strong and sturdy.

"Henri," I say. "And sorry about that."

"Steve. And no worries: I know I'm old as balls. It just stings when other people notice it too," the man goes on to say, scoping out the room of contenders with a mix of disdain and apprehension. "North America's design prodigies, if you'll believe the pamphlet."

I get his point. It's not just that we're the only two wearing suits in a room of about forty. Only a handful of the other applicants look like Canadian high school students. They look closer to the disaffected twenty-something-year-old New Yorkers you see hanging around St. Marks Place in the summer, arms full of sleeves and sides of heads androgynously shaved. Misfits by design. Some are rocking high fashion at the moment, and I wonder how the girl in nine-inch stiletto heels that look hand-crafted even made it up to the building.

The majority have some headphones around their neck or a tablet on their lap, not looking to socialize. I wonder if the mind game of meeting the competition is why McGill's interviews are structured in such a bizarre way. No back channels and informal meetings: just three days across three different weeks where applicants are invited to show up for fifteen-minute chitchat with members of the staff. A great Canadian equalizer.

A small huddle of younger applicants in the corner are animatedly chatting and comparing sketches and mock-ups on their tablets. Were we supposed to bring portfolios?

"Don't worry," Steve says. "I don't have one either. The program doesn't require them. Just 'An Unbridled Passion and an Open Mind,' whatever the hell that means. Shitty slogan, if you ask me. Most of the people who bring fancy portfolios today are probably just trying to make up for shitty grades."

A short woman with long hair and a leather binder under her arm hears him as she passes us by, and she frowns. Going by his smirk, it's exactly what Steve intended. He casts me another look and follows it with the very question I'm dreading most today. "So, what's your thing?"

"My thing?" I repeat.

Steve extends his arms out and tilts his fists inward.

"This is mine," he says proudly. "Suits. Designed this one

from scratch and still had to take the GED for a chance at this freaking program."

"That's, um, insanely impressive," I say, because it very much is.

It's a very good suit. The kind you might see with a four-hundred-dollar pocket square on a mannequin in a Fifth Avenue window display, next to a headless wife and two headless kids.

Steve goes through his family history and how the DelMattises were originally in the wedding dress industry and that he learned at age nine how to hem his first suit in a family of six sisters. The McGill program is his chance to strike out on his own, even though he's got a two-decade late start and an alimony payment. He's chatting away his nervousness, and I don't mind letting him. Eventually, Steve gets called in.

"Good luck, dude!"

"Same to you, Henri Haltiwanger," he replies as he stands. "Although you understand that if it comes down to a single spot, I'd snap your neck and throw you down a ravine, right?"

"Of course." I smile. He'd make a phenomenal *Hunger Games* tribute.

The room shrinks applicant by applicant, each greeted by a rotating cast of what I assume to be faculty members, and after what feels like an eternity, it's my turn.

"Haltiwanger? Henri Halti . . . H? Henri H?" comes the would-be interviewer, reading from his folder and chewing a pen cap as he walks. He's younger than expected, with long hair tied into a bun and a stained T-shirt under his jacket.

"Here!" I yell out, standing up at the ready. "I mean, er, *présent*!"

"Sorry about the wait," he says, with what I now recognize as the default French-Canadian accent, as he leads the way to an interview room. "Every year we get more applicants willing to trek here for an in-person interview. I guess that's a good thing, but that means a longer waiting time for some. . . . New York, right? Halwangue?"

None of the butterflies I had chomping at the walls of my stomach when I met with Donielle Kempf are in session right now. Whatever the hectic circumstances that got me here might have been, something about the cold Montreal air has killed them dead.

"Yes, New York. And it's Haltiwanger," I say with a smile. "Pleasure to meet you."

"Halti? Halti! Are you there?" a stilted image of Ming in his FATE jacket says. "Where are you, dude?"

I'd been sitting in the fire stairwell of the Design School for a good twenty minutes, the bottoms of my feet still jittery from the hour-long interview, when Ming's name popped up on my phone.

"Canada," I manage. "It's a long story, but I'll be back tomorrow."

"M'kay," Ming says before following up with, "Are you eloping with Corinne Troy?"

"What? No! I was interviewing for McGill! Corinne just

came with. I'm crashing at her aunt's."

"Oh." He seems disappointed and looks over his phone's camera, out of my line of sight to someone I can't see.

"Wait, is that what people are saying?"

"In a word, yes. But that's okay! I'll find a way to put that toothpaste back in the tube. I've got you down here."

Elope? They think we've *eloped*? "I hate high school."

"Our penance for sins committed in a past life," Ming agrees. "How was the interview?"

"Good. Great, maybe?" I allow myself to be positive. "I think I gave my interviewer a link to an illegal website where he could get the Jordans he was looking for. So who knows? Maybe that was some Canadian moral test I failed, but beyond that . . . it went well?"

In the end, I tried to listen to Corinne and talk without going over every word in my head, looking for smiles and nods of the acknowledgments from the interviewer. Henri Halti-wanger Uncensored. God help us all. I rambled about designers I admire like Tinker Hatfield and Raf Simons, and the inter-viewer nodded along, jotting notes down. And in my defense, he had asked for the link to that website.

"He did say I would love their new design lab, which felt like, I don't know . . ."

More conditional tense than future tense, maybe.

I look out the stairwell's glass window and onto the McGill campus below hectic with midday activity and dark bundles of coats and backpacks leaving steps in the trodden snow behind them. "How insane would it be? For me to go to another country for freaking design school?"

"Nothing about it doesn't make sense," Ming states confidently. "Wait, why is Corinne there with you, again?"

"What do you mean? I'm crashing at her aunt's."

"Your sleeping on a couch doesn't require her to be there."

"I'm not following," I say.

He sighs, exasperated. "I'm late for class. I'll talk to you when you get back from traveling to a foreign country with a girl you've been hanging out with nonstop and who is deeply invested in your success but that you're not dating."

I roll my eyes at him.

"Thank God you're pretty, dude." Ming sighs. "Because really."

"Okay, I'm sick of people saying th—"

The connection cuts off, and I picture Ming back at FATE cackling, very happy with himself right now. Smug bastard.

I meet Corinne back down at the McGill gates, where she's waiting for me, wearing a bright turquoise coat I don't recognize and heeled leather boots that are definitely from the Terry Bien-Aimée collection. The more time I spend with her outside of FATE's uniform, the more I've come to realize that Corinne very much has her own sense of style. It's a little eclectic and thrown together, but it often all lines up into effortlessly trendy like today.

Before I can decide on the best words to use to formulate

the compliment without innuendo, she spots me and stutter-steps across the icy sidewalk, which ends with her tumbling into me instead, and the whole thing turns into a kiss right next to my lips and another quick one on my other cheek.

"Sorry!" she sputters, visibly embarrassed.

"It's okay."

Her laughter is weird and nervous. Not unlike the Cori days of crashing parties together under duress. "La bise! In Canada, we kiss on both sides, Haltiwanger! So, um, how was the interview?"

"It was good." I smile because it's increasingly becoming harder not to when Corinne is around. I go through the entire thing from Steve to Ming, to the life story of Raf Simons and his design aesthetic.

Corinne nods and takes it all in, looking genuinely happy. "See? I told you. You've totally got this!"

"We'll see."

My grades aren't as good as they could be, I think but don't say, not wanting to spoil the mood with more weird anguish. The interview is done now. All we can do is wait.

"So, what's on the agenda for today?"

"Well, I was thinking we could explore the city a bit?" she suggests with her phone already out. "If for no reason than to show you Canada isn't so bad after all."

"I'm all yours," I say before realizing the full implications of that statement.

"Good!" She nods before suddenly grabbing my hand and

pulling me in the direction of the campus exit. And then the strangest thing happens: she holds on.

Like, she's *holding* my hand.

We are holding hands.

She idly thumbs the knob of my wrist as we walk the uncrowded streets of Montreal, hand-in-hand, both pretending like we haven't noticed we've been doing it.

Someone has flipped the switch, and Montreal's weather has transitioned from eerily sunny and frostbitten to overcast and mild, but she doesn't seem to notice, pointing to a different landmark or restaurant every few steps.

"And this is where they have Les Francos de Montréal every year. Like Shakespeare in the Park but with French jazz. And right down that way is the Old Port," she says, intent on being the most thorough tour guide she can be.

Anyone else might make it tedious, but I have a feeling Corinne could make any Wikipedia-lifted bit of history sound like the most fascinating thing in the world. She's brilliant, yes—that's obvious—but also hilarious in her way, and my face hurts from laughing as she pantomimes the story of how Terry and Chantale got into a heated—allegedly vicious—argument over whether or not the Coca-Cola here tasted slightly different from the one in New York.

"How often do you come here?" I ask.

"Well, before my mom made any money, back when she was an adjunct and a freelancer, summer trips to Aunt Terry's were the only vacations we could afford." Corinne smiles at the memory in that charming way of hers, flipping through a mental flip-book of fond memories.

"To be honest, I think they both miss each other a lot," she continues. "The snide remarks are just their defense mechanisms."

"We all have them, right?"

She looks at me strangely but says nothing as we keep walking. Palm Tree would enjoy this walking path. We pass a sneaker store, and I slow down to take a photo of the window display for Ming.

"Only you could make the most romantic neighborhood of Montreal about footwear," Corinne says, sucking her teeth.

I put my phone away and look around with a frown before turning back to her. "This is the most romantic neighborhood in Montreal?"

"Er, I mean more or less. Eye of the beholder, I guess."

And there it is again: there's this strange, unnamed thing between us now.

"And is this supposed to be?" I ask, clearing my throat. "Romantic?"

Corinne's eyes widen for a split second, but her stalwart chin comes right back up. "Cobblestone streets are coded into the genetic material of the western definition of romance," she says coolly.

"Corinne," I say, raising both eyebrows. "Is this a date?"

"No!" she practically shouts.

"Okay," I say. "Because, you know, I wouldn't mind if it was that. . . . A date," I say.

She looks up at me, eyes wide.

"I'd really like that, actually," I go on.

She keeps staring at me. A part of me still thinks I should drop it and pretend this conversation never happened, but here we are.

"I know you like me," I say.

She scoffs. "Is that right?"

"At least a little bit, right?" And when she's quiet for so long, it starts to get terrifying again, I find myself prompting. "Corinne . . . ?"

"I'm thinking," she finally says. "I don't want to get hurt, Henri. Even if you don't mean to. What if it's, like, in your genome? As a guy?"

"I won't hurt you! I'm not a hussy, Troy! I categorically do not hussy!"

"You occasionally hussy."

"Corinne," I venture as purposefully as I can, for my own sake more than hers.

"What?"

"Would you like to go on a date with me?"

Eleven seconds of silent signature Troy blinking this time, but who is counting?

"Like, right now?"

"Right this very moment, yes."

"Where would we go?" she follows up. "Just, um, so I have all the facts here."

"Oh. Uh, I'm not sure," I say, looking around. "My brain hadn't gotten to that part yet."

All the cobblestone streets of Montreal look like pathways to equally unknown destinations at the moment. "But you're the one who says it's the most romantic spot in the bilingual capital of the country. I'm sure we can find a Starbucks that has stools or something. You gotta have faith, Troy."

I extend a hand toward her, which she looks at for a minute before her face breaks into the biggest smile I've ever seen.

"Okay. But for the record, this isn't a sex trip," she says.

I laugh. "Got it."

"But I'm open to it being a kissing trip," she says, and I find myself pulled forward by the side of my jacket. Corinne Troy then kisses me. Fast and hard, clanking our teeth together, and almost knocking me down in all the meanings of the term.

In hindsight, always in hindsight, I find myself thinking that of course this is how our first kiss would go. And pretty soon, we're just that pair of degenerate American teenagers making out on a crowded sidewalk of Montreal, Quebec. As degenerate American teenagers do.

I've had a few make-out sessions here and there (a guy-in-high-school amount, not a hussy amount), and it is, hands down, the best kiss of my life.

I look at Corinne afterward, and everything about the moment feels like a postcard: the lint caught in her pink hat, the flush of her cheeks, the way she's scanning my face and biting the inside of her cheek as if there are a million things in her head that she's trying to hold back right now. Or is that me?

We can do this. After all, normal people do this all the time, no? And they even manage to hold on to it without fucking the whole thing up, right?

We eventually break for oxygen, both smiling and giddy, out of words as if the kiss said it all.

"So, date?"

"Date."

We keep holding hands and head down a random street of Montreal in search of who knows what, and frankly, who cares?

TWENTY

As the train pulls away from Montreal on our return trip to Manhattan the next day, its giant FARINE FIVE ROSES neon sign receding into the distance, I realize I really enjoy this skyline.

Montreal is nothing like Manhattan; it's smaller and more concentrated, and unlike the city that never sleeps, Montreal feels like a city that's gotten a good night's rest and woken up in time for a bike ride alongside the Saint Lawrence River. But, all things considered, I can really picture myself going to college here. I could learn enough French to impress, graduate in three years, at almost no cost compared to the US universities that don't offer scholarships or needs-blind admission. In a world where Columbia didn't exist, where that sticker wasn't on our fridge, I could almost imagine McGill being my dream school.

Corinne bundles up and cocoons in the aisle seat next to me, having no interest in the view. She doesn't snore, but her entire body goes limp and heavy the moment she drifts off.

I text Ma that we're on our way back and send her a few select photos of Montreal. The street known as "Little Haiti," with blue-and-red flags on every storefront. A long, blurry shot of the local theme park La Ronde, situated on its own little island off the side of Montreal and that's closed for the season. The cobblestoned Old Port.

She sends me a string of happy emojis, which means she probably doesn't have time to engage too much at the station.

The remaining nine hours of train ride are long and eventless, which only adds to the length. I have enough time to get through *Americanah* by Chimamanda Ngozi Adichie for World Lit class and all my calculus problem sets. Corinne clearing her throat in a very unsubtle way when I get one wrong is surprisingly helpful.

Penn Station is exactly how we left it, indifferent to homecomings and buzzing with energy. Somehow that's where it hits. I came back with all my homework done, a Tupperware of sugar cream pie, and . . . a girlfriend.

"If you're changing your mind, you have to tell me now, okay?" Corinne says on the escalator up. I can't tell how long she's been watching me like that.

"I'm not changing my mind," I say, wondering if she can actually hear my thoughts.

Our Montreal date had stretched from the afternoon into the pitch-black evening, which had been made purple by all the lights and bright white blankets of snow. There was this

201

kind of quiet magnetic pull about the whole thing. It's like she rips me out of my own head and back to earth with her. It's like everything that is normally worrying becomes vaguely inconsequential in the backdrop of this little spark that dances between us when we talk and turns into a static shock the moment our hands touch. So, yeah, the question was certainly rattling around my head; it was just a matter of finding the right words. And the balls needed to actually voice said words.

Want to just . . . do the thing? was my initial phrasing.

The thing?

You know, I said, wrist flailing between us. *The official whatever . . . The thing!*

She blinked, smiled, blinked again, and looked away in that exact order before finally speaking.

"I mean, I think I know," she said. "But I am not going to say yes to a shrug, Halti."

I groan in spite of myself. Around FATE people simply announced they were boyfriend and girlfriend on Monday morning. It was something that traveled through the grapevine. No transcript was ever released after the fact, so how did you go about doing the actual asking?

Any chance you have a stack of flash cards for me on this?

Nope. She grinned.

Corinne, you awesome human being, will you please be my girlfriend?

She smiled and an eleven-letter word came tumbling out.

Sureyesfine.

By the time we'd made it back to Terry's that evening, Corinne and I were boyfriend and girlfriend. In celebration of the news, Terry had an audio recording of *Angels in America* blaring across the apartment until all the lights were turned off and every ass was, as Terry said, "in its own corner, thinking of Jesus."

We kiss again, for the first time on American soil.

Unlike anyone else I've ever met, this girl could so very easily make my heart her complete bitch.

"This is unacceptable, Jacques!" echoes through the lobby of the Wyatt as soon as Corinne and I step in. The closer I get to my doorstep, the more I feel yesterday's cross-country exhaustion in my bones. I'm ready for an American nap until I recognize the voice. Mrs. Cloutier.

"I'm late for a call with my dad," Corinne whispers, checking her watch. Every tenant is used to looking the other way after overhearing Cloutier berating this or that building employee.

"I'll text you later."

After a quick peck on the lips, Corinne bullets up the stairs. She stops midway through and backtracks down the same staircase, her footsteps lighter than a mouse's, and kisses me again. God, will that ever stop feeling so amazing?

Once I hear her footsteps disappear, I sigh and approach the corner where I know I'll spot Mrs. Cloutier berating her favorite punching bag.

"Honestly, I don't understand what's so hard about that, Jacques," her voice whines.

"We're trying our best to pinpoint the problem, Mrs. Cloutier," Dad says, polite and contrite. He's crouched on all fours, work gloves on, applying plaster to a caved-in corner of the wall that's recently been scuffed by the Pattersons moving furniture.

It's not an uncommon scenario: Cloutier happened upon him working on one building issue, which of course is the perfect opportunity to bring up all her woes from the fourth floor.

"Your best on these matters is known to leave something to be desired, no offense." She sighs. I sneak behind a pillar and lean in to avoid being seen.

City life tends to breed rudeness. Or at least a level of comfort with open displays of rudeness. Mr. Sung upstairs, for instance, might rank at four out of ten in friendliness. He nods approvingly when the dogs I happen to be walking are well behaved, but he will audibly give a sniff of disapproval when they're yapping while he's squinting at some figures on his phone.

The Anish family on the fifth floor also isn't friendly. Two out of ten. I don't hold it against them; it's not in their nature to be neighborly. Curt head nods are all you'll get from them. There's something comforting about running into them in the lobby: no expectation of chitchat.

The Pennebakers toe that thin line between courteous and friendly. It depends on the day they're having.

Until very recently, I would have qualified Chantale only as "professionally courteous," as if there was an HR department recording all our interactions. Six out of ten.

Mrs. Cloutier, however, is strictly vile. Zero out of ten, and I don't say this lightly. She is a co-op board harpy with entirely too much time on her hands and not enough relatives checking in on her well-being. Right now she's hovering over Dad like a bird of prey who's come across a juicy mouse she's too full to eat but not too full to paw at for a few minutes.

"And while I'm down here, I'll remind you I saw another one," Mrs. Cloutier continues, apparently in no hurry to go home tonight.

"We're spraying twice a month now, ma'am. That's what is budgeted for by the co-op."

"Well, don't you have some connections? 'Hook-ups,' as they say? I am not comfortable seeing cockroaches around my kitchen every week, Jacques. This must be remedied."

"Yes, Mrs. Cloutier."

"Can you offer me any solution, or are you just comfortable nodding at your failures? I don't know what you're used to here, on the ground floor, hygiene wise," she says, glancing over to our apartment down the hall to cement her point. And oh, my God, go fist yourself, lady.

Dad's neck is clenched throughout the rest of the interaction, and eventually, Cloutier seems satisfied when he promises to stop by her unit the next morning. Her good-night comes in the form of a loud and heavy sigh, followed by an "honestly!" under her breath.

"Doesn't it make you angry?" I ask, finally, as we both watch her disappear into the overcast street. "To be talked to like that?"

"Every time." Dad sighs, hands on his hips and fingers digging into his jumpsuit as he does that thing where he invites calm back into his body. "But this isn't my life's work, kid. It's just work. Although, glad your mom wasn't here for that one."

"I'm sorry, Dad," I say.

"Why? You didn't raise that horrible woman."

He's trying to laugh it off but is still visibly upset. His tell is in his immediate aligning of his tools by his side, diligently placing them back into his toolkit, each still shiny and rust free despite years of usage because Dad takes care of meticulously polishing them at least once a year.

"Maybe Cloutier would stop if you—I don't know—stood your ground more?"

Maybe there is another way to go about life beyond keeping your head down and getting pummeled until the Cloutiers of the world are satisfied.

Dad sighs and steps down, pausing to look at me through the steps of the folding ladder. "Do you think I wouldn't like to tell Cloutier that no other unit on her floor has cockroaches? That maybe the reason she has them is because of Mr. Cloutier's study, which she condemned without emptying after he left, meaning that the thing that's causing the cockroaches is probably in there, inside her own apartment?"

It's not every day that I trigger a rant from Dad, who continues to talk as he maneuvers into the pantry for a new light bulb and then proceeds back up the steps to screw it in.

"And when I go up there tomorrow and suggest checking

that room, she'll rudely tell me to mind my own business before being overwhelmed and canceling the whole thing, sending me back here until the next time she sees a cockroach and storms down here."

He exhales as if to stop himself from revisiting years of similar grievances and indignities. "Do you honestly think I wouldn't truly, sincerely enjoy telling that woman to go somewhere and do something? Hmm?"

I don't know what to answer to that so I just focus on folding the ladder for him. It's not fair, I want to say, but the *no shit* is already echoing in the back of my head.

"You're very smart, Henri," Dad says, clasping my neck and flicking the switch a few times as the light blinks over our heads. "There's no use complaining about it and wishing the world was different. This isn't how we change things for ourselves."

Right. *Punctuality. Work Ethic. Education. Not Counting Other People's Money.*

"I still hate it," I mutter.

"I know. So . . . Montreal? Don't leave me hanging: how was the trip? Good?"

"Yeah, it was cool. It's a cool city. Parts of it felt like a less crowded corner of Manhattan almost. Y'know, with a bunch of French thrown in there. I could really see it, actually. I mean, see me, there," I venture.

Dad hums, throwing himself onto a seat at our kitchen table and leaning back to sigh heavily.

"It's not Columbia, Henri."

And there it is again.

"Look, it's good you have options—that's very mature of you—but you won't need them," he says, all fatherly and comforting. "Columbia is almost here. All your hard work's about to pay off. I know it is."

Right.

"You're on top of things at school, right?" he asks, raising an eyebrow.

"Of course."

"Grades and everything?"

"Dad," I say, filling my voice with as much easy confidence as I can right now. "Everything's good. Montreal was just a backup. Mr. Vu says it might even make me more competitive for Columbia. It's all about CU, baby!"

He smiles back and seems to believe me. And just like that, the past three days feel like an optional quest in a video game when I should have been focusing on my main mission all along.

TWENTY-ONE

I n the fairy-tale version of our lives, kissing Corinne would have been the happily-ever-after moment. But this is reality, and happy endings aren't that easy. In real life, there are . . . complications. There's no textbook for relationships, no *What to Expect When You're Expecting* for teen romance. I mean, what does this new status even really mean? How do I turn on boyfriend mode in between my early-morning dog walks and our jam-packed lives?

Not to mention the Chantale of it all. The *So, I hear you're dating my daughter, Henri* talk that I can feel coming at any moment. She hasn't mentioned anything, but I can see it in her eyes whenever we cross paths in the lobby of the Wyatt. Forget asking her for a Columbia recommendation now. She's just getting used to the idea of her daughter dating the dog walker.

And then there's the question of next year. In hindsight, starting a new romantic relationship a few months before graduation might not have been the best idea. March is just around the corner and with it the news that will determine our collegiate futures—and everything else.

But maybe I'm getting too ahead of myself.

Luckily for me, Corinne has taken the reins of removing all uncertainty from this new situation in the most Corinne way imaginable, which she unveils when I meet her outside her chemistry lab for lunch together.

"I'm already afraid . . ." I say, raising an eyebrow as she reaches into her bag.

"Precepts!" Corinne clarifies as we melt into the prelunch crowd. We now walk closer than we did before. I've never done this before, but it's not altogether unpleasant. We're a good height match. I'm taller, yes, but it's not awkward to look at each other while walking. A few eyebrows were raised at first, but a week in, we've steadily become just another hallway couple.

"Neither of us is well versed in functional relationships, albeit for very different reasons," she goes on to explain. "So this is a way to avoid some of the most common mistakes known to our demographic."

"Can you whisper that? Because my boner is, like, throbbing." I laugh, earning me a light shove into a locker as she keeps flipping through the green flash cards. "Okay, okay, share the wisdom, Troy. How do we keep this thing from crashing and burning, according to *Teen Vogue*?"

"I used many sources, and *Teen Vogue* has pretty incisive political coverage these days, by the way. It was all very insightful. . . ." She looks up from her cards and looks around the halls for a moment before pointing to Mark Iglesias and Robby Demers, hands in each other's back pockets, literally nestled into each other as they walk. They're considerably slowing down foot traffic but don't seem to care, basking in their two-years-running Prom Kings romance.

"None of that. I can walk fine without my hand in your back pocket. And vice versa, I assume."

"Your loss, Troy. My butt game is strong."

"Oh, I'm aware." She smiles ever so slightly, still reading her card. "But that's what rooms with closed doors are for, Haltiwanger."

The rest of the precepts are very reasonable if not outright welcome in soothing some of my lingering dating anxieties.

1. We're both busy and don't need to freak out if we don't see each other every day.
2. Asking for space is okay.
3. Check in when unsure of their feelings.
4. No calling each other "partners" because we're not running Mergers & Acquisitions here. We're not even eighteen: let's calm down.
5. Be there instead of being sorry.

"I don't quite get that last one," Corinne admits, frowning at her own handwriting. "But it was up-voted to the top of this thread online, so I assume there's wisdom there."

As we settle on a slightly frosted table in the quad, I glimpse another set of pink cards at the bottom of her bag and have to wonder if her notecards might be less of a life hack and more of a compulsion. There's an argument to be made that snuggling in the quad and sharing the same side of a picnic table is somewhere on the spectrum that leads to walking with hands in each other's pockets but, shit, I'm not about to be the one to point it out.

"Number six: digital communications. You, um, don't have to text or call me every day if I'm traveling," she says, leaning her head against my shoulder as she reads. "I refuse to be that obnoxiously needy girlfriend that needs 'check-ins' or anything."

"But . . . we can, right? It's not a rule that we can't? Like if we want to. Or if I want to text you."

She turns around and stares at me for a second with a smile flickering. "Yeah, sure. I mean, these are more guidelines than rules. If you want to call me, I won't . . . not answer or anything."

"Good." I smile and lean in to kiss her.

Sidebar: Corinne is a very, very good kisser. A tip-of-your-toes and giggling-for-no-reason-each-time type of kisser. She could teach a tutorial.

"I was looking it up the other night, and Princeton dorm staff actually lets residents borrow cots when they have people visiting," she says, putting her head on my shoulder. "I mean, those things have to be stained to high heaven, but it's good to know, right?"

Hm.

"If I didn't know better, I would say it sounds like you're talking like someone who already knows where she's going for college. With geographic certainty."

Her eyes widen for a split second, and her recovery is even worse; she's actually biting her lip now, aiming for casual. Someone seriously needs to teach this girl how to lie before we graduate high school. It's irresponsible not to.

"Corinne, did . . . did you hear back from Princeton?"

She concedes a tight and contained smile that soon explodes into a booming shriek. "I'm going to Princeton!

"I'm going to fricking Princeton!"

Corinne slaps both hands to her mouth and whisper-shouts it a third time, although basically at the same volume as before. She cringes at her own words and then looks at me like I'm a puppy whose tail she accidentally stepped on.

"Congratulations!" I smile, though I get the distinct impression that, in trying to make it feel natural, it's coming off like a strange Photoshop job right there on top of my chin.

"Are you . . . upset?" she asks.

"Of course not. I'm *so* happy for you. Why didn't you tell me, like, immediately?"

She smiles. "Sorry. I guess I thought telling you would be a bit—I don't know—insensitive. There's an inherent competition to college applications. Even if two applicants aren't courting the same school. It breeds jealousy—which stems from the Latin *zelus* for 'passion'—which is in turn largely accepted as irrational, especially in cases of—"

I bring her in for a kiss because I suspect she will otherwise never physically stop talking. There's suddenly a strange swell of pride in my stomach. My girlfriend is officially a Princeton-bound genius.

"You're going to be great," I say. "Really, Troy. You're going to set that stupid campus on absolute fire and then take over the world with full Ivy League entitlement and all."

"Thank you." She smiles.

First Ming, now Corinne. Of course she got into Princeton. Corinne Troy was always getting into Princeton. No lackluster letter from Mrs. Carroll writing off all Corinne's moral uprightness, honesty, and focus as "intensity" was going to keep her out.

She is intensely amazing, after all.

TWENTY-TWO

It's spring break, and Corinne is leaving for Switzerland to-night. She'll be gone all week. Her mother is sweeping her off to Geneva, of all places, where Chantale is to be the key-note speaker of some academic conference. If I were paranoid, I would think Chantale was padding her daughter's calendar to spend as little time as possible near the dog walker from down-stairs, but Corinne assures me that's not it.

"Trust me: there's always a new conference on the calendar after she walks in on me video-chatting with Dad." Corinne sighed when she told me. "Some children of divorce get two Christmases. I get room service, a few very nice mother-daughter dinners, and reassurance that I'm her priority."

Ming and I agreed to send her off together. Even though Corinne and I are now dating, the three of us make for a pretty seamless tricycle whenever we hang out. After dropping off my last dog of the day, I pull out my phone to check the Columbia portal on my way to meet with them.

Henri Haltiwanger's application is still PENDING. This time, however, I notice the time stamp at the bottom of the screen.

Last Accessed: Browser
Location: United States (NY) / 986.15.72
Time: 11:23 a.m. (7 minutes ago)

I don't know our IP address by heart, but it can only be one person: Dad. After all, we set up the account together. He's been good about not bringing up college at dinner, only casually bringing up my day at school, but it's obviously on his mind almost as much as it is on mine.

It's not just me. College is all that any senior student of FATE Academy can talk about this week. Save for those who already know where they're headed, or Marvyn the Unbothered, we're all vibrating at the same frequency of anxiety. You recognize it when you see someone taking a moment alone to stare at their phone with a furrowed brow. I really felt for Trevor O'Keefe after catching him slam his head back into a locker and shove his phone into his pocket. Trevor is the ringer of the wrestling team, known for his temper on the mat. If he had gotten rejected from Cornell, a chair would have at the very least been thrown across the hall.

In the computer lab, online application portals can be spotted being furtively logged on to and then xed out of in frustration when the "pending" status hasn't been updated. We all know we get an automatic email notice the moment decisions are out, but manually checking the portal makes us feel like we're at least doing something about our fate.

This state of anxiety is only worsened by the students who have already been admitted into their dream schools. For instance, Ayo Ikume letting out a shriek in the middle of calculus and then rushing off screaming, "Fuck yeah, Harvard!" was just fucking obnoxious. Her sister, who is a Harvard senior, allegedly pulled some on-campus strings and got a glimpse of the incoming-student-class list. She spotted her sister's name in there and let her know with a discreet photo. Strings and favors.

The rest of us are all lobsters in the pot, starting to notice bubbles at the top of the water. Anyone who has any strings is pulling them now, casting Hail Marys wherever they can. Rejections across America are being released in waves.

Now Ming comes out of the subway entrance, tucking a book on Mandarin into his back pocket. He's wearing only a light jacket tonight, considering how warm it's been lately. Except for a couple of pitiful sprinklings of cold rain here and there, it's looking more and more like this truly was a snowless winter for New York City. Thanks, global warming.

"I know that face." He winces. "Any word from the Big Uptown C?"

I tilt my phone his way, displaying the "pending" on Columbia's mobile portal. Ming pats my back as we start walking toward the Wyatt.

"Hang in there. What about McGill?"

"Design School decisions aren't out until April." I shrug. "That's still a ways away."

"Sheesh. Get it together, Canadians," Ming says. "This is why we make so many jokes about you."

Apart from everything Corinne and the sensory memory of Aunt Terry pinching my cheek, Montreal now feels like a tangent: some road I always knew I would never quite end up following. How does McGill compete with the Ivy League campus half a mile away that's been etched in your brain since childhood? I could walk there with my eyes closed.

I can't help myself and manage another refreshing of the portal on my phone as we walk. Still "pending," which Ming notices.

"I'm excited to come over, by the way," he says, rubbing his hands together as we get to the Wyatt. It's a valiant attempt at a topic change, I'll give him that. "Don't think I don't get the irony of having had to wait for you to date someone who lives in your building to get an invitation, pal."

"It's like any other building, you weirdo. Also, you're still not seeing my place."

"Had to try. Anyway, you are being way less Halti weird and jittery about it. This whole girlfriend thing? I hereby approve of its effects on you."

"Is that right?" comes Corinne's merry voice. She appears on the landing, pulling her rolling luggage behind her. "I can finally take him off probation, then."

Her pink beanie has been switched out for the turquoise one I got her last week. I suspect she only ever wears it for my benefit, but it's still appreciated by this first-time boyfriend gift giver.

"Mom, I'm headed down!" she shouts behind her.

I meet her halfway down the stairs and, after a quick peck on the cheek, carry her deceptively heavy luggage down the rest of the way.

"Look after him while I'm gone, okay?" Corinne instructs Ming as he hugs her both hello and farewell.

"Will do," says Ming, nodding solemnly. "Although I can't promise he won't give himself carpal tunnel syndrome refreshing his Columbia page."

Corinne softly kicks at my leg as I put down the cinder block of a suitcase.

"You text me the second you hear, okay?" she says, sounding concerned. "Good news or whatever."

"Or whatever." I Smile.

"My. You have a full goodbye party, Corinne," Chantale says, coming down the stairs with a leash-less Palm Tree behind her. His tail is wagging up a storm at all the confusion. He's not traveling with them, and I'm taking care of him all week, with extra walks and playdates at the Troys' budgeted into my payment.

"Hello, Mrs. Troy."

"Hello, Henri and . . . friend." It takes a lot to make sunglasses and a neck pillow look elegant, but Chantale's, monogrammed in Ls and Vs, are certainly doing the job.

"Mom, this is Ming," Corinne introduces. "He goes to FATE. Ming, this is my mother, Chantale."

"Hi, Mrs. Troy," Ming says, ever the polite young man. "It's a pleasure meet—"

"Yes, hello, Ming." Chantale nods curtly. "The car is outside, Corinne. I will not be running through JFK unless Chadwick Boseman himself is waiting at a gate."

"Here, let me help!" I say, quickly picking up her luggage and bringing it outside. Ming picks up Palm Tree and watches me operate with his lips pursed. Bastard.

After the bags are handed to the driver, Corinne and I linger on the sidewalk, not quite sure what to say. I hadn't planned for such a large audience when wishing her goodbye.

"Take lots of pictures, okay?" I try. "And don't be self-conscious about taking selfies. Like, it's the currency of the world, so go hog wild."

Chantale raises an eyebrow behind her large white-rimmed sunglasses.

"Okay, well, bye," Corinne says before pressing her lips into mine with her eyes closed, causing our chins to bump awkwardly. Did I mention the audience?

"I'll . . . not *not* miss you," she adds after pulling back. If dark-skinned folks could blush, she would be a freaking berry right now.

"That was certainly very chaste," Chantale notes, eye on the door. "Enjoy your spring break, Henri. I know Palm Tree is in good hands. I've already wired you the payment for the week."

"Yes, ma'am."

It's hard to pinpoint what, if anything, Chantale thinks of Corinne and me dating. She nominally approves, I guess, in the sense that she hasn't had me disposed of in the middle of the night or locked Corinne in a tower just yet, but it's different when I pick up Palm Tree now, as if she's making sure I'm not sniffing around her daughter's underwear drawer. After telling her we were dating, Corinne reported that her mother's only reaction was: *I see no reason to actively disapprove at the moment.* Direct quote. How utterly terrifying is that?

"And remember!" Corinne shouts as she steps into the car. "The moment you hear anything!"

Chantale gives us—*me*—one last look before pulling away.

"That woman is scary," Ming notes, trying to soothe Palm Tree as we stand on the sidewalk, watching them go. "But, like, in an elegant way that would make a striking sculpture, y'know?"

"Yup. Now, try dating her daughter."

Three days into spring break and I officially, aggressively miss my *girlfriend*. It's a surprising turn of events, all things considered. My schedule, which used to be packed from six a.m. to midnight, now feels luxurious and pointless, with huge chunks of time to wander around the city and think about what Corinne is doing across the ocean and six hours in the future.

After walking my dogs in the morning, I find myself listening to designer podcasts, refreshing my Columbia application, followed by my McGill application—albeit that one is more out of a weird curiosity more than a compulsion.

Corinne's email updates are consistent, but she's busy and probably doesn't have time for lengthy exchanges, so I offer only short replies with maybe too much punctuation. *That's so cool!! That looks delicious!! LOL.* I make sure to send her photos of Palm Tree in various states of adorableness. Palm Tree on the street, Palm Tree climbing up the stairs, Palm Tree snoring in my lap.

As it turns out, texting with your girlfriend is nothing like the mindless group chat memes with various people around school, which I've now mostly muted. (There are only so many times you can see SpongeBob SquarePants cluck like a chicken before it loses its luster.)

Ming does his best to make good on his promise to Corinne to look after me, but most of his free time is unexpectedly monopolized. Somewhere along the way, his mother realized that this was her baby boy's last spring break in New York City—nay, America!—and booked the entire family for every exclusive cultural event she could find this week, from The Shed down in Hudson Yards to Symphony Space on the Upper West Side. Tonight, I believe it's an annual John Lennon Tribute with Music Without Borders.

Unfortunately for Ming's mother, the event happens to be held one block away from a secondhand sneaker store we've been to before, which is the location from where Ming is currently streaming a series of poorly framed close-ups of Jordans.

I send him a quick text reminding him that the concert started fifteen minutes ago, and the live footage abruptly cuts off. I can't help but smile, imagining Ming running through traffic right now. One more thing that's coming to an end in a few months, I think with a twinge.

I end up spending my evening in at the Troys' with Palm Tree and go through a few more rounds of clicker exercises with him.

It's a long shot, but I'm hoping to surprise Corinne when she gets home with the gift of Palm Tree having fully mastered Down, Fetch, and Roll Over. So far, however, the results have been inconclusive. The clicker is a method of puppy training that associates a unique sound from a cheap plastic clicker with positive reinforcement. The dog learns to associate the command you give with the click and displays the desired behavior, in expectation of a treat that comes a second later. But Palm Tree does not seem to naturally recognize the click sound as something particularly worthwhile. To his puppy brain, it's just one of the many strange noises and honks of this giant concrete city.

"Hey, did you know that Columbia University is where the Pulitzer Prize award ceremony is held every year?" I say while he finds a renewed interest in his tail. "Like, *the* Pulitzer Prize?"

By the nonreaction, it looks like Palm Tree did know and found the whole thing pedestrian intellectual pageantry. For a prepubescent canine, Palm Tree is a very good conversationalist.

Tok.

Palm Tree suddenly whips his head around at a strident sound that my clicker did not make. There it is again.

"Yeah, I heard it too. What is that?" I wonder aloud.

I've been hearing it since the Troys left. An occasional *tok* that sounds like a table-tennis ball bouncing off a wall. I've checked both the oven and fancy fridge and neither of them seems to be the cause.

Tok.

There's no pattern to the sound. Some days it never occurs and others, I'm bombarded with two or three in a row. Today, I follow the sound to one of the few rooms I've never been to before. I know it's not the master bedroom, and the door is slightly ajar, which makes taking a step in not feel quite so much like a violation. Indeed, it would be weirder if Chantale Troy *didn't* have a home office filled with shelves of books, folders, and dusty cactuses. There are multiple mug water rings around the desk.

Oh, duh. An email alert dings.

It's a clunky and older model laptop that was probably too bulky to travel with. I imagine that Chantale had it so that it never goes to sleep and simply forgot to close it before leaving.

Tok. I shake the mouse to wake the screen and upon closer inspection, it's a custom email in-box notice. A new email comes through, and yup, another *tok.* I lean into the screen, curious but careful not to touch anything. People get anxious letting someone else hold their locked phones, so it's safe to say that the same level of privacy applies to someone's personal email account.

Man, Chantale is nearly as organized as her daughter. Her in-box is a web of folders, subfolders, in-progress drafts, and color-coded labels. Students. HR. Administrative. Assignments. One labeled BS.

Oh. It's not her personal email at all. This is her work email: @columbia.edu.

Columbia. Dot. Edu.

There it is.

For months, all I've wanted is a recommendation from a Columbia Someone. And Chantale is certainly that, so of course it's crossed my mind. But she's a.) terrifying, as we've already established; and b.) if her review of me dating Corinne was as tempered as *I see no reason to actively disapprove*, imagine how lackluster a college recommendation would be? *I see no reason to actively reject Henri Haltiwanger, nor do I see any reason to accept him.*

But here is her email. Open. There is her keyboard, just waiting to be typed on. I think of how easy it would be—unethical, if not downright illegal, but very *easy*—to send an email from her account to someone in the admissions department.

What was that thing Marvyn had once said? *The whole place runs on emails and favors, Haltiwanker.* Violation; *definite* violation there.

I could write it, I realize. That glowing, amazing recommendation letter I couldn't secure from voice-of-her-generation Donielle Kempf or the real Dean Chantale Troy . . . I could write it for myself, right here, right now.

The dominoes fall uncomfortably too quickly in my mind.

I find myself sitting down at the laptop and moving the cursor around before I even realize what I'm doing.

"Jesus, what the hell am I doing?" I stand back up as quickly as I had seated myself. Palm Tree is by the door and takes a moment from gnawing on his back thigh to give me a curious look.

"Don't look at me like that, dude," I say. "I didn't do it!"

I quickly collect my coat and shoes and make sure his bowl of water is full.

"I'll see you tonight, okay, bud?" I put Palm Tree in his crate and slam the door, fully shaking myself out of the potential lapse in judgment.

Decisions had better come out soon, because college admissions are officially driving me bonkers.

"I'm home!" I yell after tumbling down the stairs back to the ground floor and catching my breath outside our door. My skin is still vibrating at a weird frequency from being in the Troys' apartment and at that laptop.

"Ma?" I call out after spotting her bag by the door. "Ma? Are you here?"

"H-Henri? No, wait, don't come in—"

"Holy crap."

She's standing in the middle of the living room, looking at herself in the leaning full-length mirror we keep in the corner. There wouldn't be anything unusual about the sight if it wasn't for the fact that she is currently fully dressed in New York fire-fighter gear, watching herself in our small space. Everything about her uniform feels new and crisp. Heavy and durable. The sort of black and striped yellow coats you glimpse on the street whenever a shrieking fire truck rushes by.

"Holy shit, Mom!"

"Don't laugh," she warns. I would never dream of laughing right now.

"You look . . . badass," I manage once I recover, needing a moment to take it all in.

"Yeah?" she says, pulling up her visor to smile at me. "I kind of do, don't I?"

She really had done it. I don't quite know when exactly it happened, but somewhere along the way, this pipe dream became her reality. Our reality.

"Are you, um, allowed to bring that home?"

"Probably not," she admits as she removes the vest, revealing what are now full muscles through her undershirt. "Definitely not. But there was a photo shoot for this article in *AM New York*. 'Midcareer changes' or something. They let us bring the new bunker gear off-site for it this morning. I took a little detour home to—I don't know—bask for a minute."

She folds the heavy-looking jacket and hangs it off her arm before turning back to the mirror and posing like it's a magazine shoot. She laughs at her reflection, giggling in a note I've never heard before.

"How do I look? Halloween costume or badass firefighter?"

She's still staring at herself, smiling as she holds on to the straps of the reflective trimmed overalls, in an undershirt.

"Unquestionably badass firefighter."

"My wedding dress was borrowed," she continues, folding the uniform with reverence. "This . . . I earned it, you know?" She catches my gaze in the mirror. "Ah! *Pa gade mwin*, Henri! Don't look at me. It's silly."

"No, Ma," I say. "Not silly at all."

My skin feels like it's crawling again.

"Anyway, reverie over," she says, getting to work removing her boots. "I don't need an offense on my files before even starting the job. Want to get started on dinner while I drop this back off at the station? How do mashed potatoes sound?"

"Um, good," I say. "Hey, Ma? I left something at the Troys' upstairs. I'll be right back, okay?"

"Your girlfriend is traveling until Friday, right?"

I stop with my hand on the knob and whip my head back at her. "How?"

She rolls her shoulders. "I know I've been busy, but I'm not your father, fool," she says, having more difficulty removing the second boot. "I know when my son gets his first girlfriend. You miss her?"

"I haven't been keeping her, Corinne, a secret," I say more defensively than intended. "It just didn't . . . y'know . . . come up, I guess."

"It's okay." She smiles. "My son is a private person. My husband too. No one at the station ever shuts up, ever, so it actually balances out pretty well for me."

Her eyes narrow in on me with that motherly concern I can't quite handle right now. "Are you all right?"

"I'll . . . I'll be right back, okay? Potatoes sound great. I'm proud of you, Ma!" I say, and slam the door before she has a chance to reply.

I take the stairs up to the top floor two by two, trying to beat some clock in my mind. I think back to those elementary school presentations when you talk about yourself in broad terms that don't account for an inner life just yet. *What's your favorite color?* Red. *What is your favorite food?* Fries. *What do your parents do?* My dad is the superintendent of our building, and my mom is a goddamn firefighter. This is now a fact of life.

Dad let his dream of jazz clubs and fame die somewhere along the way, but Ma made hers happen. It doesn't matter what certificate she still needs to complete or the sick days she fudged at her last job to make time for the early days of the training program: that's who she is now. At some point, she saw an opportunity, an opening, and jumped headfirst into it. She made her reality.

And that's what I'm going to do.

I walk into the Troy apartment and pet Palm Tree, who seems confused to see me back so soon. Sorry, buddy; not right now. I quickly make my way to the desk, settle in, and open the laptop again with the reverence of a treasure box.

Pleasedon'tbepasswordprotectedPleasedon'tbepasswordprotectedPleasedon'tbepasswordprotected.

Ding.

Thank God. The computer comes out of sleep, and there are maybe half a dozen new email notices in Chantale Troy's in-box since the last time I touched this device.

I technically have all the time in the world but do not wish to linger. More than anything, I want to be downstairs again, washing and peeling potatoes in our kitchen sink.

I first read a few professional emails that Chantale Troy has sent out over the past few weeks, quickly getting a sense of her writing style. She does not use contractions. There are no semicolons. Her sentences are short and to the point. She starts every new piece of correspondence with an *I hope all is well*, no matter how prosaic or dry the rest of the email reads.

I focus on the craft and the details and try not to think about the violation. Thankfully, there seems to be nothing personal in her email account. Only departmental exchanges, friendly correspondence with some students, and perfunctory ones with others.

After soaking up enough of it, I open a new email draft, locate the name of the person best suited for this request—Michael Connelly, Dean of Admissions—and quickly begin typing as Palm Tree stares me down from his doggy bed in the living room.

"Don't look at me like that," I say guiltily, earning me no reaction from the dog.

The email is easy enough to draft. It's everything I had hoped Donielle Kempf would have said on my behalf.

I hope all is well! I wanted to bring your attention to a prospective student I recently met! Talented high schooler, inspiring to see, hard worker . . .

I avoid mentioning anything too specific, like FATE academics, or veering too far away from Chantale's academic tone. This is an informal nudge with all the institutional power that the right elbow can convey. I sign it all off: *With Regards*, capitalized R.

When I'm done, I sit back and stare at the screen, my finger hovering over the Send button. This is wrong. I know that. Jumping over turnstiles to get into the subway. Opening people's kitchen cabinets when returning their dogs in their absence. Falsifying a letter of recommendation to an Ivy League college from your girlfriend's mom.

Wrong and illegal. Wrong and invasive. Wrong and illegal, invasive *and* gross.

But this whole world is wrong and unfair, isn't it?

Sometimes, the only way to climb out is to realize that there are people you can use as steps. That's what Lion had said, right?

Everybody else uses what they've been given. Some people have money; others have connections, influence, or ridiculous supercomputer brains that can get a perfect score on their SATs in the middle of a yawn. Worse still, they have second chances: another train of opportunity they can catch, just minutes behind the one they just missed. They'll reapply after a gap year; they'll go to Dartmouth and transfer in a year. They'll afford grad school in four years.

I have only these, right now. This computer and this email. That's all. And paper-thin walls through which I can hear Dad and Ma talk at night about my bright Columbia future. I'm not gambling the rest of my life on a single email I did not send.

SEND.

After a breath, I ignore the bile in my stomach and focus on steadying my hand from shaking, removing it from the mouse, one finger at a time. It's done.

My mind reboots itself now on autopilot. I get to work clearing my digital fingerprints, deleting the email from the Sent folder. I then refresh, hoping for a quick reply from Michael Connelly so I can also delete that before Chantale sees it. The variation of a *Thank you, I'll keep an eye out on his file.* A simple receipt of politeness that hopefully doesn't allow for any back and forth.

I don't think of Chantale Troy, the woman whose status and reputation I've wrongfully used for my benefit.

I don't think about the invasion of this home that suddenly feels completely foreign to me again. I don't think about Palm Tree now napping with his tongue out. I don't think about Dad, Ma, or even Lion. I don't think of the row of flash cards neatly assembled on a dresser a few dozen feet away, or of their owner.

I refresh over and over again, for what could be an hour or ten minutes, ready to sleep here if I have to until . . .

Hi, Chantale,
Henri sounds great! We're down to the finish line in the upcoming class selection, but I will absolutely keep an extra eye out for the name. All the best, MC
Sent from my iPhone

Oh, my God. It worked. It's not an in, but it's close. Closer than I've ever been.

I delete the email before it can linger for a solitary second at the top of the in-box and again delete it from the Trash folder.

Later, I preheat the oven in our empty apartment, waiting for Ma and Dad to come home. I wash the potatoes, carefully peel them, and all the while think about Michael's email.

This is what I've always wanted. I should be happy, right?

So then why do I feel nothing?

TWENTY-THREE

The little angel and devil on my shoulders—so loud and strident while I was typing that email yesterday—have now gone eerily quiet. They've relocated and are currently hanging upside down from my bedroom ceiling like bats, watching me without engaging. The two share a conspiratorial look whenever I'm about to fall asleep, jolting me back into full awareness, afraid of what they might be planning.

Upon closer inspection, the angel looks like . . . Greg? Or maybe Mr. Vu? A combination of the two. He's dressed in coordinated suspenders, hat, and a loosened bow tie dangling from his neck.

The devil is completely nude and has features somewhere between those of Lion and Donielle Kempf. He occasionally throws me a wink. It's an unsettling creature. But then again, I guess that's the point.

I punch my pillow back into shape and wait for my eyelids

to get heavier and heavier. Eventually, I snap awake when my morning alarm begins to wail and am simply left to stare at the blank bedroom ceiling again.

I don't know if that qualifies as a nightmare, but yeesh, let's not do that again.

I slip into my dog walking sneakers, put on the cleanest Uptown Updogs hoodie I can find, throw on a coat, and head out to collect Pogo from Mrs. Ponech's first. Today, I leave my phone behind. I haven't checked the Columbia portal once since yesterday.

After Pogo, I pick up Shadow, and we end up jogging for two full laps around our usual path, at full speed. Today, I manage to keep up with him and even feel like I could run another five miles after dropping him off. Running shuts off the brain, and my synapses are in dire need of shutting down. I swing by a pet store and spend twenty bucks on puppy toys for Palm Tree before heading to the Troys'. If it's emotional bribery, the giddy border collie doesn't read it as much. He's thrilled at the sight of me. After a quick morning pee at the curb downstairs, he enthusiastically inhales his breakfast and loses his mind at the veritable zoo of "two for five dollars" polyester-stuffed animals I unleash at his feet.

I end up taking him out twice in as many hours, and we spend the rest of the morning going through clicker training exercises. We then play up a storm, running around the apartment chasing thrown toys like Daisy Buchanan thirsting for designer dress shirts.

"I'm the one who just got off an eight-hour flight," comes a voice at the door. "Why are you the one who looks jet-lagged?"

Neither Palm Tree nor I are entirely sure what to say to the sight of Corinne—key in hand, jacket rumpled and hair inflated by the fact that it was probably last combed a continent away—but it takes less than two seconds for Palm Tree to dash forward, yapping, tripping into his own legs to go lean into her as if he hasn't seen her in years and thought he never would again.

"I missed you so much, you absolute little monster," she squeals, picking him up and cradling him like a baby. "All other dogs in the world are so basic, I can't stand it!"

Usually the sight of Corinne would feel like home to me. But now it's as if some frame that's been off-kilter for the past five days has suddenly fallen and crashed to the floor in a million tiny pieces.

I watch her gnaw at Palm Tree's neck, and his tail wags so hard that it knocks her scarf off. It takes another beat of pure puppy-owner delight before she extends me another look.

"Hi," I say, stunned and not entirely sure that this isn't the dastardly mind game the little devil and angel were silently concocting all night. "This, um, isn't Switzerland."

"There's that expensive FATE education at work," she says, putting Palm Tree down. "Have you not been sleeping? You really do look like hell."

Never mind. No guilt fantasy at play here: this is the real Corinne.

"Why are you back so early? Is everything okay?" I say, wondering if she can see the guilt all over my face.

"Ta-da!" she proclaims, vexedly petting her hair down. She kicks off her shoes. "Mom's panels were over after two days, and we had dinner together twice—twice!—with Marcel Carnis, this author she knew way back when and who was trying to get into her pants."

"Corinne! Ew!"

"Well, he was! Kept saying how 'dee-lightful' I am. They were palpably horny for each other. By the end, I was pretending to be sick and spending the day on my own."

"Okay . . . ," I trail off, still unsure of so many things right now—not the least of which being Chantale and some international lover popping champagne in a hotel suite. "And?"

"And fine, whatever, I missed my boyfriend, all right!" she says. She has her chin up and defiant, her hands on her hips, daring me to say something. "And . . . and . . . I don't know! I was just bored in a hotel. Museums are weird alone! People just keep trying to talk to you. Like having a vagina puts you in permanent need of a tour guide."

"Please don't say vagina."

"Why? *Vagina.*"

She puts her boots together by the door as she talks and then bends down again and moves them two inches to the left and then back again. Why is she so nervous?

"We're seniors," she continues, and I can see the bullet points of some definite list being checked off in her mind as

237

she goes through them. "And whatever happens, we—meaning you and I—don't necessarily have that much time left in this current iteration of, well, life. And . . ."

"I missed you too." I smile.

The thing about Corinne is . . . Well. It's hard to pinpoint, exactly. She's been so many things in such a short time. The intense girl sitting in the front row of classes, the neighbor who lived right upstairs, the blackmailer, the Uptown Updogs client, the social understudy, the friend, the college road trip planner, the Girlfriend.

I expect Corinne to be blunt and, at times, abrasive, to have a set of flash cards for absolutely everything, and to one day walk into Congress with a flawless suit and a pink beanie. She's also passionate, awkward, and unpredictable, and it all amounts to something wonderful.

So it's not surprising that when she steps forward and kisses me, everything else blurs into the background. I'm not sure which one of us nudges Palm Tree into his crate as she leads us both toward her empty bedroom. There's no one in this entire apartment to stop us.

That's the thing about Corinne. She could convince you she's made entirely out of academic prowess and conviction. So much so that you'll swear to the stars that there's not even a speck of anything messy about her, and then she'll be on top of you on a fluffy purple comforter, her curls loose around her flushed cheeks, leaving you absolutely reeling.

I did something, I say in our oxygen-deprived pauses, still standing close and breathing hard. *I did something, and I'm so sorry.* Or maybe I just think it really hard, hoping she'll just guess and stop it all.

"I . . . ," I say, pulling our faces apart. "Corinne, wait—"

"I have condoms!" she says abruptly, reaching for a drawer by the side of the bed. "I've had them for a while."

"What?!"

She laughs and shakes her head. "You're going to make a puritan-ass father one day . . . but that day is definitely not nine months from now and definitely not through my cervix. So that condom is nonnegotiable, pal. I also have lube, three kinds, actually."

"Cor . . ."

"There's no shame in needing lube, Haltiwanger. It's not just for the guy."

Everything about this feels off. Or actually it feels exactly like a conversation about sex with Corinne might go, but God, why today of all days?

"Why do you think I came home?" she says, suddenly right up against me, slipping her arms around my waist. "Empty apartment, parent an ocean away . . . You can't tell me this isn't a golden opportunity. Get creative, Haltiwanger!"

Her voice is giddy and teasing. I know that tone. Anyone who's ever watched a television show with two chiseled twenty-four-year-olds pretending to be teenagers in a room alone knows that tone. If this had happened before Switzerland, I would have been the happiest guy in the world. But Chantale's computer being so close feels like some sick Tell-Tale Heart mocking me from the other room.

"Corinne, I don't know. . . ."

"Y-you don't want to?"

"No!"

In half a second her face crumbles, actually crumbles, before instantly rebuilding itself more closed off than before, and I hate to have caused that.

"I mean, no, I don't not want to," I sputter. "Because I would! And I do. It's just . . ."

Fuck, she actually looks embarrassed right now. I can't let her think that I wouldn't do . . . that with her. Because, Jesus, I would. At the drop of a hat. On a subway. Like, physically on top of a moving subway. Why is this happening today?

"I just . . . I don't think it's the right time."

"Oh. I just thought . . . Okay."

"I mean, you just got back! You're probably tired, and . . . I want it to be perfect. When it happens."

She nods. "No, no. I get it."

We sit in silence for a while. Her hands are on her knees and her shoulders tighten as if she's in some horrible waiting room she wants to escape.

"Corinne, I really don't want you to think that it's in any way you."

"I don't. You know, I should probably unpack some stuff. . . ." She turns away, clearly trying to break the uncomfortable energy in the room.

"Oh, right. Okay," I say, pulling myself off the bed, trying not to be too relieved at the dismissal. "Text me later? Please."

"Yeah," she says.

She walks me to the front door and stares at me for a moment. Her face isn't betraying any emotion, which for someone as expressive as Corinne feels like the biggest tell possible that this is all profoundly fucked.

I eventually give her a peck on the cheek.

"I'm glad you're back," I reiterate. "You have no idea."

She smiles, sheepish and uncertain, but at least it's a smile. I head back to my place, somehow feeling even worse today than I did yesterday.

TWENTY-FOUR

T hings have felt off with Corinne ever since that afternoon in her apartment. We haven't even really talked about it. Corinne ends up blowing it off like it was no big deal. ("I shouldn't have pushed so hard. It was poorly planned. Can we please move on? I really don't want to talk about it anymore.") No matter what I say, I can tell that she blames herself. And I can't do anything to fix it because if I told her the real reason I didn't want to have sex that day, I'm pretty sure she'd never speak to me again. And possibly prosecute.

Columbia should be sending out their acceptances any day now. I haven't heard anything about the email, so I figure that is that and I'm in the clear. Life just feels like it's suddenly on the express train. FATE has started its annual march toward senior prom, all the extracurriculars are in full swing with final performances coming up in May, and championships are on the docket. Mostly, it all finally starts to become inescapably real. . . . The dreaded high school finish line.

The debate finals are in two weeks, right here at FATE, on the same stage where Grant Hickman projectile-vomited three cans' worth of energy drinks at convocation last year, which is both a dramatic homecoming of sorts and also kind of underwhelming. It's hard to feel some Rocky culmination of a full season of debates and weekly practices all happening on the second floor, next to the good bathrooms.

This, however, has not deterred Greg. Today's practice was two hours long and our last one before the debate "Season Finale," as Yadira calls it.

"I'm *not* drinking this," I repeat more firmly, pushing the drink back toward Greg because *no*. Whatever mixture Greg had found online smells like asparagus boiled in maple syrup, which has then rotted inside a salmon.

"It's great for vocal cords. All-natural ingredients," Greg insists, removing another bottle of the yellow-brown mixture from his backpack and pushing it alongside the first one on the desk in front of me. It's soon joined by a third and fourth.

"Chug the whole thing down the moment you wake up," he reiterates. "Every morning until the debate."

"You're going to run a morally questionable government program one day," Yadira says, after sniffing the first bottle.

"Do you guys want to win or no?" Greg sighs, exasperated. "A coughing fit or scratchy throat will cost us crucial points—especially when the other team sounds like a freaking a cappella group."

Yadira and I share an apprehensive look.

"Don't act like you haven't both seen the clips."

We have. Not only are all of Spence's orators loquacious bastards known for their delightful delivery, but their debate team consists of a dozen or so rotating members. Every meet a handful of alternates and cheerleaders could be seen on the sidelines, cheering for their Spencey brethren. The onstage lineup itself changes at every meeting, curated to pounce on the well-researched opposing team's specific weaknesses.

"Ugh, fine!"

Yadira relents first, hooking each bottle with her index and middle finger before dropping them into her oversized purse. There's no denying that we all want to win—as badly as Greg, if such a thing is even possible.

"If I die, I'm haunting you first." I sigh, placing the concoctions into my backpack, ignoring Greg's satisfied smirk.

"This is it, guys! It all comes down to this. We have to give it our all!"

"Wooooo," Yadira says, stretching her lack of enthusiasm with every O.

"Okay, I suppose we're done for today," Greg mumbles, reviewing the bullet-point checklist scribbled on the board as Yadira and I make a point of getting up and stretching.

"Oooh! One more thing."

"Greg, I will hurt you," Yadira warns, sunglasses already on.

"It's a quick one! How do we feel about our wardrobe choices for the big day?" He fidgets with his jacket lapel as if considering how much work it would be to petition FATE's administration for a new, snazzier uniform before the weekend.

"The uniforms? The mandatory uniforms we have to wear? Mandated, Greg. I feel mandated," I answer, defiantly making a point to turn my phone back on. He was adamant that we unplug for practices this week. *(5) missed emails.*

"I guess you're right," he says, though he does not seem satisfied with this outcome.

Three spammy emails.

One party invite from Evie: her cousin is launching a new app in Tribeca this weekend or something. We've been tentative around each other since our breakup, if you can even call it that. While I contemplate forwarding this would-be peace offering to Corinne, I open the last email, received fifty-three minutes ago.

It's a link to the Columbia portal.

Dear Henri,

Congratulations! It is my pleasure to inform you that you have been selected for admission to Columbia University. As a member of the Class of 2024, you will be a participant in an academic community wealthy in intellectual and personal talents of every kind—

The entire world goes quiet for a second, and when it snaps back into place, I'm standing up and Greg and Yadira are both staring at me like I'm unhinged. I must have made a sound I wasn't altogether conscious of. A loud one.

"Jesus Christ, Haltiwanger! What is your trauma?"

"I got in. . . . IgotintoColumbia. It'ssayingI'min."

"Hey! Congratulations!" Yadira says. "When?"

"Fifty-threeminutesago. I got in! IfreakinggotintoColumbia."

Yadira steps forward and gives me a tight hug before stepping back, aware of the number of boundaries crossed. Specifically, forty-three.

"Did you just hug me?" I look over to Greg. "Did she just hug me?"

"She did," Greg says, stunned himself. "I saw. Can I just give you a high five or something? I'm not a hugger."

I raise my arm over my shoulder and collect the misaligned high five.

"You can both shut up now," Yadira snarls. "I just . . . I know how badly Halti wanted this. That's all."

I did. I do.

"Ihavetogo."

"Yes, go get the celebration out of your system." Greg nods, turning away to vigorously brush the whiteboard clean. "And before Saturday, please: your words-per-minute speed is out of control. And make sure to drink the shake. First thing in the morning!" Greg shouts behind me before I can skip out of the room.

And I'm physically skipping. I need to tell Dad and Ma. And Ming. And Lion. But they're all secondary to the person that has to hear this first.

Where is Corinne right now? I scroll through our earlier exchange to see if she told me where she would be right now, but no luck. I need to tell her in person. Texting her the news just doesn't carry the same effect. There is no sufficiently happy emoji for this. Mind Blown + Smiley Face? No, I need to tell her in person.

Princeton and Columbia. We're both Ivy League–bound students now.

I check all four of the main hallways. Corinne has a free period now, but there is no sign of her in any of the school wings. I can't locate her in Freedom, Voice, Mindfulness, or Action. All of her go-to reading benches are currently occupied or empty. I quickly text her a casual and exclamation-free: **Out of practice. Wanna meet up?**

I turn a corner and, instead of Corinne, spot a self-satisfied swagger I'd recognize anywhere. Normally I'd avoid it, but for once, it's a sight I'm a little thrilled to see.

"Marvyn!" I exclaim. I crash into him, throwing both arms around his shoulders. "Buddy! Did you get it?"

"What the hell?" he says, immediately trying to wiggle free. It's not so much the sudden physical contact, considering how often he and his bros slam into each other, but clearly, the fact that it's me doing it. To be fair, it's a shock for both of us.

"Personal space, Haltiwanger! Did you lick a toad or something?"

"Did you get it? Columbia decisions are out!" I squeal, finally letting him go free. "All of them, I think. Or they're being released throughout the day. Anyway, check your email, man!"

"Oh, that."

"Congrats!" I can't help but hug him again. "Dude, where's your joie de vivre? We got in!"

He simultaneously snorts and rolls his eyes. "Three legacies on my mom's side and a recommendation from Donielle Kempf: of course I got in. It even earned a whole twenty seconds of conversation with my parents, if you can imagine," he says. "It's just . . ."

"Yeah?"

He looks at me up and down as if to make sure I'm not a doppelganger right now.

"You know I hate you, right?" Marvyn says. "That's our whole thing, Haltiwanker."

"I know!" I laugh. "I can't stand you either, dude. And now we get to do the whole thing on an Ivy League quad!"

He snorts a laugh in spite of himself. "Whatever, Haltiwanker. You'll be so busy frenching the Alma Mater statue for four years, you won't even notice me."

After another round without locating Corinne, I lean against the nearest locker and begin to type on my phone.

I have to tell Dad. It feels weird that I've known for almost an hour now and that he may be toiling away on some pipes or carrying the building trash bags to the curb without knowing.

I try to log in to the portal again to take a screenshot of my acceptance. My password spends a good minute trying to load but fails. It figures that I've run out of data at the worst possible time.

I settle for merely texting the news, sans attachments, and the reply is instantaneous. Dad is not normally an all-caps kind of texter.

SKIP YOUR AFTERNOON CLASS
COME HOME
WE HAVE TO CELEBRATE

I head out to empty my locker and grab my coat. I'll tell Corinne at the Wyatt. He doesn't have to tell me twice. And if the uppercase state of mind didn't convey it, the fact that Dad would ever advocate for my skipping a minute of school time tells me how happy he must be right now. This was always the school I was meant to attend.

"Henri Haltiwanger!"

Mr. Vu is standing outside his office. The thing is, Mr. Vu doesn't shout. Every school's teaching body can be divided into two: teachers who shout and teachers who simply do not have it in them to raise their voice. They'll give stern speeches, failing grades, or detention, but they will simply not yell.

Up until this very moment, I had Mr. Vu firmly placed in the latter category.

"H-hey, Mr. Vu," I say, readjusting my backpack strap. It's pretty obvious to him that I'm on my way out. "Okay, I know this looks bad, but my dad told me to skip, which is as bonkers as it sounds." I laugh. "You would know if you knew him. Anyway, I have some awesome news, Mr. Vu. I got in! I got into Columbia!"

"We can discuss this further in my office, Henri. I'm not asking."

I notice that his face is beet red. Is his chest heaving? Why is he so mad? I hadn't technically skipped yet. A passing freshman raises an eyebrow at the exchange and slinks into the gender-inclusive restrooms.

Vu looks down both sides of the otherwise empty hallway before looking back to me and letting out another shout, this time in the form of a low raging hiss.

"Now, Henri!"

His voice sounds nothing like the normal mixture of administrative weariness and politeness I'm used to. Right now, it's pure outrage. And with the excitement and the Yadira hug and the Marvyn hug, for a split second I'm confused about what he could be upset about. . . .

And then it comes rushing back.

Oh. That.

TWENTY-FIVE

t's not a straightforward conversation. Not from my chair, at least. Mr. Vu doesn't so much mince words as chop them into invisible particles until I'm in a cloud of "concerns," "inconsistencies," and "ethics," wondering how long I can hold my breath before taking it all in.

Michael Connelly, the Dean of Admissions, contacted him thirty minutes ago. My file had been flagged either shortly before or shortly after the acceptances had gone out but after the online list had been submitted. I imagine a perfectly embossed blue envelope with my name on it being snatched from a pile of such envelopes mere moments before the mailman rolled them out to his truck.

Mr. Vu shakes his head a lot, joins his hands together in front of him, and then quickly untangles them. As the anger seeps out of him, so does the confidence. He opens an email on his desktop and reads it out loud. I make out my name, but that's about it. I want to be paying attention to what he's saying—I need to be paying attention—but my mind is reeling.

"I'm sorry . . . what?" I ask when Vu repeats the same word enough that it pierces through the miasma.

"*Rescinded*. Your acceptance has been rescinded, Henri," he says, finding his way back to his regular hue, having exhaled all his frustration.

"No, it can't be," I finally manage to will into syllables. "I got the email, see? I saw it with my own eyes. . . ."

I frantically take out my phone and try to reload the portal to prove it to him. C'mon.

C'mon. C'mon.

After I make the third try in which the page comes up blank, Mr. Vu extends a hand forward to stop me from refreshing again.

"Never mind that right now. Just listen to me, Henri. I'm . . . I'm trying to get them to leave it at the rescinded acceptance, but this is bad," Vu says. "Do you get that? Just how bad this is?"

Words are on the margins of my brain right now, so I say nothing as I lower the phone.

"I feel like I've failed you." Mr. Vu sighs, and I hate how it sounds so close to pity. "I know you were under an extraordinary amount of pressure, but why would you do this?"

I sigh. "You know why, Mr. Vu."

Because there's no such thing as "competitive" in the end, is there? I want to say. You're either in or you're not. Everyone who "almost got in" ends up in the same pile as the people who didn't even spell their address correctly. The world is binary. Success, failure.

"How did you do it, Henri?" Mr. Vu asks. "You falsified a

recommendation but from who? Donielle Kempf?"

"Corinne's mom," I finally give, closing my eyes. I suddenly feel very tired. "Corinne and I are, y'know, together, and her mother is a Columbia dean."

"Chantale Troy." He nods slowly, with the brief satisfaction of someone solving a crossword puzzle that's been nagging at them.

"They were both out of town. I walk their dog, Palm Tree, sometimes, and Chantale hadn't logged off her computer. . . ."

The rest of the story is nowhere near as convoluted as it feels in my head. It's a very simple and straightforward series of colossally stupid decisions.

"Oh, Henri," Mr. Vu says. "That was . . . just a very dumb thing to do."

He sounds like he's trying to skirt some line of professionalism in his mind: stuck somewhere between what he wants to say and what the FATE handbook prescribes in exchanges like these.

"We take misrepresentation very seriously here," he finally says, chin slightly up and fingers laced again. "We have to, I'm afraid."

I realize then that a disappointed Mr. Vu and my record here at FATE are in free fall. The floor is still falling.

"Am I suspended?"

Am I *expelled*? Will FATE still let me graduate?

"Not at the moment, no. But we'll discuss it more Monday morning."

Is there even a tomorrow, or is the meteorite starting to pierce the atmosphere right now, headed straight for New York?

"Maybe you should take the afternoon off, after all," Mr. Vu says, catching a glimpse of the phone in my hand. "Go home, talk to your parents. I expect they might have been contacted by the university too by now."

"And Dean Troy?" I ask, already knowing the answer.

"Oh, *she* has definitely been contacted."

My body seems to understand that I should be moving now, which is how I find myself at the door of Mr. Vu's office, feeling my phone vibrate with yet another text.

"Henri?"

"Yes?"

"I'll send Columbia an email on your behalf," he says with a weak smile. "I don't know if it'll do anything, but . . ." He sounds genuinely concerned, which is nice, I suppose. "You're a good kid. I know that."

"Thanks, Mr. Vu," I say, without smiling. I'm not that, but it's a nice thing to say.

Once in the hallway, I get another text from Dad: a string of question marks that look like they're vibrating.

Ma is coming home from work too! We have to celebrate!

Crap. She just told me not to tell you she was coming home! Never mind!

Pretend to be surprised, OK, college boy?

So my parents don't know yet what happened.

I realize now that this isn't rock bottom. Rock bottom will be seeing the looks on my parents' faces when I tell them what I've done.

TWENTY-SIX

When I was a kid, riding the subway home from school was the highlight of my day. I liked people, the very concept of them. Making eye contact with them, asking them something about their clothes or where they were going, and watching their faces brighten as they opened up. It was a game to see if I could make smile the grumpiest elderly man with a dusty bow tie if I performed for him long enough.

All children are charming as an adjective, but you're charming as a verb. Ma had once said that with a sigh while we waited on the platform. I had locked us in conversation with a stranger who was carrying a vase of fresh flowers, and we missed our stop on the express. I aced the following day's surprise grammar quiz.

Dad was always less patient about my subway antics. On weekends, I would ride the green line with him while he picked up supplies and tools from cheap East Harlem appliance stores.

When the train was running late, I would sometimes get antsy and amuse myself by stepping too close to the yellow line, and he would yank my arm back the moment my toe even crossed over.

No! That's dangerous, Henri!

Once, I even saw a dog. Future lectures, seated at the kitchen table, would convince me that no leash-less beagle was, in fact, darting down the subway platform at the time, but I will swear until the day I die that there was absolutely a dog on the platform that day. He looked happy and friendly, and I instantly took off after him, darting between bystanders and jumping over a bench to go after it. I would catch glimpses of its tail wagging between legs. The fact that I was never, not ever, supposed to let go of Dad's or Ma's hand became an afterthought: I just wanted to catch that dog.

However, by the time I made it to the other end of the platform, it was gone, and everyone was looking at me from a distance. I realized why when I finally stopped panting and could hear the panicked and angry roar of Dad catching up to me. I didn't watch a minute of television for a full month after that. Which for a first grader might as well be a year. I thought Dad hated me. The older I got, the clearer it became that of course he didn't. Dad wasn't raging; he was terrified, maybe a little embarrassed, but there was no rage.

Today?

Today, Dad *rages*.

He ends up refreshing the portal more than I did. It's as if the words I'm saying—half explanations and apologies—aren't computing. Background noise to the important task happening on the family computer. Ma doesn't say anything; she slumps down in a chair, having heard every word Dad hasn't and now seems to be processing. She's tired too, fresh home from the station. Normally she would have been asleep an hour ago. I'm so sorry, Ma. My stomach churns all over again.

"They—they can't just accuse you of something like that," he says after firmly shutting off the computer, galvanized to now go jangle a second locked door.

"Dad—"

"No, Henri. *No.* This isn't fair. We'll get a lawyer!"

"It's not an accusation, Dad. I did it. They just caught me."

This seems to be the first thing that snaps him back to reality. He's left scanning my face, and his jaw is clenched, as though he's searching for a sign that this person he's staring at is categorically not his son.

"I'm so sorry, Dad. . . ."

"You had it, Henri!" he yells as I sink into the kitchen chair right next to Ma. "Everything we've been working for was in your hand, and you ruin it by doing something so incredibly stupid and—and so *wrong*!"

The rest plays out exactly as expected, with Ma holding her neck, her lips tight, staring at us in disbelief from the other end of the table while Dad paces around the space, sucking his teeth and waving his arms at the heavens, all Haitian and no hint of Americanized chill. There's a stain on his jumpsuit, and his sweat pits are visible through the fabric like he was already having a crap day before this fell in his lap.

Ma chimes in with a quiet "You didn't have to do this, Henri," but it's a teacup against the maelstrom. I want to explain how I *didn't* have it in the palm of my hand, that like everything good in life, Columbia was a crapshoot and that all I did was take a shot. A shot that cost me everything.

"*Fah respow*, son," Dad says, slipping into Creole like he does when he can't keep his cool. "The one thing, Henri, and you failed at it. . . . Just like Lionel!"

Fah respow.

It's Dad's favorite Haitian saying, which translates to something like "Earn your respect." It's the first lesson I remember from him that didn't relate to which way to screw in a light bulb or how to take a transfer bus to avoid using multiple MetroCard swipes on the subway.

It doesn't matter if a store owner glares at you from the moment you walk into the store all the way out the door or if a cop calls you "boy" and asks to see your backpack but not Ming's. As long as you know you haven't done anything wrong, that there's nothing in your pocket, no stain on your hands, you're "fucking untouchable" is how Dad had phrased it, dropping me at my entrance exam for FATE years ago.

"I'm sorry," I say again. Haitian relatives I've never met are sitting in a line in tiny crooked frames along the kitchen wall, and all look appropriately somber for the occasion. They watch the proceedings with dour frowns because no Haitian ever smiles in portrait photos, ever.

"You're not like those other private school kids, Henri! You can't live life cutting corners!"

"Yeah," I mumble too loudly. "Their parents would have paid someone else to do it."

"How did we raise someone with such low character?" Dad continues, looking to Ma for his next wind.

"That's not fair, Jacques," Ma says.

"You see character in this, Mimrose?"

She looks at me like she knows exactly when I sent that email. Like, she heard my footsteps going up to the Troys' that day.

"We put a lot of pressure on him," she finally says.

"Are you saying this is our fault?!"

She shakes her head. "This is a hard city to raise kids in, Jacques. You know that. That school, the dogs, college applications on top of it. It's a lot."

Dad shakes his head so vigorously his neck might snap. "No! No! Absolutely not! The son I know would never do somethin—"

"Don't talk like I'm not freaking here!" I yell out, feeling something come to a boil.

Both their heads whip at me. Projecting has never been a problem for any Haltiwanger man. Especially not one with Greg-supervised debate training.

"Do you know how unfair the admissions system is?" I sputter. "Everyone gets people to write letters on their behalf or hires tutors or authors to write their admissions essays! The system is rigged!"

"Ah, yes." Dad snorts. "The system where you luck your way into a full ride to a phenomenal school where you're not bullied, have rich friends, and everyone loves you! The one where your classrooms are filled with top-of-the-line computers and you 'just chill' with the children of millionaires when you're not playing with dogs."

Did he seriously think that? Was that really what he pictured? That this has just been easy for me? That going to FATE has been *fun*?

"It's not a fun thing to go to school with the kids of millionaires, Dad. Not when you have $38.43 in your checking account! And whoever told you that picking up dog crap at six a.m. every day is fun was choking on some amazing edibles!"

He shakes his head, and his voice lowers for the first time. "You're so young."

"Yeah, well, that doesn't stop you from putting it all on me every freaking day because it's easier than trying on your own, does it? At least I tried to do something instead of just waiting for—I don't even know what—my son to buy me a mansion?"

"Henri!" Ma chimes in, aghast and suddenly wide awake.

"You lied; you stole that woman's name!" Dad throws back, and thank God we're on the ground floor, muffled by street sounds, otherwise that banshee Glanville might have already called the cops. "Where is your character that you can't see how wrong that is?"

"I said I was sorry already! God! You want to go to Columbia that badly, go fill out a fucking application and see how easy it is!"

It's mean. And vicious. And I immediately regret it.

I barely have time to register whatever is happening on Dad's face that we're both startled by one of the two ceramic bowls from the kitchen table shattering against the wall next to me.

"Do not *dare*, Henri," Ma says, her voice operating at the same volume as it always does with the only exception being that all the muscles in her arms and every vein and tendon are tensed and flexed in outrage.

"Mom—"

"No, you don't get to speak that way to him," she says, locked on me. "Not ever."

There's no follow-up, no waiting for me to reply. It's an edict from her that won't be crossed. Her face only softens once it turns to Dad.

"Jacques."

Dad's head jerks away when she reaches to touch his cheek, and he instead provides a tight smile. "I'm fine. I'm late."

"Apologize now, Henri," Ma warns.

"Dad, I—"

"No," Dad says, preempting me. "It's done. It's all done."

He slams the front door behind him without granting me another look. Ma shakes her head and just stands there for a moment, eyes shut and chin pointed to the ceiling as though she wishes she was in the middle of a burning building right now.

I stay quiet. The opposite hasn't been working in my favor

today. After a beat, Ma collects her coat and phone, and I can't tell if she's going after Dad or if it's time for her to check in at the station. She throws one last look at me.

"*Dumb*," she says before slamming the door herself, leaving me alone with all the crooked and unimpressed relatives, and that pit of shame in my gut.

TWENTY-SEVEN

The Manhattan skies are overcast like it might snow, briefly and wetly, but hours from now, maybe even into the night. It's the perfect weather for the writers sitting in coffee shops alongside Columbus Avenue to be looking out the windows in search of inspiration. I clock their faces on the walk home, in no great hurry to enter our apartment right now. I've been walking around my neighborhood for the past twenty minutes trying to clear my head, but I just keep replaying my fight with Dad over and over.

I turn the corner to our street, and that's when I see her. Corinne.

An hour ago—less, even—I wanted nothing more than to see Corinne. To tell her about Columbia, to pick her up and spin her around. Now, the sight of her standing right outside the Wyatt with a phone at her ear and Palm Tree at the end of a new leash is the last thing I want.

Palm Tree starts barking happily the moment I turn the corner, and she spots me. And the way Corinne's brow knits in confusion, I'm not sure I'm her favorite sight at the moment either. How much does she know?

I walk the rest of the way to her and wait for her to finish her call, shuffling my feet.

"I'll see you later . . . ," I overhear. "And Mom? I'm so sorry."

I'm sorry. I'm sorry. I'm sorry.

Okay. I can do this. I can do this. I can explain this.

"Hey, I texted you this afternoon," I say as she puts the phone away.

She doesn't recoil when I lean in to kiss her hello, but it's nothing like we usually kiss—with a smile or awkward pucker when there's someone around. Instead, she stares at me like she's trying to read my thoughts.

"Mrs. Raphael turned Lit class into a study period, so I took PT to the vet for his checkup," she says. There's a delay in her voice, as though she's still processing. "That was my mom just now. She's still at work dealing with . . . Henri, is it true?"

Despite how unlikely it was, part of me hoped this conversation wouldn't happen. I don't want to do this. I know how this ends.

I sigh. "Yes. But Corinne, I—"

"So, you actually did this?" she asks again, tugging the leash back slightly when an impatient Palm Tree that would normally have been picked up jumps for my knee. "You . . . wrote a fake recommendation letter from my mom? My mom who trusted you? What is wrong with you?"

So everything; she knows everything.

"When?"

I take too long to answer, and Corinne being quicker than me is nothing new. "When we were in Switzerland, right? When you were alone in our apartment . . ."

I don't say anything.

"What the hell, Henri! Do you have any idea how much of an invasion that is?"

"I'm so sorry."

"You used me!"

"I didn't! I just . . . I was up there with Palm Tree, and your mom's computer was on. . . . Her Columbia email account was open, and . . . and—I don't know—it was just . . . impulsive."

It's not the full truth, but the details won't matter right now. She's standing farther away from me than she was when we first started talking, and I need Corinne to know that I'm not whatever hustler she's picturing right now, smirking while going through her mom's office drawers with gloved hands.

"There's nothing impulsive about opening someone's email account and writing a recommendation letter on your behalf and sending it out, Henri. Those are at least seven or eight decisions!"

Her voice is louder than I thought it could even go, and the two guys coming out of the building across the street look at us. They share a quick raise of the eyebrow, probably imagining some juicy Jerry Springer drama.

If only. This is just the great disappointment of my existence rolling downhill and collecting moss along the way.

"My mom worked hard for her job, Henri! She's the first Black woman to have that job—ever!"

"I'm so sorry, Corinne. I never wanted this to blow back on your mom. I just—"

"Oh, we're back to you!"

"N-no! I just . . ." I look down. "I just wanted it so badly, Corinne."

"I don't care, Henri! God!" Corinne exclaims, now furious. "I categorically do not care about how this affects you right now! My mom trusted you in our home, and now she has *this*, this nonsense red mark in her file about being a liability because her daughter's boyfriend hacked her email account? Do you know how humiliating that is?"

Corinne shakes her head at me. She lifts Palm Tree up and bundles his leash under him. "You know, all the magazines said the same thing about, whatever, starting relationships. *How* is important. Meet-cutes, being set up by friends that know you well, finding the right dating app . . ."

I blink, unsure where she's going with this.

She sighs, sounding more sad than angry. "Our meet-cute was blackmail, Henri. I *blackmailed* you into hanging out with me. What did I expect?" She pauses. "Did you know about my mom's job all along? Is that why you . . ." She waves her arm in the space between us to cover something she can't put into words right now. "This?"

"No! No."

"You know . . ." She laughs sadly, ignoring me. "Right after the moment my mom told me what happened and I saw you come down the street, my first thought was: that explains it. That explains all of it. He didn't want to sleep with me because he felt guilty." She stops and inhales sharply, suddenly looking angrier. "Actually, maybe even that would be giving you too much credit. Now I wonder if it's because you never had any feelings for me at all. And I was just part of this gross con. Was all of this just to get my mom's recommendation, Henri? You'd date her weird, loner daughter and she'd be so grateful, she'd stake her career to get you into your dream school?!"

"No, no, Corinne—that's not it." I want to be offended. I want to say I would never con someone into trusting me, into liking me. But I do that, don't I? That's what I do all the time.

"I fell for you, Corinne. For real. You've got to believe me." I look her in the eyes. "I love you."

It's the first time I've said it, and I know it's not the right time, but I'm desperate, and I need her to know how I feel.

Corinne is quiet for a moment as the words hang in the air.

When she finally speaks, I know that this is over. "I hate how powerful people think those words are? Okay, so, you . . . that, and now what? It's all forgotten? Never mind everything you did? How can I believe you? You lie to everyone, about everything. You're a *liar*."

"I never lied to you!" I know that's a lie.

"You said you wouldn't hurt me. You said that! And I was dumb enough to actually believe it."

She keeps staring at me, and I feel like a cluttered desktop folder being right-clicked and slowly moved to a trash bin in her mind.

"I know what I look like, okay?" she finally says, shaking her head.

"What?"

"I'm not size-zero Evie freaking Hooper, and that's fine! But I— This was always . . . poorly thought out."

Where was this coming from?

"This is insane, Corinne!" I manage to choke out. "I think you're gorgeous! You know that."

"Oh, *fuck you*, Haltiwanger," she snaps. "I know I'm amazing, Henri. I don't need pity from—"

She stops herself short and looks directly up at the sky as if to hold back the slightest bit of tears from forming and locks back down onto me with that pure Troy resolve, eyes completely dry.

"You know what? I am so done with this conversation."

And with that, she hurries up the stairs to the Wyatt, with a confused puppy in her arms panting happily as he catches another quick sight of me.

I stand there, watching as she disappears inside the building.

Somehow, nothing about this outcome feels surprising. This visual of Corinne walking away from me, looking disgusted, feels like an inevitable outcome that was etched in stone since the moment she stopped being Corinne Troy and just became Corinne. There was really no other way for this to end. I just hadn't expected it to end so soon or my chest to feel like it does right now.

TWENTY-EIGHT

This time, the lobby of the River Heights building is filled with boxes. Not the kind the tenants of the Wyatt use in their moves—the repurposed online-retailer chunks of cardboard scotch-taped and weathered on all sides—but pristine and reinforced white boxes with purple lettering that matches the lettering on the backs of the purple T-shirted movers, all either Black and Latino men. They move like it's choreographed, passing the boxes to each other like dancing henchmen in a cartoon musical.

"Out of the way, kid!" one of them shouts my way.

"S-sorry!" I step out of the way, scanning the lobby for any sign of Lion.

"Man, when it rains Haltiwangers, it pours," comes Lion's voice as he manifests out of the sliver of the closet door that briefly reveals itself from the wall behind him.

"What do you mean by that?"

"Nothing," he says, shaking his head. "I'm still a bit drunk from Friday. Ignore me."

"It's Thursday."

"So, you see the problem." He yawns. "What can I do for you, nephew?"

It's a good question.

My thing used to be talking, didn't it? This address seemed like an obvious escape from the Upper West Side an hour ago, but now I'm not too sure. I suppose I just wanted to see family that wasn't likely to tell me how much I suck. Or maybe an audience for seventeen years of built-up Jacques resentment. But as I think about how badly I messed everything up—with college, with my parents, with Corinne—I don't really have the words now.

I expect another snarky comment when I take too long to answer, but Lion's face unexpectedly softens.

"Let's step into my office, yeah?"

He leads the way to one of the free elevators, trading a lightning-fast fist bump with one of the movers as he walks past them. Judging from the back of his neck, he might have lost weight since I last saw him, and he was already trim enough.

We take the elevator to the top floor and then a service stairwell whose door light turns green after a tapping of Lion's work ID. We step out on the roof, and it's an instant jolt to the system, which Lion absorbs with a grin.

"I know, right?"

Sorry, Montreal: there's no arguing which city has the most impressive skyline. It's the same view he'd sent me a video of after I was here last time.

The sky is already past orange, well into purple heading into navy. A grid of bright office and apartment lights steadily begins to overtake the sky's natural light as I pace around the rooftop, taking Lion through the full story.

Lion listens with a loosened tie around his neck, a lime-green e-cigarette at his lips, and the city of New York far below us. My arms wave around me. Greg would say that I'm all over the place, Yadira would note that I'm too emotional, but man, it feels good to get it all out.

"Dang," he eventually comments after I run out the clock on the topic of what a fuckup I am. "I'm definitely glad I don't live there tonight."

"I know, right?" I say. "Look, I get it. I really messed up. Like, bad. But I wouldn't have done this if Dad hadn't put so much pressure on me. It was always Columbia this and Columbia that. He sets these standards that are impossible to meet. I mean, you know. That's why he kicked you out."

Lion takes two inhales of his tiny remote, tilts his head back, and blows what I suspect is a failed attempt at a circle.

"The reason Jacques kicked me out, *Henri*, was you. Specifically, your moral virtue. Old Jacquo didn't want me corrupting his stalwart son, who was actually going places. I'm not making light of your pain here, but the irony is pretty delicious."

He lets out a wry cough and then leans forward and hawks a spit at the city below.

"His Ivy League–headed son," I correct, hoping some poor little old lady doesn't get her evening ruined by an e-cigarette loogie. "Without that, you and I are in the same canvas bag with a big F on it. Failures."

Lion stares at me with a frown, as if running scenarios in his mind.

"Okay, I want you to listen to me now. Really carefully, okay?"

He puts his hand on my shoulder to anchor us both in the moment.

"You, my dear handsome nephew, are a privileged little punk who goes to bed with a full stomach every night because his dad fixes toilets and drags leaky trash bags all day."

I try to say something, but he quickly preempts me.

"I don't care if you get pissed at me," he says. "Someone has to tell you. If someone out there gets to hold you to a higher standard, it's your dad."

He's right. I know he's right. I can blame my dad as much as I want, but at the end of the day, this was my fault. I wrote that email. I sent it. The fallout is mine to bear.

The door to the roof abruptly swings open and an older building-staff member whose uniform matches Lion's steps forward, his face flushed from climbing the stairwell. He has the loaded bearing of a supervisor. He throws me a confused look before narrowing down on Lion.

"You're supposed to be on desk duty right now, Lionel!"

"Taking a break." Lion shrugs. "Family st—"

"Family stuff, yeah, I know the line. . . . You get one break a day. One! Not one per made-up family emergency, man. C'mon! The twenty-third-floor movers were waiting to sign out, and there was no one downstairs."

"Then fire me," Lion says coolly, which causes the man's eyes to momentarily go wide with rage. Lionel is making the face, *that* face. The one that used to enrage Dad at the dinner table. Completely blank with just the very faintest hint of a smirk.

It's the confidence of the untouchable. Someone who has handed in their two-week notice and is perfectly content to be dismissed with severance before that.

Ma used to complain about how all the work ignored by the paralegals of her old office used to end up on her desk the moment they handed in their resignation to go to law school or some bigger firm. They no longer bothered to hide their online shopping. The man throws me another glare before slamming the door behind him, muttering something under his breath.

"You're starting a new job already?" I deduce once we're alone again.

"You know your uncle. Always on the come-up." He grins at me, so charming and smooth that I would let him sell me a time-share right now. "Bigger and better things ahead."

"Congratulations. What is it?"

Something must slip into my voice that puts me too close to Dad because Lion's smile withdraws into the hollowest version of itself.

"Clean up your garden, I'll clean up mine, huh?" he says, turning back to stare at the skyline. I'm not getting anything more on the topic from him.

"Look, the bottom line is that you fucked up and that your dad is right to be pissed. That was a hell of a gamble. . . . I'd put your head through a wall if you were my kid."

"Please don't have kids."

"If you're going to risk everything, don't get caught," he continues, ignoring the quip. "A faked email from your girlfriend's mom? That was fucking sloppy, dude. Kindergarten shit."

We both stare out at the city in silence until I finally pull myself from the roof's safety rail and dust myself off, knowing where I need to be right now.

"Be careful, okay?" I feel the need to add before heading out. "The new job, I mean."

"You categorically don't have to worry about me, nephew." Lion smiles, pulling me into a side hug that doesn't lessen my concern. I hope that's true and his new job is the HR-department-and-juicy-overtime kind, but I have my doubts.

"You know, these things smell as bad as actual cigarettes," I say, flicking the lumpy tube in his jacket pocket after pulling away. "Plus, you look like a complete asshole."

"That's just my bloodline," he says with a smirk.

On the way in, with a hand already on the stairwell door, I turn back and give Lion another look. His eyes are still transfixed on the city below. Maybe it's the city lights, but there's a gleam in his eyes that's as arresting as the skyline.

I try to imagine everything that a city like New York must be to someone born and raised in Port-au-Prince and promised a new life that looks nothing like what was expected once the plane landed.

It probably looks how it does to me right now. A little dimmer than usual.

TWENTY-NINE

ride the train home, and only after catching a darkened reflection of myself in the subway door windows do I realize I'm still in my FATE uniform. This is the longest day ever.

Dad's first sign of life comes in the form of a text in the family group chat: **OMW HOME**. Ma's entry comes a few moments later: **I was running errands, now at station. Home by noon. Good night, fam.**

At library, I lie. **Headed home soon.**

It's a mode of communication our family mostly keeps for basic information like **OUT OF MILK** or **1 TRAIN DOWN** and other bits of news that deserve to be passed on to the rest of the unit. The fact that Dad is choosing this platform to contact me makes the subtext pretty clear: **not ready to talk yet**. Even Dad knows the meaning of a period at the end of a text.

"Shit, shitty-ass, shit of a day." I sigh aloud at the sight of the Wyatt. For some reason, I text out the sentiment to Ming too, which makes it all feel marginally better.

Venting at Lionel had felt good in the moment, but it hadn't dissolved the pit in my stomach. Corinne's words have been eating away at me. When I sent that email to Michael Connelly, I didn't just mess things up for myself. I messed things up for Chantale too. There's one more conversation I still need to have.

And that's how I find myself ringing the bell to the Troys' apartment. It takes a moment after I say my name, but eventually I hear the bolt being undone, and Chantale Troy slowly opens the door. She's wrapped in a shawl, with reading glasses on and her hair in a purple scarf that's not unlike Ma's.

"Hello, Henri."

"Hi, Mrs. Troy."

She's always been impervious to my smiles, genuine or trademarked.

"Um, I just wanted to return my key. Your key, I mean. I imagine you want it back."

She unwraps her hand from the doorknob, one deliberate finger after another, and extends it forward. I place the lone key in her palm. Transaction completed.

"I imagine there's no copy?"

"No, ma'am."

"I will nevertheless be changing the locks. You understand."

"Right. No, I get it."

"Good night, Henri."

"I'm sorry!" I say before she can fully shut the door in my

face. "I just . . . want to apologize."

The door widens again as deliberately as it had been closing. "What for, Henri?"

"Um, what?"

"What exactly are you apologizing for? I've found that people, men specifically if we're being honest, really like to apologize," she says. "Four syllables that cover everything and prevent any introspection or itemization. So I'm asking: what are you sorry for in this instance?"

From the corner of my eye, I catch a glimpse of the little devil and angel pair through the hallway mirror, pointing and stifling their laughter at me.

"For abusing your trust and, um, invading your privacy . . . and hers too." I glance in the direction of Corinne's bedroom, wondering if she's in there now. If she can hear me.

The silence as she eyes me up and down is intentional. Chantale Troy feels no compunction to provide a reply, and by the look on her face, she would have no second thought about slamming the door in my face right now.

"Come in," she says, stepping back in. "There's something I'd like to share with you."

I sidestep into the apartment, almost tripping on Palm Tree in the process. He's currently rocking a party jacket with trumpets sewn all over.

"Hey, buddy," I whisper. "I like your coat."

He's thrilled to see me, and I very badly want to pick him up right now, but I know I've lost that right. Denied, he lets out a few happy yaps. I'm sorry to you too.

"That was not my idea." Chantale sighs, picking up her glass of wine from the kitchen counter and taking a gulp. "Corinne picked it up at that overpriced little store on Ninety-fourth and Broadway. My daughter has developed a taste for the tacky lately." She arches an eyebrow at me.

Guess I deserve that.

"There's a . . . website where you can find dog clothes pretty cheaply," I say, ignoring the growing pit in my stomach and focusing on Chantale. "I could send you the link if you wanted."

Chantale's glass returns to the counter with a clank.

"I think you've had enough interaction with my in-box for the time being, don't you?"

I deserve that too.

"How do you think you got caught?" she asks.

I pause. Of all the things I'd been thinking about, this question had fallen right through the cracks. I couldn't even begin to imagine the how.

"Columbia has an eleven-billion-dollar endowment," I say with pursed lips. "I assume they have pretty good Information Technology."

She snorts. "The money's not going to Information Technologies, believe me." Her wineglass refilled, Chantale moves to sit on the couch and crosses both legs and arms, eyeing me like the suspicious, fun-house-mirror version of Aunt Terry: elongated, stern, all boundaries and apprehension at my sight right now.

"A few weeks ago, during a very long flight to Switzerland," she starts, "my daughter laid out a thirty-nine-bullet-point plan as to why I should break protocol and use my professional reputation and limited free time to write a college recommendation for our dog walker, whom she'd found herself smitten with."

Oh. Hearing that twists the knife even harder.

"Do you know how many bullet points thirty-nine is, Henri? Quite a few, as it turns out. Especially when they each have a full flash card."

Her tone isn't quite *disdain* as much as resentment for the level of high school nonsense I inadvertently brought into her life.

"But that's my daughter. She was adamant that you deserved it despite *choking like a punk* at your first interview."

"Was that a direct quote from her?" I manage to ask.

Chantale smirks in a shrug, preferring not to answer. As far as I could tell, Chantale and her twin sister are born straightforward, but tonight's Chantale is uncensored in an unfamiliar way and that might be due to the fact that she's a little tipsier than either of us initially thought.

"At any rate, that's the reason you got caught. The first thing I did when I came home was write your letter of recommendation. I had hoped it wasn't too late. Needless to say, getting two separate emails from me was what tipped off the dean. Not to mention the excessive use of exclamation points in the first one. There's a grace missing from your forgery. It at least tells me you don't have the natural disposition of a criminal." She puts down her already-empty glass and stares me down. "I have something for you."

She goes to a braided basket on a shelf in which I know the house keeps their bills, delivery menus, and envelopes, and she collects a single printed sheet folded into thirds.

When I reach out to take it, she pulls back, withholding it for a moment.

"I'm not doing this as an act of kindness. I hope you understand that."

"Okay . . ." I take the sheet and fold it into itself once more and hold on to it, because crumbling the whole thing into my pocket would feel rude.

"This is salt. So the lesson stings. So you don't keep going through life on a ledge like this." She pauses for a beat as if interrogating her own thoughts at the moment. "Also . . . you hurt my daughter. I never thought I was cut out to be a mother, truth be told. But there's an interesting motherly instinct in me at the moment that wants to *hurt* you."

"Oh," I say, taking a cautious step backward. Palm Tree seems on alert all of a sudden.

"Like, rip-off-your-spine hurt you. It's very odd." She taps her index finger along the wineglass.

"I should probably get going now."

"Quite."

"I really like your daughter," I try, against my better judgment, once I'm at the door again. "Love. I love her."

If surprise never registers on Chantale Troy's face, let the record show that I come pretty close to summoning it tonight.

"I believe you," she finally says, looking at me with what can only qualify as reluctant sympathy. "But I think it's too late for Corinne. She's always been a once-bitten type of kid."

I nod because I know she's right. "Have a good night, ma'am."

"By the way, I explained the whole thing away as much as I could. It's standard policy for Columbia to contact an applicant's other schools at signs of 'moral turpitude,' as they call it, but as far as I can tell, this indiscretion won't be shared with the other schools you're applying to."

I can't bear to look at her. That is unexpected. That is the kindest thing anyone could do under the circumstances. "You did? Why? I mean, what happened to, um, you know, the whole ripping-out-my-spine thing?"

"An email shouldn't ruin your life. No matter how phenomenally stupid your actions were." She shrugs. "Some of those flash cards were very convincing."

"I don't know what to say. I . . . Thank you, ma'am."

"Good night, Henri."

I linger for a moment once outside the Troys' doorstep, hoping Corinne might come out at that exact moment, giving me a chance to explain things.

But that's not how things go, is it? And I'm not sure I deserve a second chance.

When I peel open the mystery sheet of paper, now wrinkled into six squares, I see what Chantale Troy meant. Each line of the printed-out letter, typed in unadorned Courier font, feels like an intentional uppercut.

To the concerned party:

I am writing this letter on behalf of one HENRI HALTIWANGER, a high school student of the Fine Arts Technical Education Academy and a class of 2024 hopeful. I understand that Henri's application is currently pending and wanted to take a moment to assure you that he is keenly interested in making the institution of Columbia University the next step in his academic journey.

I will be clear and say that I do not know Henri in any academic capacity. I understand his grades to be adequate, though not extraordinary. What I am writing to convey is my admiration for his work ethic and the character he has showed as a neighbor and dog walker to my family. His character is unimpeachable, and in a short time, he has become a trusted friend of the family.

I truly believe that he will benefit immensely from this opportunity at this stage of his academic career. He is a charming young man, beloved by his peers, and despite his many responsibilities and limited resources, I understand him to be a social pillar of his school. He is prepared and kind, and I strongly believe he will be one of those students who makes the most of the Columbia undergraduate college experience.

If you would like additional information about Mr. Haltiwanger, do not hesitate to contact me to further discuss this matter.

Kindly,

Chantale Bien-Aimée Troy, PhD

Dean of English

16th- and 17th-Century English Literature

Columbia University

THIRTY

The shattered ceramic has been broomed up when I gently open the door to our place. One dish is wet on the rack by the sink, the bathroom is warm and muggy from a recent shower, and there is a line of orange light from under Dad and Ma's bedroom door. Their TV is on low, barely a whisper. I have to tiptoe forward and lean against the door to hear.

I barely sleep that night. I send Corinne about a million texts apologizing and begging her to talk to me. **I'm so sorry, I'm such an idiot**. . . . They all go unanswered. Every motion I hear in Dad and Ma's bedroom feels like the beginning of an earthquake that doesn't pan out. And my conversation with Chantale won't stop playing in a loop in my head. Credit where credit is due, she would make a phenomenal despot. I reread that letter at least six times, and while concrete sleep never quite materializes, I somehow still find myself waking up peeling the letter from the side of my face, so wrinkled it feels like fabric to the touch. I almost miss the little angel and devil at this point.

Before I know it, the sun is beaming through my window, and it looks like we're in for one of those perfect-weather Saturdays that feels particularly vindictive from the universe right now.

My phone is buzzing up a storm. It can't be my alarm since my few weekend dog walks aren't for another couple of hours. Owners tend to enjoy taking their pets on those sunny Saturday walks themselves. I have seven unread texts, and despite my best efforts, my heart skips a beat as I scroll, imagining it to be Corinne.

MING (7 new messages)

I have to remind myself there might in fact never be another text from Corinne. I have a feeling she belongs to that breed of people who Mute, Block, Delete, and Forget, in that order.

> **I've been outside your bldg for 15 mins and still no sign of u**
>
> **wake up, u bastard**
>
> **did you leave already??**
>
> **my bagel is gone, btw**
>
> **you owe me a bagel**
>
> **make it a donut**
>
> **I changed my mind, actually: make it a Cronut**

The notices keep coming, so I go to the source and dial Ming's number.

"Hey, so . . . why are you here?"

"Good morning to you too, sunshine," comes the overly cheery reply. "Read my texts. It's very clear. I'm outside. Either come join me or expect me to start texting you that sci-fi novel I've been working on. Sentence by sentence, mofo."

He will. It's happened before. I've already glimpsed way too much of that thing.

"I'll be there in a minute," I groan before hanging up. "Find your chill."

The apartment is already empty by the time I step out of my room, and after a quick shower, mostly to jolt myself awake, I step out to go meet my stalker. There have been nine more texts since I woke up, and they've devolved into a full stream of consciousness about pastries. Ming looks way too comfortable lounging on the Wyatt's stoop in gray sweats and Tom Ford brown-leather high-tops that match his hoodie today.

"I swear, there had better be a reason, Ming."

"'Cause you had a bad day,'" comes the familiar song as soon as I step out of the Wyatt.

"Are you having a stroke?"

He holds one finger up to interrupt me and raises his voice an octave as he continues to sing. Way too loudly, incidentally.

"'You're taking one down, You sing a sad song just to turn it around.'"

"Dude! There are people around," I say, casting a look around the street already bustling with typical Saturday morning foot traffic. A woman giggles at Ming's controversial singing voice, but he's undeterred and keeps serenading with the old cheesy radio single everyone in this house has occasionally shimmied to while doing the dishes.

I can only glare with crossed arms as a smile begins to waver on his lips until he breaks down and starts laughing—cackling, really—but he straightens back up, committed to stretching the last line of his melody as long as he can.

"'You had a bad daaaay.'"

"I'm very glad you're amusing yourself," I say, though I realize I'm smiling too now. It might be the first time since yesterday.

"I heard everything, and I mean, you just had such a shitty day, dude. That was one for the records. It needed a soundtrack!"

His eyes are wet with actual tears, the little maniac.

"Plus, the Halti I know doesn't send texts like these," he finally says, recovered from his comedy, and turns his phone my way.

Shit, shitty-ass, shit of a day.

No one can say I'm not a well-spoken Negro in texting too.

"I figured it was worth following up in person," he says, putting his phone away.

"And which Halti do you know, exactly?"

Ming pretends to think for a moment. "Six feet tall, Haitian-American, closed-off, possibly sociopathic tendencies?"

"A lot of people might agree with you these days," I say.

"I heard," he says. "I'm sorry."

"I don't have any Cronuts, but there is some Haitian orange cake in the fridge, I think. Wanna come in? My parents are out."

Ming looks at the building and then back to me with a raised eyebrow like he's not sure if I'm kidding or not. "Like, into your actual apartment?"

I can only muster up a listless shrug. "What else do I have to lose?"

I don't think Ming even has time to take in the rest of the apartment before he indiscriminately begins to forage our fridge. He fills me in on how much of the school rumor mill I've powered since yesterday, and it turns out to be a shockingly small amount. A few dreary spins at the most. It makes sense. The upside of a school that traffics in rumors is that it takes a lot for consensus to hit critical mass. People want receipts these days. Although too many people saw my exit for it to go completely unnoticed.

"Wait. They think I got into a fight with Mr. Vu?"

"Well, you were hugging people left and right, went into his office, and you came out looking like a ghost, apparently," Ming says, rattling the Tupperware of orange cake slices at me for permission before diving in. I barely have to nod, and he's already in.

"Teacher-student affair was also a contender for a little while, but that was just Betsy Scavo. That girl sees the entire world in slash fan fiction and— Holy *crap* is this good!" Ming says, shoving a massive slice of cake into his mouth.

It's a typical reaction. Your standard Black household desserts will give you a full coronary by age thirty-seven, but there's no denying the addictive factor. Aunt Terry is not the first to capitalize on it. Ming continues to stroll around the apartment at his own pace. There's not much use for a tour for anyone with peripheral vision.

"The Haltiwanger Lair . . . Am I racist if I say that all your male relatives look alike?" he comments, stopping at the wall of crooked photos.

"No. I mean, yes, kind of, but it's allegedly a thing. Halti-wanger genes. I don't see it but—"

"Dude!" Ming exclaims next, catching a glimpse of my bedroom and darting right in, mouth full of more orange cake. There's no unripping the Band-Aid now.

"Yes, we're poor," I say, instinctively picking up a stray T-shirt and folding it as if the simple act will boost our household income. "The exit is that way, and on Monday we can both pretend this never happened."

It's both an attempt at a joke and the furthest thing from it, but Ming doesn't appear to be hearing me at the moment.

"I'm . . . I'm hurt." Ming points to the autographed Givenchy 1998 collection poster pinned above my desk and then to my rack of sneakers. Six well-kept pairs, detailed whenever I need to clear my mind after a long day. "You've been holding out on me, *asshole*!"

"Ming, you own way more sneakers than I do." I lean against the doorway and watch him bounce from pair to pair with the spiritual energy of a raccoon.

"Anyone can buy a sneaker and wait for the delivery guy!

But look at this! This—this is like a shrine to the New York scene." He takes out his phone and snaps a photo.

Who knew it would be this easy to impress Ming?

"You're very strange," I grumble, crashing back into my unmade bed headfirst. "Don't tag me."

Even without looking, I can hear the eye roll in his "Duh."

Not that I actually fear Ming would caption a photo "Henri Halti's decrepit living space" for the world to see at this point. Even Corinne had only ever briefly glimpsed my room despite inquiring a few times. Ming being here doesn't feel that strange, but he'd have to be blind to pretend not to see the difference between this place and most FATE kids' places. Still, there's no condescension to his voice. He's not pitying us or overcompensating in any way.

After an impromptu photoshoot that tallies at thirty-eight photos, by the sound of his phone's shutter sound, I can feel Ming settle on my desk chair and look my way, waiting for me to say something. It's barely morning, and I'm already so tired. Or maybe *still* so tired. It's hard to keep track. We're quiet for a while longer, and I hear him flip through a magazine.

"It was a bad day, Ming."

"I know. I'm sorry."

I wait, but there's no follow-up.

"You're not going to give me grief? No that-was-so-dumb rant?"

"I could, I guess, but it feels like you've gotten enough. Can I ask, though?" He flips through an open sketchbook I filled

291

back in the sixth grade. "What's the real reason you never invited me up here?" he asks. "I was legitimately expecting to find like three babies eating a goat."

It's a terrifying thing, this mix of concern and gruesomely dark imagery that Ming can manage in the same breath. I sigh and sit up in the bed, knocking Chantale Troy's letter aside.

"Well?"

I might as well take a few hairs while ripping off the Band-Aid.

I tell Ming about Daniel Halkias, and he listens quietly.

"So that's when this Church and State thing happened?" Ming asks, sounding every bit like a career therapist who runs a practice out of his brownstone.

"It made things simpler," I say, picking at a nail.

I do miss simple. Simple was fun.

"Well, to me, your BFF Daniel sounds like a big old cup of smegma who definitely didn't deserve your mom's desserts."

"Also an acceptable diagnosis." I smile.

"And by the way," Ming continues, sounding huffy all of a sudden, "I had friends before you too, y'know. Very cool ones. Taller and better-looking ones, even."

"Uh, okay. . . ."

"I'm just saying. I just don't rub them in your face because that would be gauche."

"You might have missed the point of that story." I laugh.

Ming shrugs. "Not at all. The origin story of all your neuroticism comes through loud and clear. But you should also know me well enough by now to know that I only ever judge a man by the content of his character and his footwear. Nothing else."

"Your shallowness is very woke." I laugh.

"Your character is good, is the point I'm trying to make here. You shouldn't have to go to such lengths to hide it—"

"Ming . . ."

He dramatically flails his arms. "I know, I know. I'm rich and should promptly be eaten for thinking it's that easy and talking about shit I'll never know! I'm . . . I'm just saying."

He leaves it at that, and I smile back, understanding what he means.

"Thanks."

My phone's alarm startles on the comforter, which means it's time to go.

"Well, I've got a dog walk. C'mon. Giddyup!" I say, stretching myself out and grabbing my dog park sneakers off the rack. "Tumbler's much cuter to photograph than my walls."

Work doesn't wait when it takes the form of dog bladder. Considering I might end up doing this for the rest of my life, I'd better commit to the calling. Ming still manages to stuff into his pocket one more slice of orange cake wrapped in paper towels before we head out.

"Do you think Corinne knew we'd have a Tony Stark–Steve Rogers heart-to-heart when she told me to stop by? I wouldn't put it past her, honestly."

Wait. What?

"Corinne told you to call me?" My head whips back way too fast to play it off as casual interest. Ming winces at my door like he's just stepped in something unpleasant.

293

"I mean, sort of, yeah. How else do you think I got all the details? I texted her, asking where you were last night, and she encouraged me to check in. Y'know . . . bring you these bad boys to cry on."

He wiggles his shoulders in perfect synchronicity with his eyebrows. Jesus, my best friend is truly a ridiculous human being.

"Don't tell her I told you, okay?" Ming says. "Because, honestly, I like her, but there's no denying that your girlfriend also scares the crap out of me."

"Ex-girlfriend."

"Was it a fight or a breakup?"

I think about it. "I . . . don't know. But either way, I think it's too late."

THIRTY-ONE

I s that your dad?" Ming asks, looking to the entrance of the
dog run from our bench. Another layer to the force field
between my school life and real life might be that my best
friend and my dad have never crossed paths.

The sight of Dad didn't used to come with an ominous gong,
but everything's haywire lately. For one thing, Dad has never
been to the dog run. Not once.

When I first started walking dogs after school, he or Ma
would walk with me. For both my safety and the dogs' as well.
After all, a twelve-year-old losing a four-thousand-dollar English golden retriever named Montgomery would likely result in
a debilitating family lawsuit.

Gomers, as I called him, was my first charge before his family moved to the suburbs. But even back then, Dad would only
circle the park or city blocks with me, preferring it to the adult
playground vibes of the dog run.

So the sight of him with an overcoat covering most of his jumpsuit, waiting outside the chain-link fence for me to come out, is a little difficult to process right now. He makes no sign of coming in, apparently waiting for me to be done instead.

"Yup. That's definitely your dad," Ming continues.

"Why do you say that?" I ask, leashing up Tumbler.

"You're kidding, right?"

Ming waves in Dad's general direction, and Dad returns a sheepish wave that, without taking his hand out of his pocket, is mostly an elbow situation.

"You look exactly alike. And I'm not being racist. It's just . . . "Jeez, Halti. Was your mother's genetic material just that sticky putty that replicates newspaper ink? He's like you in a time machine."

I look back at Dad, who's now looking self-conscious at the two of us studying him from afar. I don't see what Ming's talking about. There's a resemblance there, sure, people say it—Ma always insists our poops smell the same—but I suppose I've always been more concerned with the differences. Dad snores; I don't. He likes the news on loop in the background and the light above the oven on all night, a sense that the world is spinning. Meanwhile, I like the door shut and all electronics turned off when I sleep. Life on pause for five to seven hours.

Dad always wanted to move me into Columbia, and part of me likewise always wanted to see Dad's reaction when he moved me into those dorms too.

"I'm a little taller than him," I note, getting up because

there's no need to put off the inevitable.

Ming gets to his feet and dusts off the wet spring sand from his sneakers. "I'll see you later, all right?"

"Yeah and . . . y'know . . . thanks." I shrug. "For being around and all that. Don't get weird on me."

Ming beams a grin at me and throws a loose fist into my arm. "I'll get started on braiding matching Best Friendship bracelets."

I let out a groan and already know I'll pay for this in some way that might involve wearing matching sneakers to graduation in a few very short months.

"How did you know where I was?" I ask after a few moments of walking silently and keeping an eye on Tumbler's greedy little mouth.

"Your whiteboard," he says, eyeing Tumbler as we fall in tandem with the light evening crowd. "You keep a very detailed schedule. Dog name, owner name, unit numbers, dog park schedule."

"Ah." More silence. Maybe this is just the new status quo between us, this weird distance because some things can't be taken back and hugged away once they've been said.

"Why?" Dad eventually continues. "I mean, it's just for you, right? You know all this stuff by heart."

"Habit." I shrug, not wanting to credit or think about Corinne's influence on the smaller aspects of my life right now.

As if on cue, Tumbler lunges for a chicken bone some jerk threw on the sidewalk and gets tangled into his leash in the process, increasing his panic.

Before I can rectify the situation, Dad gets down to one knee and expertly untangles him, scratching him behind the ear as he confidently fishes out the gross bone from his mouth and then wipes his hand against his pants.

"I didn't know you liked dogs."

"Of course I like dogs, Henri," he answers, cracking his back and sounding almost offended. "Cats are the evil ones. I just don't . . . always get how much people in this country like dogs, you know?"

"I only know this country, Dad."

"I suppose you do, don't you?" He sighs. "Well, I grew up with five of them in the yard. Two of them were named Kat and Cink. 'Four' and 'Five' in Creole. They were happy, we liked them, but we didn't treat them like children, y'know?"

He motions to two passing bichons frises across the street from us, linked together by a single leather double leash. Both strut proudly, showcasing their matching jackets, harnesses, and boots, all in treated leather. No one can say that wealthy owners in this city don't go all out for their pups. I've picked dogs up from acupuncture sessions.

"I'm sorry, Dad," I try to say, and it comes out sounding like something between a creaky door and a cough. "I was so out of line with all . . . that. I'm grateful for everything you've done—that you do for us. Me and Ma, but especially me. I was just . . . It's just . . . I wanted Columbia too, you know. It was your dream, but it was mine too."

298

He nods and it's not without empathy. "I know you did. And I understand why you did what you did too."

"You do?"

"I've been watching you and your mom change, grow, and become these brand-new people here in this country. I think . . ." He pauses, reassesses, and then speaks. "I think I'm sometimes a little *too* good at putting my head down and toiling. There's nothing wrong with looking up."

Of course a dog would be the only witness present right now.

"When you do it the right way," he quickly adds, as if to prevent future indiscretions on my part.

"Without identity theft?"

"Yes, that." He smiles slightly. "And actually if it's all the same to you: president. Definitely president. I wouldn't mind living in the White House, if it's all the same to you." He smiles again.

We continue walking in silence until we finally reach the Hickmans' brownstone. He waits for me as I return Tumbler, leaning against the tree outside—head tilted back, hands in his pockets, the jumpsuit under his coat looking like a loose pair of gray slacks. Away from the Wyatt and at a distance, I realize there's an effortless swagger to him. It's not hard at all to picture him with his golden saxophone in hand, enthralling a crowd of jazz heads or even afropunk hipsters.

"Henri, when I said you're not like those other kids, I didn't . . . ," Dad starts. "I don't mean that you're not worth as much as them."

"It's okay, Dad."

"No, it's not!"

He stops walking and grabs my arm, spinning me around to face him.

"We never have to worry about you at school, you've never asked for an allowance a day in your life—"

"I just occasionally commit digital fraud and almost get kicked out of school a few weeks before graduation."

"Stop that. I mean it, Henri! You don't ask for anything. You're seventeen, and you work harder than anyone your age should. And I know you'll never take anything for granted like those kids. That's what I meant, and it's just—fuck!"

It's loud enough to raise the eyebrows of two passersby.

"Dad!"

"I'm not a wordsmith, Henri! I just . . . I want you to know that I adore you, kiddo," he finally spits out.

He does?

"Oh. Okay."

"It has nothing to do with what college you get into, dang it. You're not some trophy to me. You're—you're my kid, and I adore you. Your mom says I should say it more. And I think she's right."

Dehydrated people can get a heart attack if they're given too much water too quickly. That's how I feel right now.

"So, for all future records, if you rob a bank or become president, whatever the outcome: this is me saying it." He coughs. "I adore you, and I'm damn proud of you. That's the baseline."

Where the hell is all this adoration coming from? How

could he possibly feel that way after everything I've done and said to him? But then I think back to my conversation with Lion last night. Maybe he was right. After all, you don't bow down to the will of people like Mrs. Cloutier for fifteen years if you aren't doing it for the people you love. I realize this adoration is something I always felt deep down. But now it's coming out in full force.

"Where is all this coming from?" I ask when we resume our walk back home.

"I was so angry at you yesterday. *So* angry," Dad says. "It scared me a little, to be honest. Your mother wasn't around, and I hated the feeling, so I just ended up walking it off. I made it all the way downtown to that building where your uncle works."

"You did?"

Jesus. Were we clones or something?

"He put some things in perspective. Apparently, I put a lot of pressure on people."

I give a noncommittal hum, earning a side-eye from him.

"Occasionally."

I imagine Lion sighing every time he looks up from his desk to see a member of this family in need of emotional hand-holding. I wonder if Ma's ever visited him too.

If anything good comes out of this, it might be that Dad and Lionel are speaking again. Or at least spoke again.

The walk extends itself. At some point, we both take a left instead of the right that would get us back to the Wyatt. We head south on Broadway, to another little parish of Manhattan. Why did we never do this before? Just walk? Him, me, and Ma?

"I still love this city after all these years," he says out of the blue. "I can't help it. I loved New York since before I knew there was a difference between the state and the city. I loved the idea of it. There was a postcard right over my bed as a kid. Don't know how I ended up with it, but it was mine somehow. My city. Where all my dreams were waiting for me."

His smile dims. "But when I finally got here . . . I learned it wasn't my city. I was a part of it, could survive it, somehow, but couldn't say I tried to make a bigger space for myself than that. And then, in the blink of an eye, it's been more than two decades."

"I have, like, so many career aptitude tests I can forward you. FATE gives them out like hot cakes."

"Might take you up on that." He chuckles. Then he gets serious again. "So, what happens now . . . with all this?"

"I need to talk to Mr. Vu."

"Everyone deserves a second chance. The question is what will you do with it."

I take a big inhale. We're coming up to the Wyatt, and there's still another shoe that needs to drop, and it feels like there won't be a better time. Perhaps ever.

"New York's a good city," I say, coming back to what he said moments earlier. "But I think I'm ready to see something else."

"Montreal, huh?" he says.

When I stare in confusion for a little too long, he snorts.

"Do you not realize just how many sneaker magazines are highlighted and dog-eared around that apartment? I recycle at least thirty of them a year. I kind of had a hunch you didn't just pick McGill out of the blue."

Oh.

"So, that's that, huh?" He sighs, effortlessly slipping his arm around my neck and pulling me close like he did when I was younger. "Canada: the next frontier."

"We'll see if I get in after all this . . . ," I say. "It's a fucking disaster."

"It's going to be fucking amazing, kid," he says, stunning me again, as I was fully expecting to be told to watch my language. "Weird year, huh?" Dad says, looking up at the building.

"Weird year," I agree.

I have no idea what's going to happen next—with college, with Corinne, with any of it—but I do know now that I'll always have my dad in my corner. And that feels pretty good.

We cross the street and walk in, Dad's arm still loose around my neck. Maybe we're closer to the same height.

THIRTY-TWO

t's been over a week since everything happened. In the end, Mr. Vu had been firm. What I'd done was unacceptable by FATE standards. The school saw this as a larger violation of its Moral Code than, say, being caught with a folded piece of paper in an empty water bottle during a closed-book exam. I was suspended for a week, leaving Ming to put out multiple fires about the rumors of my sudden disappearance. There was the sneaker heist gone wrong, the one where I had been arrested for drug trafficking and sent to a juvenile detention center (because no Black guy can commit a sin that's not a *Law & Order* cliché, apparently), the one where I was bedridden because "Cori" shattered my heart, and the one where my parents had been caught trying to bribe the Ivy League into accepting me with $500,000 donations and photoshopped pictures of me in a rendition of Macbeth. Honestly, that one's my favorite.

On top of the suspension, there will also be a mandatory two-week intensive in Ethics during the summer semester.

Honestly, when your high school diploma is in the balance, they might have dropped me into a Siberian dungeon for a year and I would have said, "Yes, please." Two weeks of summer school at FATE, reflecting on "the great philosophers and ethicists of history, from Kant to Somerville," didn't sound so bad.

The good news is that a week off leaves plenty of time to study and catch up on papers, and this last set of high school finals will be pretty much a breeze. Luckily, between Mr. Vu's and Chantale's appeals, Columbia decided to keep my indiscretion within its ivy walls, so it wouldn't ruin my other college chances. Looking back, it's more mercy than I deserved.

Tonight's debate finals audience is, for lack of a better term, packed to the rafters. It's somewhat unexpected to pull up to FATE on a weekend night and find the school bustling with so much energy. Luckily, my suspension didn't extend to this— one of Mr. Vu's many kindnesses—otherwise Greg probably would have had a coronary. Students, parents, faculty. Most of whom I recognize but a good chunk of them belonging to Spence's side of the stage. Those are the folks with the same vaguely tribal and off-put air that Greg, Yadira, and I probably had at all our off-site competitions.

To say that FATE goes all out for these is an understatement. There's a professional photographer for the occasion, and every student already knows that these photos will be on the website and printed in high-res for all of next year's donation mailers.

"All these people are here for you?" Ma asks as she, Dad, and I take in the crowded reception hall, a full hour before the actual debate.

"No, of course not," I quickly say. "It's senior year. People get nostalgic and just start to lean into school activities."

But when I look around the room, the only person I really want to see, or maybe just catch a glimpse of, isn't here. There's no reason for her to be, really. I haven't spoken to Corinne since our fight outside the Wyatt. I even bought Palm Tree an adorable new outfit and left it outside her apartment door with a big "I'm sorry" balloon and flowers but nada. First girlfriend, first breakup, is all I can keep telling myself here. Who knows? I might turn out to be one of the great philosophers of the twenty-first century.

Every conversation we walk past is about college. Parents either bragging, defending, or trashing the schools where their kids got in, were wait-listed, or rejected. Anyone under the age of eighteen has a look of already being so totally over it now. I should be grateful. I got into City College with a very decent financial aid package. Whatever happens, that's something to be happy about. Or at least relieved. After all, there's an alternate reality in which I was expelled and am awaiting a courtroom appearance for fraud.

"Don't be nervous," Ma says. "You're going to do great."

"You know . . . there're probably going to be a few parties afterward," I try.

"Not on your life." Dad snorts.

"Not for eight more days," Ma says, stacking two sushis on top of each other and erasing them in one quick bite. She traded her monthly night off with another trainee at the fire station to free herself up, and Dad busted out his suspenders and fedora for the occasion. The fedora has been coming out a lot.

I've been "grounded" since the Columbia incident—which is apparently a thing. To paraphrase Ma: *Since it's the first and probably the last grounding of your natural-born life, we're going to make it count.* The heart-to-heart with Dad was not, as it turns out, adequate punishment for my transgressions. I'm nervous for the debate, but it's mostly the chance to do something other than go to class, FATE detention (aka "Reflection Hour"), and then straight home with brief, timed windows for my dog walks.

Luckily, Ming will sometimes tag along and even let me use his phone to catch up on the world since Dad somehow learned how to brick my phone to block everything except incoming calls. I couldn't have asked the world for a more consistent best friend.

I also shuttered the Uptown Updogs website a few days ago. The truth is that I've built enough of a client base that I don't need to recruit anymore. I don't want another big lie floating over me and don't have to wait for some other shoe to drop and screw me over. My current hustle is good karma.

"Holy crap!" I exclaim, spotting the fidgety figure behind Dad, looking around like he's stepped into a zoo. "What are you doing here?"

"Supporting the next generation, nephew." Lion smiles. "I might even make a generous contribution."

His hair is freshly faded, there's a series of gold rings on his left hand, and his three-piece black suit looks not necessarily expensive but proper and sleek in a way that catches the attention of at least one woman with a silk scarf wrapped around her arms as she walks by us.

"This place looks like it has a very well-stocked chemistry lab," he comments after throwing a wink my way.

Ma and I send him dual glares while Dad's back tenses up as he already looks around to see if someone might have overheard and misinterpreted the comment.

"Will you two relax? I'm obviously kidding," Lion says, hands up. "Auntie here mentioned it when she stopped by my old desk. I figured I'd check out this school that's caused so many woes."

"That was supposed to be between us, Lion," Ma says, earning her a mischievous "oops" from Lion. So Ma did visit Lion, after all.

"I should go find Greg and Yadira," I say, checking the clock. "Mic checks and all."

"Good luck, Henri," Dad says, grabbing me by both shoulders and rubbing them and adding a firm nod. "You've got this."

"Thanks, Dad."

It's still a bit awkward, this hyperamount of eye contact Dad's been making in every interaction with me as if to make up for years or something. Ma touches her chest, and Lion raises a single amused eyebrow.

"You two corny brothers look like one of those family insurance ads you see on the subway."

"Lionel!"

"Sorry, sorry! Sheesh."

* * *

The debate itself is not a slaughter, but after two even opening rounds, our side of the stage makes a few key rebuttal mistakes that give Spence a lead they never lose. The Spence girls play a very good game.

Considering the catering comes with a dessert course, no one is in a big hurry to flee the premises after the actual debate. Spence folks are happy to linger to take their victory lap, and the FATE faculty is happy to flex their hospitality. Plus, generally, there's nothing wealthy adults love more than to network. They cream themselves trading vigorous handshakes and referrals and jotting down information on their phones.

To be fair, no one on the Spence side of things seems to be a dick. They laugh and throw their arms around us, juxtaposing trophies, and posing for photos. It's always fun being the gracious winner.

From across the room, I can spot Lion, who has, of course, found an audience of enthralled kids looking for "hip" mentorship.

"A firefighter? Shut up. No, shut your actual mouth!" A woman is marveling at Ma's physique and keeps trying to guess her trainer, which seems to delight Ma. My face hurts from smiling and shaking so many hands. I'm a sprint runner when it comes to smiling, but this is a marathon.

I turn the corner of the west wing, Mindfulness, and spot Dad and two other middle-aged men. Their jackets are off, and their respective glasses of champagne catch the light of the dimly lit hallway. FATE conserves energy by adopting a greener, automated ambient light system after hours.

"I'm so proud of him," one of them says, the man with the same curly hair as Greg. "He hates it up there. Janet and I always tell him we don't care. That he could be playing video games in the basement. He doesn't have to be up there! But the kid just puffs up his chest and says, 'Yes I do, Dad!' Amazing kid."

"It's very brave," my dad comments solemnly.

"Your boy *loves* it up there," the other decidedly younger man says, throwing a light fist into Dad's shoulder. "You might have a future senator in him, going by the way the crowd loves him."

Senator? I'll have to give Yadira my deepest sympathies for her dad's drug usage.

"I don't know what I have." Dad sighs in response. My stomach briefly slips somewhere around my kneecaps, but he's smiling to himself and continues.

"I don't think he knows yet either, but he's starting to figure it out. They're all still so young, but at the same time, they're there, y'know? They're fully made. It's a hell of a thing to see. We just have to watch and steer when we can."

It's not just the fedora; he's even sounding like a jazz lyricist these days.

"I just know he's pretty damn great. They all are."

"I know what you mean." Yadira's dad nods in agreement. "Not that I would ever tell her. You can't lose the upper hand!"

"Not for a second," Dad agrees immediately.

"They're monsters once they have the upper hand."

"And entitled too."

"So fricking entitled!"

All right, that's enough of that. Jeez. I back away from the hallway on the tips of my toes before the fathers start to aggregate our disappointments and it's my fault for not cutting the eavesdropping on a high note. I slip away and back toward our empty, favorite rehearsal room, where Yadira and Greg are, for lack of a better word, decompressing with their shoes off and ties loosened. The silver trophy is lying flat on its side on a nearby desk.

"There he is!" Yadira exclaims. "I've been texting you."

She sounds deflated. It's a very strange aura on her typical piss-and-vinegar brand. A loss is still a loss.

"I'm . . . on a forced hiatus from the device that lets you receive text messages." I sigh, taking off my jacket. "Long story. How long has he been like that?"

Greg is in the corner leaning against a vertical mirror, lost in the reflection of his own glazed eyes.

"Since we got in here! I offered him a hand job, and he didn't even flinch like he normally does."

"Don't be crude," Greg eventually mumbles, and he sounds like he might be drooling.

"You did good, Greg!" I say, laughing and pulling him by the arm off his own forehead's reflection.

"I failed us. . . ."

"Dude! You got us all the way here. To the finals! That's not failing. We lost to a better team. Whatever. We still crushed like eight of them along the way! Trinity will be our bitch until the next presidential administration. Plus, I look better in silver than gold, so this trophy fits my esthetics."

He stares at me suspiciously and then looks over to Yadira, who nods her agreement with everything I've just said.

"You didn't drink the juice, did you?" he finally says.

"Not even a sip!" I grin. "Neither did Yadira."

"You're a narc, Haltiwanger."

Now that the debate is over, all that's left between us, I realize, are the loose strands of this weird friendship we've built alongside all the competitions, elocution exercises, and mental gymnastics we've been throwing at one another for months.

"Oh, my God!" Yadira exclaims to someone at the door that I can't see in the low light. "There's no *way* you have the room booked."

Corinne steps forward, and my heart skips a beat.

"I'm just looking for Halti," Corinne answers, purse in hand and her hair natural up in a bun. She's wearing wooden earrings that I would bet came from Auntie Terry.

She looks beautiful.

I find my foot stepping toward her in spite of itself, and our eyes meet. I hate that I can see her neck visibly tighten at my very sight.

"Hey," she says.

"Hi."

THIRTY-THREE

"Um, hi."

"Can we talk?"

"Y-yeah, sure," I manage to croak out.

Corinne and I are both very good at talking. We used to chat for hours, and I would sometimes catch someone eavesdropping on us in the subway, with a little smile because that's the energy our banter gave off. That's how connected we were.

I don't know if it'll ever be like that again, and it's a gut punch.

We look for another unlocked classroom but eventually settle for the interior quad. I might not know too much about the ABCs of relationships but am fairly certain that heart-to-hearts should not happen with a fascinated Greg rephrasing your lines under his breath and Yadira smirking in delight.

"What are you doing here?" I say as soon as we step into the quad and sit next to each other on a stone bench. "I mean, I'm surprised. But I'm glad you're here," I add hastily.

"Oh?" she says. "Okay. Well, good. That's very good. You did well up there, by the way."

"They were better."

"They were better." She smiles.

God, I missed her.

No, I miss her: present tense. I miss following her brain down whatever rant or path she's currently on and then realizing that it's already been three hours. She doesn't think so, but no one's easier to talk to than Corinne.

Columbia nearly KO'd me, but seeing her around school and watching her turn around and bolt and catching a glimpse of her running up the stairs with Palm Tree at my very sight back at the building have been a series of slow bamboo sticks carefully pushed up under all my fingernails all at once over these past weeks.

I've apologized so much recently that the word "sorry" started to sound like a phonetic bit of French I picked up in Montreal. Auto-Root. Vwa-turr. *Soh-ree*. But I need to say it again.

"I'm sorry, Corinne. For all of it. I wasn't using you—I swear. You have to know that."

She looks at me for a long moment.

"I know," she finally says. "I didn't at first. But then I talked to my mom. And I thought about what I would have done in your shoes." She gives me a small smile. "Okay, I wouldn't have done *that*. But I wrote thirty-seven different versions of my Princeton application essay. I'd be a hypocrite if I said I didn't get why you did what you did. Heck, I would probably still be under the covers with the blinds pulled down if I hadn't gotten in."

"So . . . can you ever forgive me?" I ask desperately.

"Maybe," she says.

One benefit of Corinne always saying exactly what's on her mind is that there's no doubt that she means it.

"So, what happens now? Did we have a fight, or did we break up?" I then ask, scared of what her answer will be. I had assumed the latter, considering the complete lack of contact, but maybe Ming was right.

"According to *Teen Vogue*, we broke up. Podcast-wise, according to Dan Savage, I should dump you immediately, but Girls Gotta Eat allows more flexibility when it comes to . . ."

"Fuckboy behavior?"

"Exactly."

We stay quiet for a little while longer, and eventually I feel her hand rest on my shoulder.

"If that was, in fact, a breakup . . . then I don't think we should get back together," she finally says.

"Oh," I say. "Okay." Even if I already knew it, it stings.

At some point in this hustle, things got turned around. It's pretty clear here who is the sun and who is the hapless, rotating planet with vague signs of intelligent life. Beyond Chantale or the letter or college, a part of me was always worried that at some point she would eventually see that. That I was just Marvyn 2.0, after all.

315

"Halti, listen to me. . . ."

She turns my way and swiftly grabs my hand between her own. The jolt after so much time without touching is almost too much. Her hand tightens bizarrely, and I wonder if she feels it too. Except for my parents at the playground when I was a kid, Corinne might be the only person I've ever actually held hands with.

There's a bizarre moment of suspension in the air where we just look at each other, locked in the moment, small as it is. Right now would be a fine time for someone to freeze the entire time-space continuum, I think. But no one does and eventually, words have to get involved. Words always have to get involved.

"I . . . I miss you, okay?" she says. "A truly stupid amount some days. Most days. I miss hanging out with you, and the idea that the end of school—ever—is going to happen without seeing you and talking with you is just nuts, isn't it?" She takes a deep breath.

"But I'm going to Princeton! And you're going . . ." She pauses at her own uncertainty there. "Did you ever hear back from McGill? They've started to send out their acceptances. I checked. I was . . . curious."

Her concern is flattering and feels shameful all at once.

"Still pending," I answer, preferring not to think too much about it. That rejection will sting the hardest when it comes.

"I hope you get in," she says. "I really do, Halti."

"Thanks. That, um, that means a lot."

"But I don't know how to hope for that as your girlfriend. Or how even to be a girlfriend to someone—Jesus, anyone—from another state! It's all just question marks right now, y'know?"

I know.

"And, some offense here, but I don't think you know how to be a boyfriend just yet?"

"Is it the breach of privacy and, er, online impersonation?"

She purses her lips, a tiny contained smile that's the brightest thing in the world right now. "Yeah, you really got to work on that for your next relationship."

I would put up an argument if there was one, but there really isn't, is there? I was the one to mess up this relationship before it could be solid enough to even look ahead to some future.

"But I can hope for you to get into McGill and design amazing sneakers and get all the awesome things in the world . . . as your friend."

And there it is.

Friend.

The worst word in the world.

Stupid words.

"That part we were pretty good at, no? And it's what I miss the most. So, for now," she continues. "Will you please be my friend?"

"Sure," I say glibly, holding back a snort that would be very rude right now and that she doesn't deserve. The average number of Friends on Facebook, for people who still use that monstrosity, is 338. So, fine: Corinne Troy and Henri Haltiwanger will be one of each other's 338. I have to respect that.

"*No*," she insists, tugging my arm, which is when I realize that she's still holding my hand through all of this. "Not in the fake exes-who-don't-mean-it way. Like, actual friends. I . . . don't have that many."

"Me neither," I admit. "And you're way prettier than Ming."

I sigh. It's not exactly what I want, but I'd rather have Corinne in my life as a friend than as nothing at all.

"Promise me, Halti," she adds as we stand up. "Because if you friend-ghost me after all this, so help me God, I'll train Palm Tree to develop a taste for human meat, and I'll smoke a pipe while he savages you."

"Jesus! Okay, okay, friends!" I say, meaning it with every fiber of my being. I'll try. For the life of me, I will. "Friends."

We walk out of the school together and make a point of not holding hands as Corinne catches me up on her last few weeks. As a friend. How Chantale has upgraded her "lover" to "manfriend," how Corinne met with a bunch of other Princeton-bound students from around the city to celebrate/ assess the competition.

Everything about FATE feels nostalgic. At this very moment, as I'm strolling through the darkened halls with Cori, the Fine Arts Technical Education Academy feels more important than wherever I end up. I distantly wonder if I'll be one of the alumni of note the school is always making us clap for. Doubtful with a silver trophy and a tainted record, but who knows? Life is very long. Although then again . . . it's feeling ridiculously short these days considering I'm only now getting used to these hallways.

"So, uh, what are you doing for senior prom?"

"Prom?" she says skeptically. "Were you just looking at a reflection of yourself during the entire conversation we *just* had?"

"I mean as a friend. Sheesh! I was going to pull a 'Two Wild and Crazy Guys' with Ming, but the three of us would have an amazing time together! You know we would."

She shakes her head as we walk.

"Look, I can't not go to prom. The whole system would collapse, frankly. It would just be a bunch of confused students walking around like zombies wondering where I am, and I can't do that to my people." I grin.

"I might bring a date," she says carefully.

"Bring a date!" I say, trying to sound enthusiastic. "Ming already asked Victoria Albee. Fifth wheel is a good place. I'll be the single hot guy with the safety net of a friend group; all eyes on me on the dance floor."

"You're still the freaking worst," she says, shaking her head and laughing a little in disbelief. "Well, I do have a prom binder. . . ." I laugh, and she hits me. "Shut up."

"I didn't say anything!" I say, arms up. "And who are you kidding? It would be so much weirder if you didn't have a prom binder, Troy."

She throws her head back and laughs, and it's the best sound in the world.

Chantale is waiting outside the reception hall, and I can spot Dad, Ma, and Lion at a table at the back, chatting loudly as Haitians do but scanning the room for me.

"So, um . . . I'll see you around?"

Corinne rolls her eyes as if to say, *Obviously.* Chantale gives me a quick, barely perceptible nod before slipping an arm around her daughter's shoulders.

"It was a good performance, Henri," she says coolly but not with any resentment I can actively pick up on. "Have a good night."

"You too, Mrs. Troy."

I watch them disappear down FATE's hallway and into the night while I rejoin my own tribe. There are no fist pumps or skips in my step but only because I pay very close attention to both my forearms and feet.

"Good luck with McGill," Corinne throws over her shoulder without turning back.

Ma, Dad, and I say goodbye to Lion at the nearest subway mouth (since he has "two more stops planned for this suit") and agree to grab a cab home. It's an unnecessary splurge considering the 1 train is running on time, but it feels like that kind of night.

"No parties," Dad says on the way home, "but you can have your phone privileges back."

With a few clicks, the parental locks are removed and the ocean of GIFs and memes I missed from Ming pours into my phone. The boy has absolutely not been doing any biology. I've also been tagged in a few dozen photos from tonight. It was a good night. Although there is no way Yadira or I will ever see that trophy again, going by how tightly Greg is clutching it in the video.

My in-box is at twenty-eight new emails—mostly school stuff. They tend to pile up when you don't get to check them. However, only one stands out from the in-box, and whatever sound I let out is enough to startle Ma awake from Dad's shoulder and for the poor driver to swerve narrowly from a passing biker.

Name: Admissions
Domain: @McGill.edu
Subject: Congratulations

EPILOGUE

T rains have steadily been regaining their appeal for me. For a while, between the Montreal subway, the MTA subway whenever I'm back home, and the Adirondack railroad in between, I was spending a sizable chunk of existence in tepid motion and developing an allergy even to toddlers wearing jumpers with smiling trains all over them.

Today's train is almost completely empty. I only recognize the man three rows ahead of me. Siavosh, I believe. He's an Iranian-Canadian working in the states and does this trip every two weeks. I must have on my grumpy engineering-midterm face today because he nods at me from afar but doesn't engage.

I'm grateful, considering this problem set worth 30 percent of the final grade is slowly killing me. Mechanical Engineering is profoundly stupid. Mechanics is nothing but the misshapen twin of calculus kept chained in the basement. Why do I need to understand how pulleys work to design shoes?

Occasionally, there's a kerfuffle at the border because

someone is trying to sneak into Canada or America with an expired passport, and you end up sitting without power, but it's mostly time to sleep, catch up on assigned reading, homework, or just doodle shoe ideas. Occasionally, Ming is up halfway across the globe, and we text chat like in the old days, depending on the connection.

After a few hours, the numbers get blurry, and I switch over to this essay I have to write for this Nike shoe-design internship that starts in the fall. The submission deadline is a week away, and historically speaking, applying for competitive programs has not been my forte.

The prompt is deceptively simple: "Personal statement. 800–900 words."

Dear Nike Design Internship,
~~I greatly appreciate the fact that you don't ask for~~
~~recommendation letters.~~

Eighteen minutes later, I'm still no closer to cracking this code.

"Next stop: Saratoga Springs!" the conductor announces.

I get off with my backpack and a nod goodbye to Siavosh. It's so cold out now that my glasses are dangerously close to developing a layer of frost. Another life update, subfolder "FML": there are glasses now. I've apparently been staring at a lot of screens for the past eighteen months. Ma says I pull them off well, and I don't get the *Thank God you're pretty* thing anymore. Well, I get it less.

I cross the street from the station and settle in at the Haitian bakery, Sak Pasé. How a Haitian bakery ended up in Saratoga Springs is a testament to the American dream. I take a booth and order two slices of orange cake and a large coffee from one of the servers I don't recognize today.

Twenty-eight minutes later, a college girl bundled up to high heaven walks in and beams a bright smile to the cashier. The eager cashier immediately offers her a menu, and by the look in his eyes, he would go in for half a spleen too. I can't help but smile. Sorry, dude.

"Oh, that's okay." She smiles. "I know it by heart, thanks!"

Before the guy can work out another way to keep her attention, she's already back on her phone, walking this way. The ability to write essays—actual essays—on her phone while walking is uncanny. She kisses me, and I can feel the smile despite her hurried tone.

"So, I've decided," Corinne says as she begins to unpack a startling amount of books and work, considering we have only four hours today. "I'm done with you."

She removes her hat and sighs in frustration and slides over to my side of the booth. And just like that, another day-trip to Saratoga Springs, roughly halfway between McGill and Princeton, has already paid off.

I once opened a calendar and tried to backtrack to the exact date Corinne and I officially "got back together," and ultimately couldn't narrow it down to a single date or event or even a spoken request. It just happened.

Was it all the midnight phone calls freshman year when college was either living up to or falling short of all our FATE-sponsored expectations?

Or was it bumping into each other in the lobby of the Wyatt, both getting in late for the holidays and ending up walking the width of Manhattan with a seventy-pound Palm Tree?

Or was it the sudden flare-up of jealousy when Marvyn visited Princeton with his lacrosse team and tagged me in the photo of him and Corinne at a party?

Was it the fights or misunderstandings, because there are always a few? Or maybe the fact that we always answer the texts that come after?

In the end, that "We went to high school together" line we give over red Solo cups in basement parties or champagne flutes at Princeton events always feels both like the most complete version of the story and a lie that doesn't cover the gist of it. That's how lives meld together, I suppose: they melt and meld and then they are one.

"Oh, yeah?" I ask. "Two years and you're out?"

"Give or take some high school shenanigans."

The signature pink hat still hasn't changed, but at some point last semester, the high hair turned into middle-of-the-back cornrows.

"The train arrived twenty minutes late! That's very valuable LSATs study time. We had a good run. Let's wrap this up."

"If you think it's best," I concede. "How's the new room-mate?"

Corinne makes a face, scooting closer under my arm. "Black but apolitical."

I let out a full cackle. "That's going to be so much fun! Please record your conversations. Did she not know she was moving in with the treasurer of the Black Student Union?"

Corinne shakes her head and steals a huge sip of my coffee.

"Get your own!"

"Screw off," she says, nibbling orange cake with her fingers. "How's the Nike application?"

"Good!" I Smile.

She pokes me at my rib, nearly spilling coffee. "The lies, Haltiwanger. The lies will get you!"

"I wrote one sentence in two hours and then crossed it out, so technically that's progress."

She reaches out and pokes at my cheek in admonishment.

"You know our deal, Haltiwanger: you have two more weeks and then I'm taking charge of that application. I told my mom about the internship, by the way."

"Corinne," I whine.

"She approves! She even offered to write you a recommendation letter if you need one."

I raise an eyebrow.

"And then laughed at her own joke for like five minutes."

"That wedding is going to be *fun*," I groan in dread. After a lot of discussions and family dinners, Chantale Troy's mysterious international lover—Shamus—is now officially moving into the Wyatt with a very shiny and expensive wedding ring as his offering to the gods. Palm Tree likes him, which is veto enough for me. I'm convinced that being included in this wedding party by Chantale is simply payback for my past high school sins. Auntie Terry said we're both in the same boat on that front.

"My friend Aaron thinks there's something incredibly messed up about the fact that we haven't broken up yet. Statistically, it is an anomaly," she says.

"I hate us," I say.

"Oh, we're the worst," she agrees, settling back into her seat, eyes already on her book, lost somewhere in Wollstonecraft feminist theory.

And we're both smiling right now, though neither of us even realizes it.

ACKNOWLEDGMENTS

It turns out that being an author just means stumbling into old platitudes that used to make you roll your eyes—and realizing they've been true all along. *Kill your darlings; avoid unnecessary adverbs; your second book will be harder than your first.* True. True. Dear GOD, so very true.

To say that writing this book kicked my butt would be an understatement. Second books are a beast, folks. I still can't fully explain why.

No matter how much I love Henri and Corinne—and I do—it took forever to lock into their voices. At some point, Corinne was a spoiled brat in a penthouse and Henri, the quiet dog walker hired to teach her responsibility. That version of Halti was a classist grump with a serious chip on his shoulder about the rich. Most of the story ended up taking place during mandatory puppy walks. I'll be the first to say it was a bad draft all around. And that fully written version of the story is sitting somewhere on this very laptop, smirking at me, bloated from the eight months of my life it ate up! That jerk cost me a full half-inch of my vertical hairline.

I can't account for how they'll be received, but I'm happy to say that Henri and Corinne are their truest versions within the book you're holding and for that, the following people have my eternal gratitude:

Alessandra Balzer. I still don't have a manager and don't quite know what a manager does, to be honest, but I assume it is for those unlucky folks out there who do not have an Alessandra Balzer in their lives to hold their hands through every step of the book-making process. (Tee-hee, suckers.) She is the best editor you could hope for.

And I've also been blessed on that front with the amazing folks at Alloy Entertainment. I owe Viana Siniscalchi, Sara Shandler, Joelle Hobeika, and Joshua Bank my firstborn and that is all there is to it. They'll refuse because they are very nice and sane people, but I'll place it in their arms and dash off. Viana: don't let Josh raise my fictional offspring as a disgusting Rangers fan. (Hmm, maybe writing these at three a.m. wasn't the best idea.)

I'm also forever grateful to Caitlin Johnson, Andrea Pappenheimer, Kerry Moynagh, Kathy Faber, Nellie Kurtzman, Ebony LaDelle, Sam Benson, Sabrina Abballe, Patty Rosati, Mimi Rankin, Katie Dutton, Jon Howard, and Stephanie Macy.

I don't know all the hands this passed through except that they are all deft and incredibly talented at their specific crafts. I tend to picture HarperCollins as an assembly line of hyper-literary raccoons, which now just sounds adorable. Little glasses on their noses and everything . . . Where was I? Oh, right. Acknowledgments.

Charming as a Verb wouldn't be complete without that jaw-dropping cover, courtesy of Chris Kwon on design and queen Steffi Walthall on art. I mean, my God. Flip to the cover and bask for a moment.

And thank you, book reader, for reading. Without someone picking up that little box of pages at the end, the whole endeavor would have been for nothing.

The end!

Fin!

Rasengan!

Valar Dohaeris!

Avada Kedavra!